THE PIRATE BRIDE

Also available from *New York Times*
bestselling author

SHANNON
DRAKE

and HQN Books

The Queen's Lady
Beguiled
Reckless
Wicked

Watch for her next sweeping tale in fall 2009

SHANNON DRAKE

THE PIRATE BRIDE

HQN™

ISBN-13: 978-1-60751-241-7

THE PIRATE BRIDE

For Bobbi Smith—
wonderful writer,
amazing friend.

THE PIRATE BRIDE

PROLOGUE

Victory and Defeat
The West Coast of Scotland
1689

"THE CHILD! For the love of God, Fiona, you must save the child."

The wind was stark and cold. Fiona's vision blurred, and she could do nothing but feel, and what she felt was a cold wind blowing. All her life, she had loved her home. The rich colors of the braes, the hard rock of the cliffs and crags, and aye, even the wicked cold and bitter wind that came with winter. Despite the chill, a day such as today often meant the coming of the spring, when the earth would burst forth with a wild beauty that was beloved by those who knew it and held in awe by those who did not. Aye, good God, but she loved her home, all the brilliant blues and mauves of spring, and the rich greens of summer…even the gray of an angry and overcast winter's day.

All swept away now.

By the bloodred spill of life that had been the final result of William III's so called "glorious revolution."

"Fiona!" She felt her husband's hands on her shoulders, shaking her. She opened her eyes and stared into his, and she knew then that she would never see him again. They were to pay. The Highland Scots were to pay for their opposition to William, for their loyalty to the legal king, James II. Catholic or no, by God's right, he should be king. And the Highlanders had proven their mettle—as they had so many times before—but it had been in vain, and now they were to be thrashed ruthlessly and without mercy in return.

"Ye've got to go now, my love. I'll be with you soon enough, I'll warrant," Mal told her, his eyes shifting from hers as he smoothed a stray lock of hair from her forehead.

"Ye'll not see me again," she whispered. At first she didn't feel the pain of that realization, only the whipping of the wind. But then she saw the endless blue of his eyes, the rich waves of his nearly midnight hair and the rugged planes of his face. His mouth was broad, his lips generous. She thought of his smile, of his kiss.

And suddenly the pain was like a knife ripping through her. She cried out and fell to her knees, and he quickly knelt down beside her, ignoring the men who awaited him, both his cavalry and his foot soldiers. It was not so regimented an army as the one that came after them, or the one they had so recently and brilliantly beaten with skill and daring. They were Highlanders, clansmen, and aye, they could feud, but when they fought together, it was as brothers. Still, they had their own minds and did not always need orders. But they had their hearts and souls when their weapons were poor. They would die for one another, in a bond not often found in the paid ranks of the enemy's army.

"Fiona, come." He reached out to help her to her feet. She saw his hands as they took her own, and they were wonderful hands, strong, long-fingered, capable of holding her with passion and a child with tenderness. She was suddenly terrified that she would shame him by screaming hysterically at the knowledge that he was going to die. And his death would be a crime against God, against nature, for he was a beautiful man in his strength and wisdom, not only in his flesh, and in the love he felt for the land and their God and all those who lived in their small corner of the world.

"The child, Fiona. You must protect the child."

She staggered to her feet, trying to see despite the curtain of her tears. She stood tall and reached a hand to the child standing near, wide-eyed, afraid, and yet so sadly old before time could make the years go by.

Mal suddenly bowed his head, perhaps to fight the dead light of destiny in his own eyes, then clasped his offspring, shaking.

Then he straightened and planted a last, fiercely sweet kiss upon her lips. "Gordon, take my lady and my child, and see them safe."

Malcolm turned then, taking his horse from one of his men, a distant cousin, as were so many. Gordon's hand fell upon her shoulders. "To the tender, my lady, swiftly now."

She was blinded. It was the wind, she told herself, but she knew it was the tears that streamed down her face, unheeded. As they raced to the shore, she wiped her cheeks and turned, lifting her babe, looking back one last time on the man she so loved.

Laird Malcolm, kilted and magnificent, sat upon his great charger, shouting to the men around him. And from the shore she could see the valiant charge of the Scots as they raced up the hill, their battle cry upon their lips.

They would die well.

They would not be dragged to the gallows and mocked as they died. Warriors all, they would battle their enemies to the death. Mal had claimed they would triumph, as they had done before, but she knew of a certainty that this time courage would not be enough.

In her arms, her young one squirmed. Ah, but so strong and tall already! "Me da!"

"Aye, Father goes to battle," she murmured.

Then, high atop the hill, she saw the enemy.

They came in one great mass. Thousands…and thousands…

She turned, tall, straight, no tears flowing down her cheeks now. With Gordon helping her along, she hurried to the water, where the tender waited. An oarsman, cloaked, his head down, sat ready.

"Hurry, man, hurry!" Gordon cried. "Ye must get her to the ship."

The oarsman rose and cast back his hood, and she looked in the man's eyes. Her heart leapt to her throat as she saw his face.

"Nay, I shall not," the oarsman said.

Gordon drew his sword, but the oarsman was ready. As fine and experienced a warrior as Gordon, his hand was already at the hilt of his sword beneath his cloak, and when he lifted his blade, it was to slice Gordon through.

She no longer felt or heard the wind. Her vision was clear now, and all she saw was red. A sea of it before her...

Madness struck her then. She reached for the dirk in the sheath at her waist, and she attacked.

The oarsman screamed in pain and rage, and responded instantly.

Fiona never felt the steel as it ripped into her. She heard her heart, though. Thumping, erratic and fast, pumping out her life's blood....

Her heart cried out. *Malcolm, my love, it seems that in truth we do not part after all today, for there is a heaven for those who have been just and strong....*

"Mother!"

Her child! Her precious child! She tried to cry out, but she had no breath.

As she lay dying, she heard his laughter.

And then there was screaming. But the sound did not come from her. As the world faded, she was dimly aware that the oarsman was pushing off from shore, and her child, still so young, yet old enough to see, to know what was happening, was being swept away by sheer evil.

CHAPTER ONE

The Caribbean
Pirates' Alley
1716

"OUTGUNNED, OUTSAILED, outmanned, out...blasted! Damn it all! Bring her about and set to speed. Full sail," Logan Haggerty cried, teeth grating, eyes narrowed, fury all but blinding him as he stared at the pirate ship headed his way.

"Captain, we *are* at full sail, and blimey, we're tryin' to come about," Logan's first mate, Jamie McDougall assured him. Jamie was an old salt, an honest merchantman impressed into the navy, he'd moved on to piracy and then been pardoned back into the King's own service. If there were a trick to be played upon the brine, Jamie knew it.

If there were a way to outrun a pirate, Jamie knew that, too.

If they were sunk through the greed and egotism of the aristocracy, well, Jamie would know that, as well.

Logan had informed the duke that there were pirates in the area and explained his own disadvantage due to the lack of manpower he had aboard, should they be boarded. He had explained, as well, that the weight of their cargo would drastically affect their speed and maneuverability.

But the duke hadn't cared.

Logan had ten guns.

The pirate had twenty he could easily count, perhaps more, and Logan's spyglass assured him that the crew upon the pirate vessel numbered at least two dozen men.

He traveled with a crew of twelve.

The vessel bearing down on them, sporting a scarlet flag, was handsome indeed. She was a sloop, sleek and fast, riding across the waves as smoothly as if she were soaring through the air. She had a narrow draft, and would easily be able to escape larger ships in the shallows. The craft was well-fitted, he could see. Besides the larger cannon pointing their way, he could see that the upper deck was fitted with a row of swivel guns, and those with many barrels.

She was a beauty and had been altered for her life of crime. Three masts, when many sloops offered but the mainmast, and with sails that caught the slightest breeze. Her tenders were situated behind the swivel guns, allowing no space for weakness. She was small, sleek and strong.

He had known better than to enter pirate territory, but pride had been his downfall.

Ah, yes, his own pride, even more than that of the nobility he mocked, who had tempted him into daring this voyage despite his original vehement refusal to accept the assignment.

And how had the duke managed that? Logan mocked himself then. Why, because of Cassandra.

Sweet Cassandra. He had been sure he could win her love if he just had enough money. His bloodline was noble enough, but his circumstances were far too impoverished to secure her to him. But if he made a success of this mission, he could return triumphant and regain all that his family had lost. No, that had been *stolen* from them. If he could challenge the sea and make this voyage, he would be worthy. *She* was the prize that mattered if he succeeded in this breakneck dash to bring the gold of the temple of Asiopia to the colonists in Virginia.

Now he realized that he had been a fool indeed. And why? What was it about the woman that had so beguiled him that he would attempt such a reckless endeavor? He had spent his life knowing he must make his own way, and he had known both harlots and great ladies. He had shown them courtesy one and all, but never had he felt such a tug upon his feelings, or this desire to settle down. It wasn't that she was a tease or temptress, that she made demands or ever threatened to play false. It was the laughter in her flashing, quicksilver eyes, the gentle touch of her fingertips, and, most of all, the honesty in her every word and action. He could love her; really love her. There was more, as well, of course, which he could admit in his own heart. She would be the perfect mate for him. She was the only child of a respected and wealthy family. With her name joined to his, he could reclaim all that had once been his family's, rebuild the Haggerty fortune. She was everything he could have hoped for in his life's partner.

He could not blame her for his own willingness to take this risk. He did not even blame her father, who merely wanted security for his only child.

If there was any blame, it fell only upon his own shoulders.

A mocking inner voice taunted him for a liar and a fraud.

He had said that he sailed because he needed the money, but that wasn't wholly true. He was always eager to sail the seas. Eager to find one man.

And that man lived upon the seas, outside the law.

Logan even claimed that he sought justice, not revenge, though were he honest with himself, he would have to concede that vengeance, too, was in his mind and heart.

He should have carried more guns, he told himself now. He should have brought more men, but he needed men he trusted for the battle he hoped to engage, and such men were hard to find.

Still, if there was any blame for his current predicament, it was his.

These were dangerous times to sail the seas. When England and Holland had been at war with Spain and France, many so-called pirates saw themselves as fighting a righteous battle. In an English ship, he would have been at the mercy only of a French or Spanish ship. But when the combatants had come to terms in 1697, privateers littered the sea.

Many had nothing to go home to.

Many had no desire to go home. Waging war upon the sea had become a way of life.

And many others saw that a fortune might be won if a man were brave, reckless and ready to risk his life.

Never before had the Caribbean been so overrun with thieves.

He rued fate and the wretched, greedy men who had lured him to go against his better judgment.

Damn them, he thought.

No.

Damn himself.

A man could not be led to such a place unless he chose his course.

So much for common sense and strength of purpose. He had fallen. And his own reckless desires had damned these good men along with him.

Here on the waves of the Caribbean, he would be the death of them all. They couldn't outrun the pirate ship, and they sure as hell weren't going to bring it down. He wasn't a coward, but neither was he a fool. Lust and greed were about to kill him and, worse, all these good men.

"M'lord Captain?" Jamie asked. "What is your command?"

"We must rely upon this pirate's honor," Logan said, knowing he must sacrifice pride for the sake of his men's lives.

"What?" Jamie demanded. "Pirates have no honor."

"Aye, they do. More than many a supposed great man," Logan said. "Send up the flag. Demand parley. I will negotiate with her captain."

"Negotiate?" Jamie protested. "There can be no negotiation—"

"If not, we are dead men. Bring our flag to half-mast. I will deal our way out of this," Logan said.

"Deal with a pirate captain? He'll skewer you through."

"Not if he wishes to keep the respect of his men," Logan assured him. "For the love of God, man, we are running out of time. Do as I say."

Despite Jamie's protest and the wary looks upon the faces of his men, in twenty minutes time they were broadside the pirate and not a cannon had been fired. Logan stood with his men, staring across at the handsome rigging of the pirate ship, while the crew of privateers stared at them, grinning, totally aware that they had the upper hand.

Grappling hooks and strong rope bound them as tightly together as lovers locked in an intimate embrace.

"Your captain, my fine fellows!" Logan shouted. "Where is your captain? I demand to see your captain."

"You *demand?*" one peg-legged man jeered.

"Indeed. It is my right to demand negotiation, not *even* though you be pirates but *because* you be pirates. If you refuse me, you are cursed and damned, and well you know it."

He had counted on the superstitious bent of sailing men, and he had not been mistaken. The surly crew muttered softly and looked uncertainly from one to another.

Then, through the crowd upon the deck, strode the

captain, a slender young man, clean-shaven, with rich dark hair curled beneath a broad-brimmed feathered hat. His coat was red velvet, and beneath it, his shirt was white as snow. He was tall with features that belonged on a Greek statue rather than a rogue at sea. He wore great black cuffed boots, and despite the elegance of his countenance, he walked with assurance, and the pistols and knife sheathed at his broad belt meant business, as did the long sword that hung by his side.

"Good heavens, men, don't let this gentleman disarm you so quickly. He is cleverly attempting to save his own hide," the pirate captain chided, stepping forward. "But not *even* because it is his supposed right to negotiate, but *because* he deems himself so clever, I am willing to take the time to have a word with the man."

"Whatever your reason, I appreciate it, good Captain…?" Logan said, waiting for a name.

"My flag tells it all," the captain said. "I'm known as Red Robert."

"You are an Englishman," Logan said, as if to remind the pirate he had attacked one of his countrymen. Though the days of so-called privateering were behind them, many a sea robber still did not prey upon his own kind.

"I am not an Englishman, I assure you."

Red Robert had apparently made his assessment already.

His name, Logan reflected, was bandied about in many a tavern. It was one that caused even the brave to tremble, for the stories that went about were fearsome.

He had not expected a man who looked so young. Then again, pirates rarely survived many years, at least, not at piracy. They were killed, or they took what riches they had obtained, changed their names and created new lives on distant islands or in out-of-the-way towns.

Logan spoke again, aware that he had to do so with a certain eloquence if he intended to achieve his goal of keeping his men alive, whatever his own fate.

He took a step forward. "I, good Captain Robert, am Logan Haggerty, Lord of Loch Emery, with no emphasis on the title, for were it worthy of great land or riches, you'd not be finding me here upon the high seas. What I seek is the right of man-to-man combat."

"Hmm, do tell," Red Robert said.

"If you best me with your sword, you have gained a good ship and great riches without spilling an ounce of blood other than my own, or chancing the loss of treasure to the bottom of the sea, and without risking the lives and limbs of your men."

"And if *you* best *me,* m'lord?" Red Robert inquired with polite amusement.

"Then we sail away."

Red Robert seemed to weigh his words with gravity. But then he said, "Surely you are jesting."

"Are you afraid?" Logan demanded, assessing the pirate captain's slender frame and apparent youth, which made a strange contrast indeed against the hardened edge of the sea robbers surrounding him.

"This is not a profession for one who is afraid," Red Robert returned casually. "Don't be deceived by my youth, *Lord* Haggerty. I am more than proficient with my weapons."

One well-muscled man standing at the pirate captain's side—not much older, but far stronger and broader—whispered in Red Robert's ear, causing him to laugh.

"This may be some trick, Red," one of the other men warned, a fellow with long gray hair, a large gold earring and his fingers twitching on the hilt of the knife at his waist.

"No trick," Logan said quietly.

"No fear, Hagar," Red said, acknowledging the man who had spoken. "And no deal." He turned to Logan. "However, here is what I do offer. If you best me, you do not sail away free. After all, m'lord, you surely knew you traveled dangerous waters." When Logan would have spoken, Red Robert raised his hand. "Your men live. They may sail away free with half the treasure. But you remain with us, a willing prisoner, to be held for ransom."

"I've told you. My title means little."

"And so the daring voyage you attempted today?" Red Robert mocked.

Logan stood his ground without reply, though his heart seemed to shrivel at the thought of never seeing Cassandra again. Still, his men would live to sail away.

If he could win.

And, God help him, the fellow was lean, which would make him quick. Agile. A deadly foe.

Though far broader in the shoulder himself, and not without a fair share of power in his arms, he was agile, as well. He'd trained with some of the finest swordsmen money could buy, since it was only recently that the family fortunes had taken such a sad turn.

His men. He had to save his men, God help him. He'd had every right to gamble with his own life, but he had been wrong to risk theirs, as well. And if he could best this captain...

"I will be your willing prisoner. But I would ask, then, that even if I lose, you take the treasure but give my men the tenders so that they might make safe landfall."

Red Robert shrugged.

The tall, dark-haired fellow at his side protested. "No."

The captain turned on him with such a fierce look of displeasure that the man stepped back and hung his head. "Brendan," Red said warningly.

The captain had a curious voice, Logan thought. He seemed eternally soft-spoken. Strange, for someone who needed to bellow orders against the wind. There was a husky, almost whispered quality to his voice.

"Aye, Red," the man named Brendan replied, but despite his immediate acknowledgment that Red was captain and his orders stood, he was rigidly disapproving.

"It is done," Red Robert said.

"This is madness," Jamie protested softly to Logan. "A trick, certainly. They will not let us go. They will not forego half of such a treasure."

"It *is* madness," Logan agreed. Madness from the moment he had agreed to transport the treasure. Madness? Aye, from start to finish, but here was his chance to at least save those he had dragged into folly along with him.

"Madness, but I believe this pirate will stand by his word."

"My deck, m'lord Captain, is the larger," Red Robert said. "We shall hold our contest here."

There was some muttering upon the pirate's deck.

And some protests from Logan's own.

Red Robert lifted a hand. The muttering went silent. "We shall fight until first blood," he called out gruffly.

"Are you afraid of Lord Haggerty's prowess?" Jamie shouted out.

Logan wished the man silent. They were hardly in a position to aggravate their opponents.

"I don't intend to sacrifice a fine ransom or ready muscles for the oars," Red returned, unruffled.

"Well?" demanded one of Red's fellows. "Do we get on with this or not?"

Logan leapt nimbly upon the ship's rail to make his way to the other ship's deck. Alone among the ruffians and sea robbers, he stood his ground. He stared at the slender and oddly aesthetic pirate, then dipped a deep and sweeping bow. "At your convenience, Captain."

"Clear the deck," Red Robert said, and it wasn't a resounding, thunderous shout, but a quiet command, still instantly obeyed.

"He needs a second!" Jamie McDougall called, and leapt across to stand, white-faced, fists clenched, at Logan's side.

Jamie McDougall was a good and loyal friend,

Logan thought. They had a long history together. Jamie would not, apparently *could* not, leave him now.

Red Robert pulled his sword from the handsome scabbard belted about his hip. He swept a courtly bow to Logan. "At your convenience, m'lord."

"Nay, sir, at yours," Logan said softly.

It might have been a casual meeting on the street. At first they circled one another carefully, each trying to assess the measure and mettle of the other man. Neither of them appeared the least concerned. Logan saw a smile twitch at the pirate's lips. This close, he saw that the captain was indeed very young.

He wondered that the pirate captain, however youthful and—perhaps?—inexperienced he might be, had not shed the crimson coat. He was clad in shirt and breeches himself, allowing a far greater freedom of movement.

But his opponent seemed perfectly comfortable in his coat.

He certainly wasn't about to suggest his opponent remove it. Why offer his foe any advantage?

"Get 'im, Red!" cried gray-haired Hagar, and a chant went up among the pirates.

Not to be outdone, Logan's own crew called encouragement to him.

"Take the sea robber, m'lord! Take him!" Jamie shouted.

"Red, watch his footwork," warned the man named Brendan.

"He's a scurvy sea rat, m'lord!" cried someone from his own deck. Richard Darnley, Logan thought, a good young sailor, and a man intent on making his way in the world.

Young and stalwart. A man who deserved a long life and the fulfillment of his dreams.

Red Robert continued to assess him.

And then they met.

Slowly, almost politely. A touching of the swords. A meeting of the eyes.

Then they began in earnest.

Logan felt the clash of steel vibrate all along his arm. A quick return, another, then another.

For a moment he felt he had the advantage, but he quickly realized he had thought too soon.

His opponent leapt nimbly against the starboard hull, then pushed off and nearly caught him dead in the chest. Logan managed a jump to the side, instinct-driven, and he was certain that saved his life. But it had been close. Far too close. They were fighting only until first blood was drawn. But had the pirate made good on that last lunge...

It wasn't to be a gentlemanly duel, Logan realized.

"M'lord, watch the wretched sea robber," Jamie warned him.

Logan came on hard with a series of quick thrusts and slashes, forcing his opponent back again. Just when he thought he had the pirate nearly cornered against the master's cabin, Red Robert once again made a sudden sweeping leap that sent him bouncing off a storage bin. This time when he came about, it was to nearly sever Logan's head from his body.

Instinct had driven him to duck, keeping life and

skull intact. Barely. His opponent was as adept with a sword as he'd claimed, and clearly not at all afraid of shedding blood or lopping off limbs.

Logan caught a glimpse of the pirate's eyes.

They were narrowed and deadly.

The chanting, the jests, the encouragement, the hoots of derision, all seemed to be getting louder and louder, like a growing storm.

The pirate's face was flushed. Red Robert wore his name well at that moment, Logan reflected, hoping he was seeing a sign of weakness. Perhaps the pirate had been a bit too impressed with his own skill. A more than respectable skill, certainly, but no man was assured of victory.

He had to take the advantage now, Logan knew. A very large part of excellence in swordsmanship lay in the mind, in creating a strategy for using a man's talents most effectively. A heavy man used his weight and strength, a nimble man his agility. To best this pirate, he had to assess each leap and slide the man might take beforehand, then be somewhere else when the strike came.

Once again the pirate took to the air, this time landing atop a rum barrel. And in that split second, Logan anticipated the man's next move, a rapid leap that would bring the pirate behind him.

Logan whirled around. In that brief moment, he prayed he hadn't anticipated in error and that the pirate would not come down behind his current position.

He didn't.

Too late, Red Robert saw that his move had been predicted.

He landed facing Logan.

And Logan set the point of his blade against the pirate's throat.

Blue eyes gazed at him with fury, and yet he was certain the pirate was not so much angry with him as he was with himself for being outmaneuvered.

"Good calculation," Robert said, barely managing to unclench his teeth.

Logan withdrew the point of his sword and bowed. As he stood, he found the pirate's blade at his throat.

It was his turn for anger.

"You, Captain, are not a man of your word. I have bested you."

The pirate gloated. "First blood. You did not draw blood."

"Only because I chose not to cause injury. But an agreement has been made, and I am an honest man."

"But I am a pirate."

"A pirate's honor is said to be greater than the average man's."

"And what do you know of a pirate's honor?" Red Robert demanded.

"I have sailed these seas for many years."

Red Robert's sword began to drop.

Still angry, Logan reacted, slashing hard against his opponent's blade and all but sending it flying. He quickly nicked the fellow's cheek; a tiny dot of blood appeared.

"First blood," he said icily.

Red Robert didn't even blink. Nor did he touch the drop of blood upon his cheek.

He merely turned away, striding toward the door to the master's cabin, where he paused, looking back and speaking to his men. "The cargo of our Lord Captain's ship shall be evenly divided. His men may proceed upon their path when our split of the goods has been taken."

"What of the captain himself?" Brendan asked.

"Take him below to the brig, of course," Red Robert said. Those icy blue eyes met Logan's across the deck. "He is an honorable man. He will go without skirmish, as he has sworn, I am certain."

"And if I were not a gentleman? If I were to protest now?" Logan inquired.

"You drew first blood, but I'm quite certain you realize I do not exaggerate my ability at swordsmanship," Red Robert said tightly. "I am equally adept with a cat-o'-nine-tails. But that's really no matter, is it? You gave your word. And you are a man of honor."

The pirate captain turned to enter the cabin.

"Wait!" Logan demanded.

Red Robert turned back.

"I would request a moment with my first mate. To give instructions."

"As you wish."

"You're not afraid it's a trick?" he could not help but ask.

"Why would I be afraid? I repeat, you have assured me that you are a man of your word."

Red Robert stepped through the cabin door.

Logan stood tall and straight, watching the door close. He felt as if he were trembling inside, but he could not—would not—let it show. He had achieved his aim; his men would live. They would sail on to South Carolina.

"My lad, my fine lord," Jamie said, and it sounded as if he were choking. He did not stand on ceremony. He gripped Logan's shoulders tightly, staring into his eyes with misery.

"Jamie, my good fellow. I'm quite all right. You will sail on with the others and see to my release. I believe our patrons will be glad half their treasure has survived, and you must ensure that we receive the promised cut. Forty percent. Don't take less."

"Aye, captain."

Logan saw that Brendan was leading a ten-man crew across to his ship.

Even from this distance, he could tell that his own men were tight-lipped and stiff, barely moving.

"Help with the divide," he called out, his voice strong. "We have made a deal, and it will be kept. Hinder no man of the pirate ship in his effort to take what is his."

"Ye heard the captain!" Jamie roared.

"Go, my friend. See to it," Logan told him.

Jamie nodded, deep sorrow in his eyes. The old salt actually looked as if he were about to cry.

"I have survived thus far," Logan assured him softly. He forced a cocky smile. "I guarantee you, I shall continue to do so."

"I will find a way to kill these blasted brigands," Jamie swore. "I'll not rest 'til I've met whatever ransom this pirate requires and seen you freed."

"You are a good man, Jamie. We will meet again."

"M'lord…"

"Tell Cassandra…" Logan began.

"Aye?"

"Tell her that I am deeply sorry. But that…that I pray—no, I demand!—that she choose whatever path now lies open to her for happiness."

"Nay, my lord!"

"You will tell her so, Jamie. Swear it to me."

"I cannot—"

"You can. You must. Swear it, Jamie."

Jamie hung his head. "Aye, Logan. As you wish."

"Go with God, Jamie."

Jamie, a fierce and bitter look upon his face, glanced toward the captain's cabin.

"I pray that God will be with you, for surely he has abandoned all other men here."

"He helps those who help themselves, so it is said, and I am quite capable of helping myself, as you know, my friend."

Jamie nodded tightly, then turned quickly and moved on.

Logan remained.

Feeling the breeze.

The sea…the air…the sweet cry of the wind. They all meant freedom to him. He had never realized just how much until this moment. Amazing how he had never before realized how much he had loved freedom.

But then…

It was a long time since he had been a prisoner.

That had been another lifetime. But he hadn't forgotten.

After all, that memory was half the reason for the fool trip that had brought him to this fate.

"M'lord Captain?"

There was just a hint of mockery in the words.

Brendan stood at his side, watching him. The fellow neither smiled nor goaded him as he continued. "I'm afraid your presence is required. In the brig."

Logan nodded.

The man carried shackles, he noticed.

"There is no need for those," he said. "Merely show me the way."

The man did so, first looking toward his captain's cabin, then sweeping an arm toward the steps that led down to the hold.

With one last glance at the brilliant blue sky, Logan headed for the steps.

They seemed to lead to blackness, to an abyss.

But one no darker than his heart.

To take risks was one thing.

To lose all…

Quite another.

His men had lived. And he thanked God that in all his years, even through his bouts of rage-inspired madness, he had never forced others to perish on any quest of his making.

He had never meant to sell his soul.

But as he descended into the darkness, he wondered if he had lost it anyway.

CHAPTER TWO

THE SOUND WAS haunting, would always be haunting...

There were hoofbeats coming like thunder. A slow rumble at first, like a tremor pulsing beneath the earth. With the first vibration, it seemed as if the birds screamed, followed by the rushing of the wind. The sound of the hoofbeats grew louder, the quivering of the earth, deeper. Then, a mere heartbeat later, the pounding hooves came ripping through grass and dirt, striking sparks off rock, shaking the world.

By the time the horses raced into view, there was screaming everywhere. People were running, desperate.

The thunder was upon them. As loud as if a bolt of lightning had struck the ground and blasted a hole through the globe.

Then...

A sword, glittering in the sun.

The blood, a cascade of it, gushing, flying...turning the blue day to red.

And the bodies...

Red awoke gasping, stunned and frightened, but aware that someone was there, someone with strong hands, and a frantic and yet somehow reassuring whisper.

"Stop. Don't scream."

Red let out a shaky sigh, gulping for air, but remained silent.

"You haven't had the nightmare in a long time."

Red nodded.

"It was the fight," Brendan said.

"I don't know what it was," Red said curtly.

"I do," Brendan said. "It was the duel."

Red was silent.

"Do you think he knows?" Brendan asked anxiously.

Red straightened and rose, escaping Brendan's touch, to pace the confines of the master's cabin.

"I don't know."

"You scared me to death, you know," Brendan said, getting to his feet, as well. He caught Red by the shoulders and looked into those striking blue eyes. "You could have been killed."

"I could have been killed a dozen times over the past few years," Red said.

That was true enough.

Brendan released Red and began pacing himself. "The fellow is clever, too clever. I mean, what fool transporting such treasure would dare such a brazen ploy? God knows, most pirates would not have bowed to such a bargain."

Red sank down on the elaborate sofa that flanked the handsome mahogany desk. "No?" The reply was dry. "I seem to recall successfully using a similar ploy against the great Blackbeard himself."

Brendan paused and stared at Red. "Blackbeard told me he was amazed when he met you, fascinated, and that he thought you such a *pretty* boy it amused him not to kill you. He seemed quite baffled by his own response."

"I beat even the great Edward Teach fairly," Red told him indignantly.

Brendan shook his head. "Only because at first he was laughing so hard that he underestimated you. He knew you were a woman, Bobbie. He admired you tremendously."

"A good thing, since he is still a friend and has kept my secret," she said sharply. "And that is the thing, Brendan. Most the fellows we run into are vermin-ridden and desperate men, keen on making their fortunes—yet easily swayed by a bottle of rum and a whore. But even those filthy, rotten-toothed knaves usually have a certain honor. Honor among thieves, if you will. But they have shown more honor than most of the supposedly respectable noblemen with whom we've come in contact. They adhere to the pirate's code of ethics. We did nothing less today."

"I fear he knows," Brendan said darkly.

"So what? Our whole crew knows," she pointed out.

"The whole crew worships you. You saved them from certain death," he reminded her. "An act you might have found yourself hanged for, by *law.*"

She shrugged. At the time, there had been nothing else to do. That had been her first act as a pirate. She had done exceptionally well, taking everything into consideration. "We might have died, as well. There was no guarantee for the future when we began. We were already impersonating others, even then."

A quick smile curled Brendan's lips. "You did go from being Lady Cuthbert to Red Robert with amazing speed. You could have done remarkably well on the stage."

Red had been smiling, as well, but now her smile faded. "Aye, and what good would a life on the stage do me? I'd be considered no more than a harlot at that, either."

"You would live to a grand old age, perhaps," Brendan said.

"That wouldn't be living. Brendan, I cannot forget…"

"That's evident. Your screams are terrible. I thank God I was able to transform that closet around the corner into a first-mate's chamber. If you scream so and I cannot stop you before you are heard, we will be in serious trouble."

"The nightmare hasn't come in almost a year," she said.

Brendan went to his knees at her feet, touching her cheek tenderly. "We are living a dangerous lie. A very dangerous lie."

She touched his face in return. "I'm all right. I swear it. I will not dream again."

"You can't know that! We need to—"

"Turn back?"

"Aye, Bobbie, we must turn back."

Roberta stood again. "I will never turn back."

"But, Bobbie…"

She stared at him, minus the dark wig, minus the boots and knives and pistols, the coat and the plumed hat. Her real hair was red, and it streamed down her back in soft glistening curls in the glow of the lamplight. She knew that, minus her trappings, she appeared almost frail and ethereal. She knew and loved her own crew, especially Hagar, who had been their friend before. They would never harm her, and they would die before they saw her harmed. But her facade was a strong one, because it was necessary. And no matter how she appeared in the dead of night, in truth, the ruthlessness she showed in pursuit of her cause, the strength and determination, were now the reality of who she was.

"There are no buts, Brendan. Now, beloved cousin, we both need to get some sleep."

"I still fear he knows," Brendan said dourly.

She smiled at him sweetly. "Then he'll have to die."

"I STILL SAY YOU take too many risks."

Logan was startled, in his prison below the deck, by the words he heard so clearly. He'd spent the last two days in a small hold, walled away from the cargo. At some point it might have been private quarters for a ship's officer, but now it was barren of anything—anything at all. It was a ten-by-ten wooden space, but there were two small horizontal windows, perhaps ten inches long and three inches high, and he had listened at them constantly, hearing whatever he could of the crew's conversations.

They hadn't said much. But after two days of solitude broken only by the arrival of a tray of food three times a day, along with fresh water and a small portion of rum, any conversation was, if not elucidating, at least momentarily entertaining.

He'd wondered frequently just how long his imprisonment would last. It was certainly not the worst punishment he might have received. No whips had been brought against his back, he hadn't been starved, or threatened with death or mutilation...but the monotony, after only two days, was numbing. He'd spent his first hours seeking a means of escape, then sought for one again, even when he realized there was but one door and it was kept closed by a massive lock. The crew were diligent and took no chances. Several armed men came to the door each time food was delivered.

He spent hours mock-dueling with himself with no sword, hours pacing the small confines, and hours thinking. The thinking he tried to stop. It led him nowhere.

This time, though, it was very late in the night, and the ship had been quiet for hours. And the voices he heard now belonged to Red Robert and his first mate, Brendan.

Red let out a soft chuckle. "Ah, but what is life *but* risk?"

"Yes, but up until now you've had a plan, and now...now you're risking your life."

"Brendan, stop this obsession. We risk our lives every morning when we awake and take a breath."

Brendan let out a sigh of aggravation.

"You shouldn't have kept the prisoner."

"I should have killed them all?"

"No." There was a silence. "Damned good ship, though, and you let it sail away."

"We don't need another ship."

"We didn't need a prisoner."

"What difference does his presence make? We may find someone willing to pay for his release."

"Right. He was out on the seas stealing from the ancients when we came upon him," Brendan said dryly.

"A man has to make his own fortune, but that doesn't mean there isn't someone out there willing to pay for his release."

Brendan grunted. "He'll go mad by the time you let him out."

"No harm has been done to him."

"Imprisonment can destroy the mind. You've left him with nothing. Not a book...not a thing. He can't even practice tying knots."

"Give a man a rope, he may hang himself," the captain pointed out.

"He's able-bodied."

"Too able-bodied," Red snapped.

"He could work."

"And he could escape. *Kill* someone and escape."

"He wouldn't," Brendan said.

I wouldn't?

"Oh?" Red asked.

"He's a man of his word."

"And he's given his word not to escape?"

"You haven't asked him for it."

"He isn't being tortured," Red said impatiently.

"He could be useful on deck."

"We don't need a deckhand."

Brendan sniffed. "We're not a large group, you know."

"Nor can we be."

"So we can use another deckhand."

Red groaned and fell silent.

"Look, when this began...I understood. But now... what exactly are you looking for?" Brendan's voice sounded both sad and serious.

There was silence, then a soft reply. "Revenge. It's what keeps me going. It's my only reason to stay alive."

He heard footsteps; then the captain called to one of the men, checking on the ship's heading. They were going in a southwesterly direction, and Logan couldn't help wondering why.

He leaned back against the wall thoughtfully. The captain was indeed young. But for one so young, there was something ageless in his outlook. Revenge, not life, was not the most worthy prize. How had one so young come to hate so much?

Maybe it wasn't all that difficult. Such was the wretchedness of life that many were born to endure. Some rose above it. Some barely survived it.

Some died.

And some became cutthroats, thieves and pirates.

But Red Robert...something about him was different. He was so small and almost...effete, extremely adept of course, but hardly...manly.

Logan leaned back in deeper thought, and in a few

minutes he knew he had to be right about the conclu-
sion he had come to.

But...*why?*

And just what revenge could drive someone to such
desperate measures?

Logan was cuffed when he was taken from his
cubicle in the cargo hold. Brendan apologized, as two
men took care of the actual shackling. "Sorry, my
friend. But we respect your talents, and thus...well, I'm
sure you understand."

Logan nodded gravely. "Thank you, *my friend.* I
will take that as a compliment."

Brendan shrugged. He led the way past the first
hold, with its guns, powder, crates of cargo and supplies, and crew hammocks, and then topside. Ah,
topside. Fresh air. It was clean and clear, and the breeze
was soft and beautiful. No rain was on the horizon, and
no storm clouds threatened the heavens. He was glad
for a minute just to stand there, to feel the embrace of
the sun.

But then a hand was clamped on his shoulder, and
he was led toward the aft cabin. Brendan knocked on
the door and received a crisp "Aye" from Captain
Robert.

Brendan nodded to Logan, indicating that he should
enter. As the door closed behind him, Logan found the
captain, fully dressed in breeches, shirt, vest, coat,
boots and hat, seated at a large mahogany desk and
writing with a quill pen. He did not look up at Logan's
entry, nor when he spoke.

"It's been brought to my attention that although your

welfare certainly means little enough, you might be of use on deck, though I confess I do not trust you. That being said, my mate seems to believe you would be willing to give your oath that you would make no foolish attempts at escape, were we to set you to work topside." The quill was set into the inkpot. The captain looked up at last. "Quite frankly, if you did try to escape, we would have to kill you. Not a great loss to us, I'm afraid, but as you are certainly adept with weapons, I would be loathe to lose a loyal crew member over you. The choice is yours."

Crisp words, hard spoken, no humor on the face, the facade quite effective.

"I don't even know where we are. I'm not at all sure where I could escape *to*. The waters of the Caribbean are warm, but vast," he replied.

"That's not exactly an oath. Try to escape now, and yes, you would die, one way or the other. And, as I said, it means little to us, since there's no guarantee we can gain any reward whatsoever for your life." The pirate was staring at him intently. Those eyes were…

Deep blue. And haunting.

"I give you my word, Captain, that I will not try to escape while working topside," Logan said, his tone as level and emotionless as the captain's.

The captain assessed him with a direct and emotionless stare. And then…just the slightest hint of a smile. "Good. It's laundry day."

"Laundry?" Logan said incredulously.

"Aye, laundry."

"But…we're at sea."

"Aye, that we are."

"But you'd be wasting good water!"

"What I waste is my concern. There is a Bible on the edge of my desk. Place your hand upon it and swear you will not try to escape." Again, a subtle smile upon the captain's lips. The young face could be gamine-like, delicate...beautiful, beneath the attempt at ruggedness. "*And* that you will do laundry." Red picked up the quill again and began to write. "And bathe."

"Bathe?" Logan inquired politely.

"There's a breeze today, you may have noticed. Otherwise, the Caribbean is quite hot. What many of my associates upon these seas have not noticed is that we seem to avoid the dangers of disease with greater success than others because we make every attempt to keep this vessel free from vermin, such as rats, and the lice that are prone to so enjoy the human scalp and body. When we are at anchor, by the islands, my men are quite fond of swimming. They have discovered that saltwater is excellent for whatever may be plaguing their skin. So, you will serve—and bathe—as one of us. Or you may rot back in the cargo hold."

"Captain, bathing does not at all dissuade me."

"And laundry?"

"It will be a new...adventure," he admitted.

"Adventure," Red mused. "Well, then. Swear. On the Bible."

"Do most of your captives believe in God, Captain?"

"Most men claim not to give a damn if the devil takes them, but I don't believe you're the average man.

Then again, at the point of death, a man's beliefs have a tendency to change. I've seen many a supposed disbeliever cry out to heaven when he knows his death is imminent. So, swear or return to the brig."

He picked up the Bible and gave his oath.

When he set it down he said, "Laundry…and bathing. I can only assume then, given that I have correctly ascertained our direction, we're heading for Nassau."

"Nassau, New Providence. You know it?" Red asked politely. "You don't appear to be the type of man who spends much time there."

"I've been there," Logan said.

"Well?" Red demanded, when Logan continued to stand there.

"Will I be allowed to go ashore?"

"Yes."

"How magnanimous of you."

Red turned those striking eyes full on him. "Pirates do have honor, as you keep pointing out to me. I will see to it that everyone is made aware that you are a captive and where you belong. Should you attempt to escape, any one of them would happily kill you, because we'll have a bounty on your head, a fair sum for your return—dead or alive," Red said pleasantly.

"That won't be necessary," Logan said.

"Really?"

"I have given my word. And, Captain, if you're curious, I do believe in God, in the hereafter and in purgatory. I prefer to spend my full share of years upon this earth, but I am not afraid to die."

"Bravo," Red said dryly.

"*You* are obviously not afraid to die," Logan said.

Red once again set down the quill. "You said it so well, Lord Haggerty. I would prefer to spend my time upon the earth, rather than beneath it—or as fish food, as might well be my fate. But I am not afraid of death. You may go now."

"I am handcuffed."

"So you are."

"It's difficult to do laundry in handcuffs."

"That matter will be rectified."

"Captain Red Robert..." Logan said musingly.

"What now?"

"You, too, do not seem to be the type of...man to spend time in New Providence."

"And why is that?"

"I've not seen all that many well-bathed gentlemen upon the island."

"I have certainly never claimed to be a gentleman, much less do I claim the title of 'lord.'"

"I definitely do claim it—it just doesn't mean a great deal."

"Many a man buys his bath on New Providence," Red said impatiently.

"Yes, and many other things." Logan grinned knowingly, as one man to another.

"Are you talking just to annoy me, or to avoid doing laundry?"

Logan smiled. "Well, it *is* in the articles of piracy that there should be no women aboard a ship. Bad luck, you know and brawls between the men."

"If you're asking me if you can buy a whore on the island, Lord Haggerty, you might want to recall that you are a captive, and as such, you have no coin."

Logan was still grinning. "That would be 'no,' then?"

"Do you wish to return to the brig?" Red demanded.

"Not at all. I am quite intrigued by the concept of laundry."

"Aye, I don't imagine a lord knows much about it."

"I pronounce it 'laird,'" Logan said, surprised by his own sudden irritability.

"A Scotsman, then?" Red said politely. "I had noticed the accent."

"Indeed."

Red stared at him. "No better than an Englishman, I'm afraid." Red's voice rose. "Brendan!"

The door opened; Brendan was waiting.

Logan cleared his throat and lifted his hands. "You have my word," he said seriously.

"Captain, seeing as the man has sworn, may I remove the shackles?"

Red Robert had returned to the quill and paper but gave a slight nod.

Brendan grinned. Logan realized the captain's right-hand man liked him, or at least respected him. He realized, as well, that Brendan bore a resemblance to the captain, or vice versa. They were both far too young for this life.

Then again, few grew old in it.

"Laundry, I'm afraid," Brendan said.

Logan shrugged. "Lead me to it."

SHE HEARD LAUGHTER on deck.

Laughter!

Red stood and walked to the cabin windows. Shifting the drape slightly aside, she stared at the improbable sight on deck. The men were teaching their prisoner the art of laundry.

He had already found himself a comfortable niche within the group, which told her that he was either a fearless idiot or very brave indeed. Either way, he was dangerous.

There was a knock at the door, which opened before Red could find out who was there or ask him to enter. It was Brendan.

"Aha!" he said. "You're spying on our captive."

"I'm the captain," Red said irritably. "I can spy on anyone I want."

"The captain." Brendan laughed, then sat, placing his feet up on her desk, at ease and amused. "He's quite a man, is he not?"

"Interesting, at least."

"And a good swordsman."

"Yes, I noticed." A finger rose to her cheek, as if on its own.

"It's a nick. It won't scar."

"I am scarred to the quick as it is, Brendan."

"Ah, but that's your soul, not your flesh."

Red shooed him away from the desk and sat herself. "We're heading for New Providence."

"Aye, that's been your course. But—"

"We can sell this new cargo there."

"We can get more for it in the colonies."

"I don't want to travel so far with this much treasure. Word of what we have will get out, and we'll be under attack by every untrustworthy sailor out there. It may be considered ill luck to attack a fellow pirate, but most of the time our peers are greedier than they are superstitious."

Brendan was silent for a while before changing the subject. "I know I have been tormenting you lately, but you must know this life we lead can't go on forever. How long do you plan to carry on this charade?"

"As long as it takes."

He leaned forward. "It grows more dangerous every day. And I don't like going into Nassau. It's a lair of the worst filth known to humanity. The fellow sharing your rum bottle one moment will gladly share his dagger the next."

"That's why the entire crew is careful and ever watchful of one another's backs," Red said.

Brendan shook his head. "You want to go to Nassau to see if you can't find out where *he's* heading."

"Of course."

Brendan fell silent again.

"Will you please stop fretting?" Red finally demanded, aggravated.

"Lately…lately I've been afraid, I admit. Look, we've done well…we could find some place, assume new identities…we could live decent lives. Real lives. There are places in America where we could disappear."

"It isn't about money, Brendan."

Brendan shook his head. "Bobbie, you know the

kind of man he is. He's going to be killed by someone, somewhere."

"Oh, really? He's managed to spend nearly two decades making his fortune off the terror and tragedy of others. Besides, I would prefer to kill him myself," Red said sharply. "And stop calling me Bobbie, please. I'm Captain Red."

Brendan looked aggravated. "You're Roberta, Bobbie to me, no matter what charade we're playing. We've survived this far together, but we used to be...you used to listen to me. I have a terrible feeling we've taken things too far."

The set of Red's features was stubborn. "Brendan," she said, and there was steel in her voice, as well as a certain compassion, "if you wish to quit, you may do so. I can set you ashore at a safe harbor of your choosing, and you can take passage on a ship to the colonies. You can claim to have been the victim of a kidnapping for all the time we've been at sea, God knows, it will not have been the first such time that has happened."

"Bobbie, God knows I have fought, and fought hard, at your side. I have risked my life, just as you have risked yours."

"No one has fought harder," she agreed.

"But I can't help but admit to this strange desire to survive."

"I want to survive, too. Instinct, I suppose."

"There is a life out there for you...somewhere."

"Brendan, what, in all the time that we have shared together, have I known that might be construed as an actual *life?*"

She saw the pain in his eyes. Brendan had shared so much with her from the beginning. Terror. Poverty. Servitude, threats, abuse, and an elite governing body that had turned its collective back upon them. She had finally discovered the only true kinship she had ever known among the pirate brethren.

Brendan rose suddenly. "Who knows? Maybe if our wretched old mistress had sent you off to a decent and compassionate—albeit old and disease-riddled— man, things would have been different."

She cast him a furious stare.

"What a wonderful suggestion, Brendan. I could have lived a wretched life as a syphilitic whore and then died a wretched death. I'll take a sword," she added softly.

"Bobbie—"

"Stop calling me Bobbie!"

"The men know your name."

"Our prisoner does not."

"The prisoner you've been spying on. If you're so intrigued, come out and join your men, Captain Red Robert."

"If you wish to be nothing but a pest, you should leave and enjoy the company of the prisoner and the men," Red said irritably.

"I'll do so," Brendan said, and grinned.

When he was gone, Red stared at the door, wondering why she felt so ridiculously annoyed. And worried. Brendan's certainty that they had taken their act-turned-real-life too far was beginning to make her uneasy despite herself. She gritted her teeth, looking at the lists she was preparing regarding the division of their take. The words seemed to swim before her. She was getting cabin fever. She had stayed locked up in her small realm on the ship for too long. She needed air.

Brendan's accusations were true. She *was* obsessed. But *he* was out there. And she meant to find him, to kill him, or die in the trying.

Blair Colm.

So many years had passed. But if she closed her eyes…

When she slept too sweetly…

She could see it all again as if it had happened just yesterday. They'd been but children then.

There were men who fought because they fought for a cause. Others sought riches, titles, to better themselves in life.

And some were simply cruel. Some enjoyed watching the pain they caused others. They considered it only a bonus that slicing men, women and children to death often came with a reward, as well. Blair Colm was one of those men.

It was amazing that she and Brendan had survived….

But there had been so many others to kill.

And so they had been sold into indentured servitude in the colonies instead.

She had hated Lady Fotherington almost as much as she had hated Blair Colm. Prim, bony, iron-haired, iron-willed, she had thought that indentured servants did best when beaten at least once a week. To her way of thinking, certain nationalities created beings of lesser value, and Roberta and Brendan were certainly that.

Red looked at her hands, and sniffed. It had not been difficult to play the part of a man as far as the delicacy of her hands went. She had spent her days scrubbing…anything from the hearth in the kitchen to Ellen Fotherington's hideous feet. The only kindness she had ever known had come from Ellen's spinster daughter, Lygia. As tall and thin and bony as her mother, she rarely spoke in front of anyone. Red had finished with her tasks late one night and slipped into the office that had belonged to the late Lord Fotherington, and had found Lygia there, reading. Red had been terrified, certain she would receive an extra beating, but the great rows of books had beckoned to her forever. Stammering, she had tried to think up an excuse, but Lygia had actually smiled, and the smile had made her, if not beautiful, compelling. "Shh. I'm not supposed to be here, either. I am supposed to follow other arts, such as music and dance, but I do so love my father's room. If only he had lived…."

He hadn't lived, however. He had died of a flux. And so Ellen Fotherington had come to rule the mansion in Charleston, where she entertained statesmen, lords, ladies, artists and the gentry. She ordered the finest merchandise from England and France, and tea all the way from China. She ruled her house like a despot, and her only regret in life was that her daughter resembled *her,* and not her dashing husband.

The promise of a fortune should have seen Lygia

well married, but she had read too many books over the years. She refused. She refused the young swains who were not old and ugly, but were only after her money. She refused the fellows who were so old they did not deem her ugly. Her mother had forced misery upon her, just as she did her servants, indentured, most of them, and little better than slaves. But Ellen had never been able to whip or bully Lygia into marriage.

So Red had been blessed with one friend. One who virtually gave her the world, because they shared a passion for books.

Ellen had a way of truly making slaves of her servants. If their time of servitude should come to completion, they were accused of taking something, using something...doing something. And so they owed her more time.

Red had seen many die in her service.

They had died because they had no hope. Their eyes had died long before their bodies had given out. Their spirits had perished. Mortal flesh could do nothing more than follow.

Ellen Fotherington did not hack people to pieces. She did not steal their birthrights. She took what made life most precious: freedom, and their very souls.

In Red's case, she had determined to curry favor by shipping her to France and giving her to a hideous little count with gout and a dozen other wretched diseases to use as he wished. Under lock and key, Red was sent back across the Atlantic.

It was then that Red Robert, the most deadly pirate on the high seas, had been born.

Red lowered her head, inhaling deeply. She steadied herself, and then almost smiled. The captain of a merchantman they had once seized off Savannah had told her that Ellen had died. Slowly. Painfully.

She did believe in God.

And it might have been the only time she had ever believed that God also believed in her, no matter how unChristian such a thought might be. Ellen, who had paraded her entire household to church every Sunday, deserved to be in hell. God could afford to be forgiving; she could not.

Still, Blair Colm, the man who had slain infants in front of her for the sake of expediency, was still alive, a fact that desperately needed to be rectified. God had allowed him to live far too long. God had allowed him to commit far too many atrocities.

God needed her help.

God had helped her create Red Robert, and so Red Robert would now help God rid the world of Blair Colm.

That was one way to look at things, anyway. It was a way of seeing the world that helped her to stay sane and committed to her path.

And now that she had started upon her path, there was no going back.

She would not give up this life—*could* not give up this life—until he was dead.

And so...

On to New Providence.

CHAPTER THREE

New Providence

To SAY THAT she glittered in the distance would be a
stretch. But there she was, big and bawdy, a place
where the shouts in the streets were loud enough to be
heard from a distance, where many a rogue kept a grand
lair in which to exercise his base desires. The wharf was
filled with boxes and barrels being loaded and un-
loaded; ships lay at anchor in the harbor, small boats
plying the shallows back and forth between them and
the shore. Women, tall and short, their skin of as many
colors as their brightly festooned clothing, walked the
muddy roads, past storefronts and taverns and huts,
most of them nearly a-tumble.

It was a beautiful day. The ship rested at anchor,
gently listing in the bay, beneath a sky that was just
kissed by soft white puffs of cloud. The breeze was
sweet and clean and caressing, at least out here, where
they still lay at ease upon the sea. Logan knew that there
were areas of New Providence where little could be
called sweet. Slop buckets were tossed out windows,
turning the roads to foul mud. And since the populace

leaned heavily toward drink, the stale scents of whiskey, rum and beer combined with the fumes of old pipe tobacco to make the resulting stench nauseating.

But from this distance it all looked merely colorful and exciting, even offering a strange charm with its straightforward, no-apology bawdiness.

A hand fell on his shoulder. "It's the isle of thieves, my friend," Brendan said.

"Aye, but honest thieves they be, eh?" Logan said.

"You've been here before?"

"I have."

Brendan stepped back, grinning as he looked at him. "What was a fine gentleman such as yourself doing among the riffraff of this island?"

"Bartering," Logan told him. He hiked his shoulders and let them fall. "I don't recall saying that I was a fine gentleman."

"*Lord* Haggerty?"

"We pronounce it 'laird,'" he told Brendan wearily.

Brendan arched a brow, his easy grin still in place. He was a strange enough fellow himself to be a pirate.

For one thing, his teeth were good.

Then again, it was passing strange that a shipful of burly outcasts should bathe and do laundry, though one of the toughest-looking of the group, Bill Thornton, known to one and all as Peg-leg, had told him that he found it amazing not to have caught the least fever nor been plagued by scabies since he'd taken up with Captain Red. In fact, the man had confessed, he was looking forward to seeing what soaps he might be able to buy in Nassau.

But Brendan...

Interesting man. As interesting as the captain. They were obviously related. Brendan was taller by a good five inches, though the captain—despite the heeled boots—was not short. Brendan stood well over six feet, and had the shoulders of a man who was long accustomed to using his muscles. He was in excellent shape. His features were nowhere near as fine as the captain's, his eyes a paler blue, his jaw far more square. At times, he brooded. When caught in the act, he was quick with a ribald comment or an off-the-cuff remark. He'd shown himself keenly interested in what was going on in the colonies, his interest greatest regarding the more southern cities, such as Charleston and Savannah.

He was friendly. And through that friendliness, Logan had come to know the others. Hagar was like a huge watchdog, a burly man, towering over even Brendan and himself. His hands were massive, his thighs were like tree trunks, and his chest could vie with a barrel. But Hagar, too, was a decent enough fellow, with a fine sense of humor. All seemed to worship the captain, rather than just honor Red Robert.

"As you wish. *Laird* Haggerty, we are about to make shore. Next boat, my good man."

The *Eagle,* as the ship had been dubbed by the pirates, who had changed her name from that which the previous captain had given her, was equipped with two tenders for loading and unloading supplies and cargo, and also boasted two smaller, sleeker ones. The tenders had headed to shore first, with Hagar in charge, and now the first of them was being lowered for those who would follow, Peg-leg, Brendan, Captain Red and Logan, with another huge crewman, Silent Sam, a strapping Iroquois, at the oars.

As the men stood there, ready to make the descent, Red Robert made an appearance in customary attire: high black boots, white shirt, brocade vest, black coat, and plumed, low-riding hat. There was a knife set in the flap in each boot, and a low-riding leather belt carried a blunderbuss and a double-barreled pistol. A sword in a leather sheath hung from the same belt.

Red Robert was prepared.

"Are you ready for New Providence, Laird Haggerty?" Red Robert asked.

"I know New Providence," Logan reminded the pirate captain.

"But it changes, you see," the pirate said. "It changes literally with the wind, for the mood of the town follows that of whichever king of thieves is in port." Red Robert nodded at Brendan.

"My *laird,*" Brendan said to Logan, offering a sweeping bow and gesturing him to precede them into the tender.

Logan nimbly crawled over the rail and onto the rope ladder that led down to the small boat, where Silent Sam was already waiting at the oars. Logan jumped the last few feet, feeling the tender rock beneath him, and easily took a seat. He watched as the others followed.

"So, you'll sell my cargo here?" he asked Red and Brendan when they'd taken their seats.

"Every man out there will know I have it soon

enough. Better to rid myself of dangerous riches. Pieces of eight are easier to manage," Red said with a shrug.

"I could have gotten you much more for it elsewhere," Logan said.

"Pity. That's the way it goes," the pirate captain replied.

Logan tried a different tactic. "This is quite a dangerous place to conduct business."

"And have you, despite your current state, come ashore for business?" Red asked.

"I have. But I'm not…" His voice trailed off, and he turned to face the wharf.

"You're not what?" He was startled as Red's gloved hand fell on his knee. The wary anger in the deep blue eyes that met his was disturbing.

"I'm not a pirate."

"The hell you're not," Red said, settling back.

"Well, he's not," Brendan commented.

"Oh, really? He is at least a thief, for was this treasure not already stolen before it came to us?"

Logan stared back at Red but said nothing.

"You do not protest?" Red asked.

"No. Point taken."

The tender drew up to an extension of the wooden dock. Hagar and several of the others were there, waiting.

"Is he here?" Red asked.

Hagar nodded. "Awaiting you at the Cock's Crow."

"Fine. And the cargo?"

"Already at the tavern, Cap'n," Hagar said. "All

know you're the rightful owner, all are considering their bids, should he decide not to buy."

"Fine. Skeleton crew is holding the ship, you know your orders." Red started down the wharf with Brendan. Curious, Logan followed.

Chickens skittered across the dirt road, flapping and clucking as they walked. *"Gardez l'eau!"* someone called out, and they stepped aside in time to miss the contents of a chamber pot. Red strode on with confidence, and Logan noticed men calling out in greeting, all with respectful tips of the hat or touches to the forehead. Red never did more than nod in return.

"Amazing," Logan said to Brendan.

"What's that?"

"I've never seen a group of such derelicts show such respect to another man...even Blackbeard," Logan muttered.

"Red took down the devil, you see," Brendan said quietly.

Logan realized that the other didn't intend for his words to be overheard and answered equally softly.

"The devil?"

"Ever hear of Black Luke?"

Logan frowned. The man had been the terror of the seas, feared and loathed even by other pirates.

Usually a pirate's intent was not to sink a ship or to kill the crew. Ships were valuable. They were usually taken and added to a pirate's fleet. Men were killed only when they refused to surrender, for the captured ships needed crews.

Black Luke had sunk more ships than most men saw in a lifetime. He had never allowed a captured man to live. He had tortured his captives. His men had not voted, as was the pirate way, nor received their fair share of any treasure. There would have been a mutiny, had they not been so terrified for their lives. It had been said that he had eyes in the back of his head. One of his men had once tried to kill him when he had been sleeping. Black Luke had arisen to grab him by the neck and throw him into the sea.

"*Red* killed Black Luke?" Logan asked incredulously.

"Yes."

"How?"

"Talent. And a hell of a lot of luck," Brendan said.

"Were you there?"

Brendan's jaw was as tight as a hangman's noose. "Yes," he said after a moment.

"I can't believe it."

"Believe it."

"I'd heard a rumor that Black Luke was dead, but no one ever seemed to know if it was true, or, if so, how he died," Logan said.

Brendan was staring straight ahead, clearly unwilling to explain.

A door burst open, and a man came flying out of an establishment with peeling white paint and shuttered windows that were open to the day. He was followed by a woman with a mass of wild black hair, bare feet, a low cotton bodice and a multicolored skirt with the hem of a dirty petticoat peeking out from beneath it.

"Take yer filthy paws elsewhere, y' varmint!" she shouted. "My girls are not cheap!"

"Your girls are whores!" the fellow yelled in return.

"But they're not *cheap* whores, and they'll not be taking on the likes of you for nowt. Get away with ye." She paused, a smile splitting her face as she saw Red. "Captain Robert," she said, her tone delighted.

"Aye, Sonya, we're in port. Is Edward about?" Red asked.

"He said ye'd be here. He's a room ready fer yer negotiating in the back. Brendan, poppet," she crooned. "And...what have we here?" she asked with a wink, her gaze moving admiringly over Logan.

She walked up to him quickly with a sway in her steps but stopped short of touching him.

"Why, it's Laird Haggerty," she said with another smile.

That stopped Red, Logan noticed.

"Aye, Sonya. A pleasure," he said, and dipped his hat.

Red was staring at him with an expression that plainly said, *Men. Naturally, he knows the island's harlots.*

Sonya frowned. "You are...sailing...together?" she said incredulously.

"Laird Haggerty is our guest at the moment," Brendan said. His tone, though pleasant enough, indicated that she should ask no more. Then he clapped a hand on Logan's back. "To the rum, eh?" he said.

"To the rum," Logan agreed. He was certain he had

no other choice. But as they entered the noisy, smoke-filled tavern, he could not help but watch Captain Red Robert as the pirate walked toward the rear of the dubious establishment.

"Sonya knows you?" Brendan asked, a wicked gleam in his eye.

"I sail to all the known ports," Logan said.

"Seeking treasure?" Brendan asked skeptically.

"I sell and trade," Logan said, and looked away. "And, of course…every sailor seeks information," he added.

"Information?" Brendan pursued.

"It's wise for all of us to know what happens on the seas. Which…captains sail where."

"Ah. Pity, you didn't hear about our whereabouts, then."

"Pity," Logan agreed.

"LITTLE GIRL! WELCOME!"

The man already entrenched behind one of the tavern's rickety wood tables in the rear corner of the place was huge. His double-breasted jacket was open, as was his cotton shirt, and grandiose lace spilled out over his velvet vest.

Edward Teach, popularly known as Blackbeard, was fond of ostentatious clothing, as strange a contrast as it made with his thick dark hair, formidable size and ruggedly lined features. He was a sensual man, with full lips, large hands and a barrel-deep laugh.

Red cast him a look of baleful warning.

"Ah, think you that the lot of drunks beyond this wall can hear a bloody blessed thing over all their cater-wauling and so-called music and whoring, missy?"

"There are always those who long to topple the successful from power, and you know it," Red reminded him, sliding the chair opposite him out from the table with her foot. As soon as she sat, he reached across the table and took her hands.

"As you wish, Cap'n Red, so it will be. In the darkest of night, in solitude and to the heavens. Cap'n Red. That be that."

"I brought you treasure."

"I steal treasure for a living, as well you know." He arched a brow. "I agreed to meet you here to consider your offer to join forces, not to buy treasure."

She waved a hand in the air. "This is an exceptional treasure."

"Oh?"

"Spanish treasure."

He laughed. "Well, it's sorry I am to say it, but the English have not come up with much treasure. The Spanish are the ones known to be wiping out whole populations and taking what they won't be needing anymore, since they're all dead."

"The English did not claim the lands where gold was to be found," she said. "But, apparently, certain English nobles were willing to pay highly for this treasure. You've seen what I've brought. The pieces and the jewels are exquisite."

"Aye, I've seen what you brought. And it's fine indeed."

"Of course. So you'll offer me negotiable gold for it?"

"I am an exceptional sea thief myself. I can steal my own treasure."

"But this one will cost you half its worth—and not a man to boot. You won't waste a ball or shell, you will not have to let loose a single cannon. You can obtain this rare treasure at an unusually low cost in time, effort and life."

"I like you, and you know it. And I think you should live and take your pretty arse out of all this," he said, nodding seriously.

She smiled. He was one of the most feared men to sail the seas. He knew what she had instinctively fathomed: perception was of far greater value than truth. Not that he hadn't slain his share of opponents, and not that he couldn't be ruthless, but he didn't kill every man he captured, and he was very fond of women. In fact, he had married many of them.

He didn't believe in divorce, but then, his marriages were hardly legal anyway. He was generous and kind with his women, though, and preferred a simple disappearing act to anything more fatal.

"I heard that you chased Blair Colm," she said flatly.

He stared back at her and sighed. "Aye, I saw the man."

She leaned closer. "The ship—or the man himself?"

He leaned in, as well. His beard, in which he took great pride, lay upon the table, with strings tied here and there through it. He liked to light hempen fuses when he went into battle, where he would appear to smoke and nearly burn, an image that filled the hearts of his opponents with terror.

"I saw the man clearly with my spyglass. He has a fine ship. A frigate. He's modified her, but she still can't handle the shallows as a good sloop can. I might have been outgunned, so I did not draw so great a vessel against me. And perhaps he has heard that my reputation is beginning to equal that of any wretch upon the seas, for he had no taste for battle, either. He caught the wind with his mighty sails, and he was gone. He knew he'd find no mercy from me."

"A frigate," Red said. She loved her sloop, but a frigate...was huge. It could carry tons of powder, shot and guns. It could not give chase into the shallows or maneuver narrow channels. But it the open, it was deadly.

"You need to be staying away from him," Teach said.

"You know why I cannot." She met his eyes and asked, "Where did you see him?"

"He was heading north along the coast. I daresay he will hover near the towns and cities where he is honored by the British. Word is that he is looking for you, too. He believes that you stole one of his most valuable possessions."

"How can anyone honor such a man? I do not believe the people can possibly know what a heinous murderer he is."

He caught her hand. "One man kills, and he is a hero. Another kills, and he is a monster. It depends on which side of the battle line one is standing. You are a monster to some. When a man doesn't see something with his own eyes, he doesn't know what is truth, so he believes what becomes legend. Ah, come, girl. The average man wants only to live in peace, so he prays that conflict will not come his way. He is willing to accept the truth of what he is told is the rightful law rather than fight for anything that might disturb his world. Your monster is considered a great military commander by those with whom he does his business in England and the colonies. All anyone there knows is that he helped win the day for King William of Orange and the great empire. Had the war been lost, he would have gone down in history as an ogre. But the English crown was triumphant, and therefore, he is an honored man. Such is history, poppet. It's the deceit I loathe. I don't set out to kill a man. I do so because he is in my way and won't get out of it. My reputation is far worse than my deeds. I prefer scaring a man into surrender. Sadly, there are good men out there ready to die for honor. I don't relish killing them. And unlike Blair Colm, I do not butcher women and children."

"As far as the women go, you just marry them," Red reminded him with a grin.

"Why waste a lovely lass?" he inquired.

"Most of the children turn to piracy."

"I ransom what children I can."

Red looked down, smiling. She wondered what Edward Teach might have become, had he not wound up sailing the high seas. He did have a personal code of ethics.

"Of course."

"And when no one wants them…I do them no harm.

And I'll have you know, they're still hanging children all nice and legal in some ports for offenses not much worse than stealing bread. I'm not a cruel man at all, when you look at the world around me, and see what is done in the name of law and justice."

"I've never said that you were a cruel man. You are a fine captain and swordsman, and you're a wicked shot with a pistol," she said in a tone of genuine compliment. He grunted his pleasure as she continued. "But you are a performer, with that black beard spewing flame and smoke."

He wagged a finger at her. "*You* are the performer." He shook his head. "And to think, if what I heard is true, that a little bit like you killed Black Luke."

She shrugged. "Have you ever seen a tiny insect bite grow infected? Before you know it, a giant roaring fellow is down and dying of fever. Size is not always the deciding factor in a fight."

"Well, I'll take your treasure. I'm quite fond of a number of the trinkets, and I happen to be decently flush with pieces of eight at the moment."

"And what of joining me?" she asked softly.

"That is another matter."

"Oh?"

"You're out for vengeance. I'm out for profit. And how did you come by this treasure, pray tell?"

"I came upon a merchant ship that didn't have a prayer against me."

"So you took the ship?"

She shook her head. "No."

"You sank it?" he asked incredulously.

"No."

"Oh?"

"We parleyed. I now have the captain with me, as my prisoner. He is a Lord Haggerty. Ever hear of the man?" Red asked.

Blackbeard leaned back, grinning. "Aye. I know the fellow. I've met with him in this very tavern."

"But he isn't a pirate."

"No. Neither is he military. He sails a merchant ship."

"Still, he is no outlaw. What was he doing here?" Red demanded.

"Business."

"Treasure?"

Blackbeard laughed. "Nay, poppet. He came to sell what makes a life fine. The finest feather pillows. Silk sheets. Porcelain from China. Tea. Coffee. Apples."

"And he wasn't simply killed in the streets here?" Red asked, amazed.

"I had the opportunity to watch the first time he came. He strode in with his crew, right bold, and when he was challenged, he demanded that he be met man to man. After he bested three of the doughtiest fellows on the isle, I considered challenging him. But, I confess, I was intrigued by his brashness in dropping anchor in the bay, and then stepping foot on land. He was well aware, however, that no quarter would be given to him on the seas if he traveled with merchandise and was caught."

"I didn't give him quarter," Red snapped.

"So he took you in through eloquence as well?" Blackbeard teased.

"He is my prisoner," she said.

"Of course."

She decided to change the subject. "So, I seek revenge, I admit it. And you seek plunder. If we were to go after Blair Colm together—"

"Poppet, give it up."

Red groaned. "Good God, not you, too."

He lifted her chin with his massive forefinger. "I will die on deck. I will die at the point of a sword, or by an enemy volley. That is how it must be. Until then, I will terrorize the sea, I will have a dozen more wives, and I will drink and challenge every man I meet, and mayhap even God. But you…that shouldn't be your life."

"Why not? I would rather die at sea than scrub another floor or be forced to bed some pox-ridden old man or die myself of his venereal disease," she said, deadly serious.

"Ah, but don't you dream of something better?" he queried.

"My dreams are of corpses on a battlefield, the blood of children slain," she said.

He sighed and leaned back. "Sorry, poppet. I'm not suicidal. I won't join my forces to yours, but I will give you gold and buy you rum, eh?"

"Cap'n Blackbeard," she said, determined not to sound disappointed, "I will be honored to lift a glass with you."

He shook his head. "Ah, and you speak like a lady, lass."

"Maybe I was a lady. Once. Past memory, past caring.

God knows, I was so young when the troops came. I remember…"

"Aye?"

"My mother," she said, blushing slightly. "Aye, she was a lady. So softly spoken, so regal…but she is gone, dead and gone, and so is the life I was born to. There is nothing to return to of the life I lived then. But…I have not lost faith in all humanity. There was Lygia."

"Lygia?" he repeated.

"The daughter of the witch who bought my indenture papers from the officer who decided I was worth more alive than dead," she said. "She was ugly as sin, but as sweet and kind as her mother was cold and cruel. We'll drink to her! I imagine she is rich now, with her mother's passing. May she find happiness at last."

"To Lygia. Bless the lass!" he said. "Rich, you say. How ugly was she?"

Red laughed, lifting her glass high. "Quite. But who knows? With enough darkness and enough rum, the ugliest lass may become the fairest. Especially if she is rich. Or so I've heard men say."

He looked at her strangely as he drank his rum.

"Curious…"

"What?"

"That it is *you* who came upon Laird Haggerty."

"Why is that?"

"Ah, poppet. I keep your secrets, but I keep his, as well."

"He has secrets?"

"He has…an agenda."

"And?"

"I just said, I keep a man's secrets."

"Edward…"

"Don't you go wheedling me, girl. I have said all I shall upon that topic. Men come to this tavern for amusement. For whores and for drink. And to listen."

"Listen to what?"

"I've said all I will say."

"But you keep giving me clues!"

"I shall say no more. Drink up."

She tried, but he had made up his mind, and he would say no more. So they drank. She would have her promised gold, and there it would end.

THERE WERE MANY MEN in the shanty tavern so drunk they wouldn't have noticed an earthquake. Some lay on tables in the puddles of their own ale. Whores sat atop the laps of others, mindless of the drunkards snoring nearby. Bodices slipped, hands ran up under skirts and ribald shouting and jokes filled the air, along with the stench of old meat, stale tobacco and unwashed bodies.

Logan turned to Brendan. "Nice place," he commented dryly.

"Aye, and obviously you know it well," Brendan said, his tone equally dry.

Logan shrugged. "You and the captain don't look the type to…appreciate such an establishment," Logan said.

"Nor do you."

"I come for business, then leave."

"There's no legitimate business done here."

Logan had to laugh. "Actually, there is. I certainly

didn't intend to run into a pirate vessel on the high seas, but dealing with pirates on land can be quite profitable."

"And very bad business, as well," Brendan commented, eying Logan carefully. "You do know something about the art of negotiation, my friend. But there are those who don't wish to negotiate. I've met many a fellow who cares nothing for human life. Expediency is what rules. Many a pirate captain would gladly have slit the throat of every man on your crew—or saved steel and bullets and simply tossed them all overboard."

"But not without great loss of life and limb, even if I would have gone down fighting," Logan informed him.

"True enough. So…" Brendan stared at him still. "A man of honor, are you?"

"And your captain's a pirate of honor," Logan returned.

"We'll drink to he—him," Brendan said, lifting his glass.

"What business has the captain with Blackbeard?" Logan asked.

Brendan looked back at him, weighing the risks of sharing information with a captive. "The captain wishes to join forces with Teach."

"With Teach?" Logan was startled. He knew himself that Teach was crafty, but not nearly so cruel as his carefully crafted reputation would have others believe. Teach didn't hesitate to kill when necessary, but he was far more prone to let a man live when possible.

He never relished killing the innocent, as did some fellows on the sea.

Knowing what he knew, Logan couldn't but feel that Captain Red Robert...should not be partnering with the notorious Edward Teach.

His honor urged him to leap up, stride into the private room where the two were meeting and demand Teach unhand the *woman* known as Red Robert. But the impulse was pure insanity, he knew. He had battled Red. She could hold her own. She didn't need nor want his protection.

And, should he attempt to give it, he would no doubt find himself skewered through the heart or the liver, perhaps even castrated, but certainly, in whatever manner, left dead or dying.

Still, it was hard to remain sitting upon the raw wooden stool where he was perched, and warning himself not to be an idiot wasn't much help. Yet surely, if there were something to fear, Brendan would not be sitting beside him so calmly, sipping his ale.

Hagar came up to the bar just then. "Brendan," he said, offering a nod to Logan. "Ye'll be needing to talk to the cap'n. Ship's carpenter has warned, we've got to careen her. Soon."

Brendan frowned, as if warning Hagar to speak softly on such a matter.

Since pirates couldn't simply take their ships into a port and have them dry-docked, it was necessary to take them to a secluded place where they could be "careened," hauled ashore and rolled to each side, so that the hull could be scraped of barnacles and tarred against woodworm. It was a dangerous procedure, for it left both the ship and her crew vulnerable. Most pirates, Logan knew, did only one side of a ship at a time. It was too easy for others to discover that a ship was lying vulnerable, and even if other privateers left her alone, there was always the law to fear. The governors of the various colonies were always pleased to increase their popularity by sending out their naval officers to bring down a pirate, and a hanging was a full day's entertainment for most.

"Aye," Brendan said, and Hagar nodded, aware that it wasn't something Brendan wanted to discuss in their present circumstance.

When Hagar moved on to answer the taunting call of a bare-breasted woman, Logan commented casually, "I take it the fellow has not long been a pirate?"

Brendan ran a finger up and down the heavy glass that held his ale. "You're a decent fellow, Lord Haggerty. If you want to live long and prosper, you shouldn't ask so many questions."

"I've given my word. I won't be trying to escape."

A dry smile curled Brendan's lips. "Aye, but you see, we intend not only to let you live, but to see to it that you are returned to your people, whether there be a fine ransom paid or no. Too much information is not good for a man who will return to the world where the king's law holds sway."

"The king's law," Logan repeated, his tone hinting of bitterness. "There are no doubt good men in that world, but I have never been deceived. Laws are made by those in power. And what men do when they gain power is too often far removed from any law of decency, justice or humanity…far from any law made by God." He turned, then slid from his stool, surprised to see that the door to the private room where Red had been meeting with Blackbeard was open.

"Where is Teach?" he asked Brendan sharply.

Brendan turned. Both the massive Blackbeard and Red were gone. The room was empty of all but its rough wood table and chairs.

"How the hell did we miss a man such as Blackbeard?" Logan asked, unable to believe he had forgotten to pay strict attention.

"He would never harm Red," Brendan said, but he sounded anxious, as well.

He might have been the prisoner, but Logan started for the door. To his surprise, Sonya was suddenly in front of him, setting her palm on his chest, splaying out her fingers.

"Lord Haggerty, don't be in such a hurry," she drawled.

He hesitated, looking at her. He'd never fooled with the whores in this place, though he'd tipped well enough for his drinks. But she knew he wasn't interested in what she had to offer.

She was trying to keep him from leaving.

"Brendan, we need to go," he said sharply.

"What?" Brendan asked.

"Sonya knows something. In fact, I'd say someone paid her to stop us," he said softly, looking into the woman's eyes.

She flushed, lowering her thick lashes.

"Nay, 'tis only that I live by the profits of this place," she said, sounding a little desperate.

"I doubt if any man is brave enough to go after Blackbeard," Logan said. "So who paid you to keep us here so that they could go after Captain Red Robert?"

She stepped away, but he caught her arms and dragged her back.

"Sonya?"

"I don't know!" she snapped. "Some fellow…he gave me gold," she said, as if that would explain everything.

He moved her firmly aside and looked at Brendan. "I haven't figured out what Red Robert is so bent on achieving, nor do I know who or why, but someone is after Red."

Brendan stared at him, then turned toward the door. Logan caught his arm. "We're in this together," he told him quietly. "And may I suggest you call your man Hagar, as well?"

Brendan, face taut, nodded stiffly. For a moment he'd had a reckless look in his eyes. He was a formidable man, tall and muscled, but agile, and his concern would have sent him off without heed, but Logan's words reined in his impulse to rush out alone. He sized Logan up carefully while shouting, "Hagar, gather who you can. We're going after the cap'n. Now!"

They moved out. There were narrow alleys to either side of the tavern, both now dark and menacing, filled with shadows and gloom. Each led into smaller, darker alleys, little craters of blackness that could hide many a sin. Ghostly laundry hung in the darkening mist of the day. A dog howled as the wind picked up, and the screeching cry of a cat sent shivers up Logan's back. A scurrying sound warned them of rats.

The day was no longer what it had been.

The clear sky had gone dark. The breeze had gone chill and brisk, whispering with the coming rain. The clouds overhead billowed and rushed.

A storm was coming, and coming hard.

A perfect shield...

For a surprise attack.

A man stood leaning against one of the supports that held the bar upright, his head on his chest as if he had fallen asleep in a drunken stupor. "Which way?" Logan demanded.

The fellow didn't move.

Logan shook him, and he opened one bleary eye. But Logan didn't believe he was so far gone.

He shook the man harder.

"Which way?" he asked again.

"I don't know."

"Tell me, or I'll slit you from the groin up," Logan said evenly.

"The alley."

"Which alley?" Logan demanded.

"The alley to the left. Cap'n Robert went that way not five minutes past. The...others came out a bit after."

"How many?" Logan demanded.

The man shrugged.

"How many?" Logan repeated, his tone still low, but filled with a menacing promise.

"Eight...ten..."

Brendan was already running into the shadows.

Logan released his hold on the drunk and followed.

And the storm broke.

CHAPTER FOUR

RED KNEW SHE was being followed, and she listened carefully.

It was exactly what she had expected. No, hoped for.

But as she pretended to saunter along, weaving a bit, as if she had drunk heavily, she listened hard and damned the weather. The rain had started. The sky had threatened that it would come down in buckets, but as yet, it was just an annoying and continual fall, darkening the world and making it hard for her to listen. She couldn't tell how many were following. She had assumed it would be just one man. Maybe two. But there were more than that behind her, she knew.

Blair Colm did not know who she was. He knew only that the pirate Red Robert had a reputation for horrible ferocity.

And that Red Robert was looking for him.

And *she* knew that despite his cruelty, Blair Colm had always been a coward.

When she left Teach, she had seen Sonya taking a coin from a man. She'd tested it, but Sonya was a businesswoman—she knew real gold when she saw it. Red didn't even hate Sonya for the betrayal. The woman's life was hard. She hated most men. She'd crawled her way to the top of the heap by lifting her skirts for sex in dark corners, turning her face from the putrid breath of unwashed men. Red couldn't hate her.

Maybe she had grown too complacent in her own skills, Red thought now. A sad miscalculation, since she had lost to Logan Haggerty. But he had been different. There was—or usually was—little to fear from other pirates. They passed at sea and saluted one another. They shared dens of iniquity, like the one she had just left. They brawled and wenched and drank, but they seldom picked battles with one another. They shared one bond, the ever-present image of the hangman's noose. No need to battle one another.

But Red had wanted to be followed, for there could have been only one reason for it. And now she knew. Blair Colm had spent a great deal of money to send men out to murder Captain Red Robert.

But now she began to count the footsteps and lament her own reckless determination to see Blair Colm dead. There were at least six men behind her. They would have to be the most drunken, poorest swordsmen in the world to fall victim to her alone. She damned her own stupidity and confidence—her belief that she could best her pursuers in any duel and demand to know from them where Colm was headed now, where he might be found.

She hadn't asked Brendan or any of the men to go with her, for a coward who had taken money to kill would not have followed her if she had been accompanied.

She simply hadn't believed there would be so many.

Ahead, a white sheet billowed as the alley widened, and she hurried beyond it, knowing she had to pick a place to make her stand.

And so she did, checking the line that held the laundry as she held her position, barely daring to breathe, and waited.

She heard the footsteps, coming closer now, moving faster.

"Where's he gone?" came a whisper, just audible in the night.

A flash of lightning illuminated the sky for a split second.

From her vantage point atop a step just beyond the line, Red saw the men. Eight. Two were leaning upon one another, and one of those two carried a bottle of rum. They weren't there to fight; they were just waiting for the kill.

None of them was well-armed. They were debris, she determined. Refuse that had found its way to the island. There was only one—a tall, muscular man, wearing a brace of pistols, his cutlass at the ready— who appeared to offer any real danger. He was bald beneath his sweeping hat, and one of his eyes was made of glass. Though the alley was dark, she could see that; slivers of moonlight caught on it, casting a glint of reflection. That was good. She would attack from the left.

Full darkness seemed to fall when the lightning dimmed. It was time.

With a violent thrust, she set the line of sheets flying. Several of the fellows were toppled immediately. She leapt from the step, her cutlass waving as she strode through the confusion. Easiest first to wind the men into the sheet. More of them fell. But then she discovered a man at her back, ready to skewer her, and when she turned to parry his attack, she saw the bald fellow moving toward her, as well.

From a window above, there was the sound of life at last.

"Glory, what be happening down there?" a woman called out shrilly.

"Battle in the alley! Close the shutters, woman," came a masculine reply.

Lights flickered from above, and were quickly doused. She could hear the slamming of shutters on both sides of the alley now. Apparently none of the residents of this sorry place meant to become embroiled.

She would not be receiving any assistance from them.

She leapt over the tangle of men seeking to free themselves from the sheets just as a third man came at her, followed by a fourth.

She slashed her blade at him, then caught hold of what remained of the laundry line and used it to swing to the far side of the alley to face the remaining three.

She sheathed her cutlass, drew her pistols and fired both simultaneously. She caught one man in the leg and winged the other in the shoulder. But as they fell, two others at last dislodged themselves from the sheets and joined the fray.

Without time to reload, she went for her cutlass again and crouched, finding the knife lodged in the sheath of her left boot. Her aim was swift and sure, and one attacker went down with the blade caught in his shoulder.

Still another fought free of the sheets. It was the sot who had been holding the rum bottle, and he looked sober now. And lethal.

She was dead, she decided, overcome with bitterness and regret. She had expected so little from life. Even so, she had not thought it would end in a filthy alley on a dead man's isle.

"Take the flanks!" the bald man called to his companions.

They planned to back her against the wall, she realized, then come at her from three sides.

She would do as much damage as she could before going down, she resolved.

Would God forgive her for the life she had led? she wondered vaguely.

Was God even there? Where had He been when her family was slain?

But as the bald man walked toward her, taking his time, grinning, she was stunned to hear the loud volley of a gun.

And suddenly the overconfident bald attacker was no longer walking toward her. His one good eye was wide, and then blood burst from his chest, like red tears, for the rain was growing harder, and it mingled with the blood.

The two coming at her from the side froze as the night came alive with shouting and the thunder of footfalls. Brendan was there, Hagar, Peg-leg —and their prisoner.

Her other attackers finally fought free from the sheets, and the wounded men staggered up, desperate to survive. She was left alone at the wall as her attackers and her crew went to battle, deadly and swift. One man tried to run, but Peg-leg was not a man who was prone to mercy. He went after the coward, and the swordplay that ensued was swift. In moments her would-be murderer fell dead in the rush of blood that spewed from his throat.

And then her crew was standing still in the dark alley, looking around, seeking new combatants.

But there were none. They were all on the ground, unmoving.

"Red!" Brendan cried and rushed forward. She saw the terrible inner battle he fought, trying not to reach for her, longing to draw her against him in relief.

"I'm well, good fellows, and I give you my deepest thanks," she said, as Peg-leg clapped her on the shoulder.

"Sorry," he said quickly, realizing how much force he had used. "Aye, but, Cap'n, you were holding your own so fine."

"So fine," Logan Haggerty repeated. She looked at him and could see the contempt in his eyes. She would have died if they hadn't come, no matter how fine she might have been doing. And he… He was a prisoner. But he had come with the others, and had fought well and…loyally?

"Captain Red, what the bloody hell…?" Hagar asked, shaking his head and breaking into her thoughts.

"Let's hope someone is alive to tell the tale," she said, and realized she was shaking. How strange. She hadn't feared death—she really hadn't—though she had hated the fact that she would die before accomplishing her goal. But now...

Now she suddenly knew how badly she wanted to live. Not for vengeance. She wanted to see the sun again, taste the rain, know the feel of the waves beneath her, plunge into a warm sea, read more books...

Feel a human touch that was gentle and tender...

Change that look of contempt upon Logan Haggerty's face.

She gritted her teeth and willed the shaking to stop. She had not come so far to be diminished by the look of a man who had unjustly condemned her as a fool.

"Find someone living in this scramble," she commanded sharply.

As her men moved about the alley, checking the downed men for signs of life, the shutters above them began to open. Lamplight flickered again, making the mist in the air shimmer mysteriously.

"Dead," Hagar announced, rolling over a body.

"This one, too," Peg-leg said.

"Not this one," Logan announced, dragging a man to his feet.

The survivor was skinny, and wore only a shirt, breeches, worn boots and a sword belt that barely clung around his narrow hips. His sword was still sheathed. There wasn't a mark on him.

"Please," he whimpered. "I caused no injury to any of you. I was...I was caught. I was tangled in the sheets."

"You played dead, you mean," Logan said bluntly.

"I...I..."

"Who sent you?" Red demanded.

"I, um...that fellow. The bald man over there. He paid us all. He found us back at Ha'penny Hattie's, and he paid us to follow him down the alley. That's all." He slipped to his knees, looking up beseechingly, his hands folded in desperate prayer. "I was just drinking me rotgut there, I swear it, and the money...as you can see, I'm not a prosperous man."

Red was about to turn away in disgust.

"But you *are* a lying one," Logan said, catching the fellow by his shirt collar and dragging him relentlessly to his feet. "Who paid the bald man?"

"I don't know!" the skinny man screeched.

"You do," Logan said flatly.

"He'll kill me!" their captive implored.

"He's dead," Brendan pointed out.

"No, no, not the bald man..."

"It's all right," Red said. "I know who sent him."

Their captive's eyes were all but bulged out of their skeletal sockets. "I didn't tell you. I didn't tell you!"

"He *may* kill you. I *definitely* will," Logan threatened softly.

Red shook her head. "Don't bother. It was Blair Colm."

Logan stared at her sharply, and she had no idea what was going on in his mind as he watched her. It seemed for a moment as if time had stopped.

"Oh, God!" the skinny man screamed, going limp.

"Is he here? Is he somewhere near here?" Red demanded.

The man slumped down again, but Logan dragged him back up. "Answer the captain," he said.

The fellow just shook his head, moaning.

"Answer," Logan persisted menacingly.

"I—I...no. He's headed north. He's heading up to the Carolinas." He looked up at them at last. "He's...he's no pirate, you know. They welcome him at fancy tables. He's free to sail wherever he chooses and...kill and loot at will. Because he does so for the governors and the Crown, and he's somehow..." He shook his head. He was no longer hoping to hide anything from them. Maybe he wasn't even hoping to survive anymore. "I have never known another man so utterly ruthless and brutal. He's invincible, and you might as well kill me now, and I can only pray you will do so mercifully."

"How will he know you were hired by the bald man?" Red asked.

"He'll know," the terrified man whispered. "There is talk. There is always talk. Tomorrow they will be talking about the fight tonight."

"How did he hire you? Was he here recently?" Brendan demanded.

"No...months ago, he paid the bald man. One-eyed Joe. That's what I heard. And he promised a great reward. That's all I know. I swear it."

"Fight?" Hagar snorted. "Intended execution, more like."

"No one thought Red Robert would go down without taking a few men with him," the fellow said mournfully. "That's why there were so many of us.

This island is hell, my friends, and in hell, people always talk, and there is nowhere to run."

Hagar looked at Red. "We can't take him with us. The man is a coward."

"I was caught in the sheets!" the fellow implored.

"Can't trust him," Peg-leg said.

"We have to kill him," Hagar said.

The man began to moan softly again.

"Oh, shut up," Brendan snapped.

A door opened somewhere nearby. People were beginning to venture out.

"Pick up the good weapons," Red said quietly, and Peg-leg and Hagar hurried to do so, before those who had cowered in their rooms above could come down and, like vultures, prey upon the dead.

Red turned. A man was working at one of the fallen assailant's boots.

"I don't have shoes," he said simply.

Red nodded. "Aye, then, take what you need—except the weapons. The weapons are ours. And see to the bodies."

She started walking slowly away.

"What about him?" Brendan called after her.

She turned, not sure what to say. She couldn't order the man's death. He was right; he was probably a dead man anyway. He was hardly trustworthy. But he couldn't really hurt them in any way.

Before she could open her mouth, he cried out, "Wait! I can cook. I'm a good cook. Meals are wretched at sea, but I can keep meat fresh longer than any man alive, I can mix grog, and I know a recipe that keeps away the scurvy, too."

"Any man can make grog," Hagar said. "Rum, lemon and water."

"But mine is the right combination. Keeps the growth from the water, makes it good and sweet for drinking. And I know spices and herbs. Take me on as a cook. Please," he begged.

"He'll hide in any battle," Hagar warned.

"He can hide down by the guns, then," Red said. "Are you capable of priming and loading a cannon."

"I am."

"What's your name?"

"O'Hara. Jimmy O'Hara. Once an Irishman, never an Orangeman. No country of my own."

She lowered her eyes for a moment. Time had passed, years, and this was a different world....

"Take him on," she said.

When she started walking quickly toward the wharf, unwilling to stay ashore and determined to take the tender back to the ship, she found Brendan by her side.

And Logan Haggerty on the other.

Hagar and Peg-leg brought up the rear, Jimmy O'Hara between them.

And now, even as the rain fell harder, the alley came alive. All those who had cowered in their rooms above were down in the street.

The bodies of the fallen would be picked clean of whatever coins and trinkets, pipes and tobacco, they might have been carrying in their pockets. Boots and clothes, if in any kind of repair, would be stripped. She could only hope the bodies would be buried, as well.

Most probably they would be, she told herself. The residents wouldn't want to live with the smell once the sun rose in the morning and the stench of decay set in.

"Where are you going?" Brendan asked softly. "I thought you had taken rooms."

"The men may enjoy their shore leave, as promised. I'm returning to the ship. Tomorrow we'll take on supplies. Then we'll head north."

"And what about O'Hara?" Brendan asked.

She shrugged. "We'll see if he can cook."

"But he tried to kill you," Brendan reminded her.

"No. He came along because he needed money."

"What if he plans on poisoning us all?" Brendan asked quietly.

She smiled. "Well, we have Lord Haggerty, don't we?"

"Ship's taster," Logan said, not glancing her way.

"Red…" Brendan began.

"Don't worry. I don't believe he's a poisoner. Neither does our good captain," Logan said, then looked at Red at last. "I strive to please."

She stared back at him for a long while. She liked the man, and she hated that she did. Pirates' honor, indeed. Logan had his own code. He could have escaped tonight. Instead, he had fought for her, and fought well and hard.

"Ransom or no, we will set *Laird* Haggerty free in the Carolinas," she said.

He was still staring at her.

"You have earned your freedom," she said simply.

He smiled slowly. "Have I?" he asked softly. "Perhaps I played this game tonight because I knew the other side would lose."

"We'd not have found you without Laird Haggerty," Brendan said. "He threatened Sonya, and then a drunk, to find out where you'd gone. And he was the marksman who killed their leader."

"You might have missed—and gotten me," Red said.

"I don't miss," he assured her.

"Too bad he isn't a pirate, eh?" Brendan said, and stepped between them, slipping an arm around both their shoulders.

"Too bad," she mused dryly.

And too bad that she was.

Better than her other options, she thought, then wished she had never set eyes on Laird Logan Haggerty and his ship.

LOGAN SAT ON DECK, idly tossing bits of dried fish to one of the ship's cats, a tabby he'd grown quite fond of. The animal was called Rat because he was so efficient at ridding the hold of the creatures who would otherwise ravage their food stores. Rat had a harem of females who did his work with him. He was a huge beast, never afraid, and most of the crew steered clear of him. Rat had an affinity for the captain, though, and Red could pick up the cat and he would purr. The animal was as loyal to their captain as the best hound could ever be.

As were her men.

Those who appeared to have come from some kind of finer life, and those who seemed to have been born swabbies.

Peg-leg was in the captain's cabin. Logan had just finished repairing a tear in the mainsail and was about to tar a gap in the hold, but even prisoners were given a luncheon break.

Especially prisoners who had been offered further shore leave but had chosen to return. In fact, being quite fond of his health, he had resisted the entertainments offered by Sonya and her fellows, and had been pleased to return to the ship. Their supplies were being loaded even now, and he had to admit that their new cook, Jimmy O'Hara, seemed to have a good idea of how to buy salt and store meat and the rest of their provisions. He'd tasted the fellow's grog, and it was damned good and even left a fellow with a stable mind. Such a man could be a valuable asset, for he'd heard of far more pirate attacks for simple necessities than he had for gold. Pirates could not put into any port. Meat went bad easily. Weevils tore apart wheat, bread and rice.

A cook—one who could keep food from spoiling aboard ship—was as valuable as a carpenter.

Jimmy had set up a grill on the deck, where he had prepared filets of local fresh fish for the crew. He hadn't lied when he said he had a way with seasonings. Old rice and fresh fish had been turned into a meal fit for a king. If a few weevils had made their way into the rice, they'd been masked by the parsley and saffron the cook had acquired.

Logan been feeling ridiculously content and sated when he had first sat down to play with the cat and rest a spell. But now the lethargy was gone. He was alert, his senses heightened, as he listened to Red discussing her plans with Peg-leg.

"We'll lose the lead we have," Red said.

"Captain, I told you before, we'll be sinking to Davy Jones's locker if we don't take the time to keep our ship afloat," Peg-leg said.

There was silence.

"You should have taken Laird Haggerty's ship," Peg-leg said with a sigh.

"No. This is a finer ship, and better equipped with guns. She was already a pirate vessel."

"Black Luke's vessel," Peg-leg muttered.

"Black Luke's vessel," the captain agreed. "She has speed and guns. She can hide, she can outrun almost anything out there, and she can dare the shallows where most others wouldn't have a prayer. No, she's our ship."

"Then we need to keep her in shape," Peg-leg insisted.

Again there was silence.

Red's regret was almost palpable when she said, "As you wish. But now we're freshly loaded—"

"And I can brace the cargo when we haul her ashore," Peg-leg assured her. "You're not forgetting what you saved me from, Red, and not forgetting that I'd lie down and die—give up me good leg, if need be—for you."

"I know, my friend, I know," Red said softly.

"'Cause you're far from a fool, lass," Peg-leg said.

Lass?

Did the entire crew know that they were sailing beneath a woman? Curious. Most pirates thought it was bad luck to keep a woman aboard. Oh, they had slipped through here and there, those females seeking something they could not find in the regimented life their sex was condemned to on land, but most of the time, if discovered, women were not welcome.

But this was unlike anything he had heard of before. This was...

Red Robert.

He winced. He had thought that, even if he wasn't blindly, insanely in love with her, he loved Cassandra. He *did* love her. Of course, he loved her. There was everything to love about her. She was beautiful, kind, patient, and she had a gentle personality that was still lively and fun. He enjoyed her company. She was so right for the life he had envisioned for himself....

And at this moment, he couldn't recall her features.

It was insane. He certainly wasn't seduced by any other woman, definitely not a hardened soul masquerading as a pirate. No, it was no masquerade. Red *was* a pirate. He had seen her command her crew. He'd fought her. He knew she could be tough, even ruthless.

But he'd seen her eyes, as well.

He'd seen the pain that slipped past the armor. What caused it?

And why in hell did he care?

He had kept his honor, as she had kept hers. He would be released. She would play out her charade until the day came when she was killed. And by then he would be a free man. With luck, perhaps even a rich one. Ready to marry. To return to Scotland and claim his ancestral home....

Did he really still want that life?

Yes. He owed it to those whose blood had been shed for it. Even if now the possibility of reclaiming his birthright would not come with arms, war and trumpets, but with a simple act of unity, forged because the rightful Scottish queen was the rightful English queen, and parliaments agreed.

His muscles tensed, as they so often did when he let himself think of the past. He understood the hatred. Oddly enough, the man both he and Captain Red so despised would *not* understand.

Blair Colm had no soul. He lived for his own selfish pleasures, for money, power and his creature comforts. His heart was ice, and he had no qualms about killing children, women, the sick, the weak or the elderly.

He enjoyed the pain of others. And despite that, it was true that he could walk about the colonies a free man. If someone were to take a knife to his throat on the streets of Richmond or Charleston, that someone would hang for murder. He'd often thought about that himself, afraid that he would not be able to help himself. That he would attack the man and kill him with his bare hands.

And then hang for it.

Then again, perhaps it was not so hard to believe after all. In his own homeland, women still went to the stake to be burned as witches, and men could still be hanged for stealing a mere loaf of bread or a few coins. As recently as the "Glorious Revolution" that had raised William of Orange to the throne of England, they were hanging witches in the northern American colonies. It was a harsh world. Perhaps it was no surprise that a monster like Blair Colm could so freely roam the streets.

Or that pirates could actually have a stronger sense of honor than so-called honest men.

He wondered why that all seemed so clear to him now.

They were still anchored outside New Providence. The storm that had broken last night was gone. The misting rain had become a deluge during the late hours of the night, but now the sky was crystal blue and beautiful, and the sea was sweetly calm.

The breeze was gentle, like a soft kiss against his cheeks.

And all he had thought he knew about the world had changed.

He wasn't seduced, but he *was* intrigued. Or perhaps obsessed.

No, he told himself. It was no such thing. It was just curiosity to know what had driven the woman to such extremes.

"Curiosity killed the cat, so they say," he whispered softly to Rat. The cat had been extremely cautious of him at first. Hostile, actually. But Logan had gone out of his way to befriend the beast.

Why?

Because the cat and the captain were close?

The door to the captain's cabin was opening. Peg-leg came out, and saw him there. The man's eyes bulged, and Logan knew Peg-leg was afraid his conversation with Red had been overheard.

Logan laid a finger across his lips.

Peg-leg frowned and quickly closed the door behind him.

"What are you doing here, man?" Peg-leg demanded, but since he was whispering, afraid of being overheard by the captain, his bluster didn't carry much force.

"Resting," Logan said, and smiled.

Peg-leg wagged a finger at him. "You…you didn't hear…" He paused and let out a gruff sigh. "What did you hear?"

"Nothing I didn't already know," Logan said softly.

Peg-leg swore.

"There's no problem," Logan assured him.

"But there is!"

"Oh?"

"Now we have to kill you, and we all like you, Laird Haggerty."

Logan couldn't help but laugh. They weren't going to kill him.

She would never allow it. She hadn't even been able to condemn a man who had been hired to kill her.

"Stop that," Peg-leg implored, still whispering.

Logan sobered; the man was genuinely upset.

"I will never tell. On my soul, on my honor, before God," he swore.

Peg-leg eased back, his balled fists relaxing.

"Do all men aboard know the truth?" Logan asked.

Peg-leg hesitated, then nodded.

"You cannot understand…."

"But I would like to."

Peg-leg looked around. The men in view were busy at simple tasks. Silent Sam was adding a layer of varnish to the mainmast, while two others were busy repairing the portside rail. A man was up in the crow's nest, sanding the wood in preparation for a new coat of paint.

"Come," Peg-leg said.

Logan arched a brow.

"I'll tell you the story of Red Robert."

CHAPTER FIVE

PEG-LEG HAD BEEN gone for several minutes, and still Red continued to stare at the door, frustrated.

She was certain that if they just sailed at full speed...

But she knew she had put off the necessary job of careening the ship because she had been too determined for too long that her quarry was just over the next horizon. It was almost as if he knew where she was and was careful to stay a step ahead.

She frowned, tapping her quill idly upon the desk. It was too bad that Blackbeard would not join her, but she understood that he was a man with his own plan, and that plan was to enrich Edward Teach. She needed to be glad he was her friend.

There was a tap on the door. She instinctively checked her hat, which kept the dark wig she wore fixed securely upon her head. But when she bade the visitor to enter, it was only Brendan.

"Small boats are arriving with supplies," he told her.

"Good. Do you have the manifest?"

"I do."

He handed her the sheet. She smiled again, thinking about Teach. He had given her a hefty quantity of gold.

She had duly purchased a hefty quantity of supplies. Glancing over the sheet, she saw that all she had asked for had been acquired, down to the scented soap. A luxury she could not afford with a prisoner on board, but...

She had sworn she would release him. And she would do so.

The sooner the better, she thought. She felt him watching her far too often. And she was afraid he saw far too clearly. She was also irritated that he continued to prove himself an admirable man.

Brendan cleared his throat.

"What?"

"A letter for you made its way to the tavern."

"Oh?" she said, looking at her cousin, who'd apparently read it already.

"It's an offer of ransom."

Her heart skipped a beat. She was a pirate captain. She had demanded a ransom for Laird Haggerty, and his men had seen to it that a letter had made its way to New Providence. Like letters had probably been sent to Jamaica and every other likely port.

She read the letter quickly.

To the pirate captain known as Red Robert,
Dear Sir,
It has been brought to our attention that you are a man who honors his word. As you are holding something dearer to our hearts than gold, we are glad to believe in his good health and safety. We

are willing to offer whatever price you require for the safe return of Laird Logan Haggerty. As this is not a business to be handled through regular channels, please reply via the same channels as this missive was received.
Sincerely,
The Right Honorable Lord Horatio Bethany, and, in the case of my illness, death, or incapacity, with equal assurance, Lady Cassandra Bethany

She hadn't realized her fingers had tightened on the page until Brendan warned lightly, "You'll rip it."

"I'll write a reply directly, assuring them that there need be no further correspondence, and that the good captain will be released at our earliest convenience."

"What about the ransom?"

She tried to shrug nonchalantly. "We are owed nothing. He proved his valor."

"But they are *offering* a ransom."

"Brendan—"

"The men will think you have grown soft."

"The men will remember how often I save their lives."

"Red, let's face it. We're really not in the business of taking ships and treasure, but even so, you have a reputation to uphold."

"And let my reputation be that I honor a man of honor. Pirate or no."

Brendan rolled his eyes. "I knew *I* should have been captain." She looked at him, arching a brow. "All right, cousin, I admit you saved my life. But you must admit that I was doing well, thanks to Lygia."

He shrugged. "Write your letter, then, so it can be left."

Brendan closed the door as he left the master's cabin. Black Luke's cabin, once upon a time.

But, when he was gone, she didn't dwell on Black Luke. She looked at the letter, and her fingers trembled. The letter had been written with love. Logan Haggerty had a home, a safe port, a place where he was esteemed and admired. He was not a man who would ever hang.

He had…

Cassandra.

Of course he did. No man who looked as he did could be without a sweetheart.

Impatiently, she dipped her plume into the ink and began to write. She would do as she had promised, as she should.

But it hurt. And she was angry with herself for that, because she was a realist, and she knew all about the harsh truths of life.

Still, she couldn't help wondering. Did he love his no-doubt adoring Cassandra in return? Did he dream of her by night, and in those dreams, did he touch her and hold her tenderly in his arms?

What would life be like if she knew such tenderness? With even just a sweet whispered hint of passion… of love?

His was a world she could never know. She must write the letter. Get the man off her ship. Remember her quest…

"THE SEA IS A HARSH and cruel mistress, we all know that, lad," Peg-leg said, looking out over the bow.

It was true, Logan thought. He knew the sea, knew it could be hard, cold and treacherous. But at the moment, it couldn't have been more beautiful. At a distance, Nassau, New Providence, even looked enchanting, the colorful shanties near the shore, the rise and fall of the landscape beyond.

"And not just the sea, but the men who sail her, as well," Peg-leg said.

Logan turned, crossed his arms over his chest, leaned back against the rail and stared at Peg-leg. "The *men?*" he asked politely. They were, after all, discussing, Captain Red Robert.

Peg-leg appeared distressed.

"Your tale?" Logan prompted. "What made Red a pirate?"

Peg-leg sighed deeply. He looked toward the captain's cabin, clearly afraid he had given her away. His look was protective and sad; he deeply admired his captain.

"I told you, I already knew Red was a woman. I will be far more likely to remember at all times to keep the secret if I can truly understand it," Logan told him.

Another sigh followed.

"Peg-leg?"

Peg-leg looked off into the distance, as if he were seeing a different time and a different place.

"I was working a merchantman at the time. The ship was under hire by a certain Lady Ellen Fotherington. Do you know the name?" Peg-leg asked him.

Surprised, Logan hesitated.

"Yes, mean old broomstick of a woman," he admitted at last. "Her husband was a fine enough man. I met him upon many an occasion in a tavern by the water in Charleston. But he died when I was young, and I met her but once or twice. She passed away in the last year, so I heard."

Peg-leg wagged a finger at him. "Goes to show, perhaps, 'tis true that only the good die young, because she was not a good woman and, sadly, she did not die young."

"She is dead now," Logan said pragmatically.

"Well, 'tis a long story, but the short of it is that she had rights over the future of a certain young woman. Our Red. Well, no matter how rich and high that wretched Lady Fotherington might have been, she always wanted to be richer. Oh, she was a harridan, and I'm glad you met her, because elsewise, I might not have the power to explain properly."

Logan knew that Lady Fotherington had been fond of taking on indentured servants, although she owned slaves, too. But she knew how to turn her indentured servants into slaves, as well, creating debts they must also pay, accusing them of some crime. Logan had seen it done all too often. Indeed, had he not found himself, by chance and good fortune, in the home of such a man as Master George Delaney, he himself might have suffered a similar fate before reaching his majority. He'd been bitter and resentful, fighting like a wild cat, when he'd first arrived in the colonies; only Delaney's kindness had changed his course in life.

"Red was a prisoner on this particular merchant-man, which was captained by a fellow named Nimsby. Nimsby was an evil man, and he was cheap," Peg-leg continued. "He was hard on his crew, though, quick to take the cat-o'-nine-tails to the back of any man who committed any infraction. He never traveled with enough men—and he never traveled with enough guns. He'd been known to carry human cargo from Africa, and he allowed little room for anything that could not make him money. I was in his employ because I'd been taken off another ship and it was sign on with Captain Nimsby or…well, take my chance with a trial and the hangman. I've not often seen trials go well in the colonies. On this particular trip, Nimsby was carrying molasses and a few other staples home to mother England before going south to Africa, then east to the Caribbean and back to Charleston again, his customary route. He'd been given quite a fair sum by Lady Fother-ington to deliver one particular piece of cargo to France—that being the woman you now know as Red Robert. It was on leaving Charleston, just out of the shipping lanes, that we were beset."

"By pirates?" Logan queried.

"By pirates led by a beast," Peg-leg assured him.

"A crew captained by Black Luke?"

Peg-leg nodded gravely. "The very same. I had seen Red, of course, but barely. She'd been brought aboard by two burly fellows who saw her into the captain's cabin, and she was kept there under lock and key."

"Did this Nimsby…assault her in any way?" Logan asked, furious at the thought.

"Oh, no. Nimsby was far too fond of gold to go against the Lady Fotherington's wishes. Red was destined for an aging French count."

"Who?" Logan inquired curiously.

"Le Comte de Veille."

Logan grimaced. The fellow had just perished at eighty-plus. He had gone through several wives, dozens of mistresses and, by reputation at least, hundreds of whores. He was said to have been pock-marked so deeply that he was barely recognizable as human, unable to walk and suffering the insanity of late-stage syphilis.

"Was she a relative? Perhaps a niece?"

"No. She was *bought*. She was meant for the bed of the Comte de Veille," Peg-leg said, horrified.

Logan shuddered, thanking God that Red had escaped such a fate. "Go on. How did a Frenchman's...mistress, locked in a cabin, become the pirate Red Robert?"

"Desperation," Peg-leg said. "And love," he added sadly.

"She was in love?" Logan asked with a frown.

"Young master Brendan is her cousin. Surely you have discerned that they are related," Peg-leg said.

Logan nodded. "She...wasn't in love with her cousin, was she?"

Peg-leg's look of absolute indignation was humbling.

"They'd been together as children, working in the household of Lady Fotherington. He'd been sent to fetch and carry and work on the merchantman, but he was an able and quick lad, and some of the crew grew quickly fond of him. He had a knack with a sword. He said there had been a groom back in the colonies who had enjoyed teaching the children the art of fencing when the old harridan was about on other business. There was a daughter, you see, Lygia. And she was the very soul of kindness. When her mother wasn't at home, she saw to it that all the children received some special treat, the slaves and the indentured servants both. She loved fencing and reading and the like, so…young Brendan knew how to handle a sword."

"And then…?"

"Then bad went to worse," Peg-leg assured him.

"Pray, go on."

Peg-leg sighed. "Black Luke bore down upon us. Nimsby felt he had nothing to fear, as he was good friends with a man named Blair Colm. He—"

"I know the name," Logan interrupted curtly. "And not only because he sent those men after Red."

"Well, then, you know he is known to travel with plenty of guns, and any pirate who has ventured to attack him has gone to the depths of the sea or had his head parted from his shoulders. His friendship with Nimsby had saved the man before, but this time Nimsby had placed himself in the path of Black Luke. Black Luke was a pirate's pirate. He didn't care who Nimsby knew, nor did he intend to sink the merchant-man. He wanted to seize her, and all who were aboard." Peg-leg took a deep breath, then went on. "When the firing started, Nimsby was preoccupied. I took it upon myself to unlock the master's cabin, and I warned the girl within that we were under attack by a pirate, and that she must look to herself. Nimsby was killed almost immediately, when cannon fire brought down the mizzenmast. Then Black Luke boarded, and we were all a-fightin' for our lives. Young Brendan was proving himself such an able combatant that he was cornered by several of the vermin from the pirate ship, and then Black Luke himself. All looked bleak indeed, I can tell you. Then, suddenly, this force of fury comes streaking out of the captain's cabin, cutlass waving madly. It all happened so fast.... There was a whir of motion, and then suddenly Black Luke was dead. He'd turned and roared he was about to cut down a little louse, thinking that Red was the man she'd dressed up to be. But he underestimated her. She'd taken her swing before he could finish his words.

"That's what I meant by love. The brigand had been about to kill her cousin, and that had given her the strength she needed. I think she was as stunned as anyone. Everyone just went still. When we looked around...there were mostly dead folks, and the ship was sinking. Without Black Luke, the pirates were suddenly trying to make it back to their own ship, but there weren't enough of them left to man her. Suddenly the girl who had been locked in the captain's cabin and come out like the wrath of God was shouting orders. The pirates who weren't dead believed that Black Luke had been slain by another pirate held captive in the captain's cabin, and they were set into the merchantman's longboats to make it to shore if they could. And Red took over this ship, just as we have her now.

Those of us on the crew who survived…Silent Sam, myself…and a few others, well, we swore to honor her, and so did Hagar, who'd been sent to tend to her and Brendan by Lady Fotherington. We'd been serving the likes of the wretched Nimsby and nearly died because he'd not had enough guns. It…was easy to serve her. And to keep her secret."

"So…none of you were pirates before?"

"The cooper and the ship's carpenter…they were from Black Luke's ship. But they were both grateful not be serving beneath Black Luke, and they proved to be fine men. So…we started sailing the seas. We made up a dandy flag, and we all vowed to go by the pirates' articles, as set down years ago by Bartholomew Roberts. We've not needed to fight near as often as you might think. Folks usually give over to a pirate ship with surprising speed.

"You must never give her away, Laird Haggerty. Never. I'd have to kill you," Peg-leg assured him, adding softly, "Or die trying, at the very least."

"I would never give her away."

"Even once you've been ransomed yourself?"

"I would never give her away. I swear," he vowed.

"Thank God," Peg-leg said, and scratched his head. "I'm not so sure I *could* kill you. You're pretty handy with a blade yourself. And you've never been a-pirating, eh?"

"Maybe we're all pirates in a way, Peg-leg, seeking something we don't have."

"Now what would a laird need with pirating ways?"

"A good question. I might ask a similar one. I don't see our captain as a greedy vixen sailing the seas for riches," he said.

Peg-leg shrugged, turning away.

"What is her argument with Blair Colm?" Logan asked the man's back.

"That is a tale I cannot tell," Peg-leg turned and said solemnly.

"And why not?"

"Because I do not know it," Peg-leg said. "You see, young laird, I did not say that I *would* not tell you, only that I *cannot*."

"If she is after him, I would gladly sail with her until he is found," Logan said.

Peg-leg studied him a long moment. "And glad I'd be to fight at your side, Laird Haggerty. But I believe she intends to set you free as soon as it might be done."

"But the ship needs careening," Logan said.

Peg-leg actually blushed a furious shade of red. "She's a good ship," he muttered, embarrassed that he had most certainly been overheard.

"So…it will be a while," Logan said.

"So it will. Who knows what may come?" Peg-leg said. "The sea…always a wicked mistress, eh? Tempting with her beauty and her promise, deadly in her vengeance."

Was he truly speaking of the sea? Logan wondered, and thought of their captain instead. Her eyes were just as Peg-leg had just described the water they sailed. As blue as a clear sky at times, then deep and indigo, roiling like a tempest at others.

"Today the ocean is at peace," Peg-leg said grate-fully.

"Aye. Today...she is serene and lovely. Gentle and sweet," Logan said. What had he been thinking? Red Robert was never at peace. She was always torn within, so it seemed.

Peg-leg studied him seriously once again. "Well, we shall see."

"So we shall," Logan agreed.

THE CARGO HOLD was filled, and the anchor was raised. The breeze was picking up, filling the majestic sails, and the ship set out to sea as if she rode above the clouds.

He worked the mainsail with Silent Sam and Peg-leg at his side. At the bow, Red Robert stood, hands clasped behind her back, as she faced the wind. She had learned to ride the waves, and she swayed ever so slightly, as if she were one with the ship. She didn't shout out orders; she spoke them to Brendan, who called them out to the crew. They were headed north, on a path that would eventually lead them up the Florida coast to Georgia, and then to the outer banks of the Carolinas. Logan was convinced at first that she didn't intend to bend to Peg-leg's plea that they careen the ship for cleaning, but as they neared northern Florida, he began to recognize a number of the islands, and he realized she must know of some safe haven where they could go to make the necessary repairs.

The day had been perfect. It wasn't until nightfall that Logan first felt the shift in the wind, which came with a sudden cooling. The day had been hot, the heat eased only by the sweet rush of the breeze. At dusk, he felt the difference, and he saw that several of the men seemed to notice something amiss, as well.

He was pondering the weather when he found Brendan at his side.

"Captain Red would have a word with you, Laird Haggerty," Brendan told him.

"Oh?"

"Captain's cabin."

He nodded. He had just donned his coat against the chill, and he followed Brendan with his shirt duly tucked, his hair queued, his vest in order and his boots polished. He entered her cabin when she bade him to and stood before her desk, waiting for her to look up. While he stood there, he examined the books lining the shelves. Most were sea charts, logs and navigational manuals, but there were works of fiction, as well. He couldn't help but wonder if Red hadn't added to the library that had once been Black Luke's.

"It has been drawn to my unhappy attention that the ship must receive maintenance," Red said without looking up. She dipped her quill into the ink and continued writing in what appeared to be a log.

"So it goes with ships," he said.

She glanced up at that. "I'm assuming, Laird Haggerty, that you have brought your ships into dry dock, but I'm afraid that's not a possibility for us, as you can well imagine. I had hoped to see you safely set upon an island in the Outer Banks within days, but I'm afraid that will be out of the question until we've completed repairs."

"I'm at your disposal," he replied with dry humor.

"Hmm," Red murmured, returning to her writing. "I received a letter today. A Lord Bethany—and a Lady Cassandra Bethany—have offered to pay for your safe return."

Logan didn't know why he found that information so disheartening.

"They are good people," he said simply.

"I left a reply. Good people are apparently not above finding those who are willing to enter pirate towns. The letter came through the Cock's Crow."

He smiled slightly at that. "Captain, I have been in that tavern before, as you know. I am glad that you will receive the ransom."

Red studied him for a moment. "I left a reply that you would be left safely ashore. We are asking no ransom."

"That's quite generous of you."

"You are apparently quite dear to Lord Bethany—and his daughter. I thought you should know."

It was curious that she seemed to be expecting something from him.

He was silent for a moment. "Thank you," he said. It was almost a question.

"Lady Cassandra Bethany. Is she your fiancée?" she asked. The tone was casual, as she set quill to ink once again.

"Not at this time."

Red looked up again. "Ah. Perhaps your beloved?"

"A very dear friend."

"A proper young lady?"

"Quite proper, yes. Why do you ask?"

Red set down the quill and sat back, a half smile curving her lips. "I'm sorry. I'm just imagining your life. The drawing rooms, the elegance. A proper young woman. Ah, but proper can mean so many things among the wealthy. Proper—she's rich. Proper—she has a title. A proper marriage would no doubt provide a wonderful advancement in your social status."

The words were like nails raking down his back. *Proper* could be all those things. But if he'd had his own doubts about sincerely being *in* love, rather than feeling an infatuation and an affection for someone, the taunting words of the captain were like knife cuts against his soul. He found himself taking a step closer to her desk and leaning both hands upon it. "She is proper in every way, Captain Robert."

Red laughed suddenly. "Does that mean she's as ugly as sin?"

He shook his head. He could be honest. "No. She's a striking beauty, truly. Eyes like emeralds, and hair as blond and rich as gold. That is the truth. But even did she not have such a lovely visage, it wouldn't matter. She has a certain purity of heart, a sweet humor, and is ever willing to help anyone downtrodden or in danger. There is truly nothing ill to be said of her."

"Well, I hope you will both be very happy. It sounds as if you make a perfect match. I had not previously imagined such a thing could really be, I admit," Red said, and the laughter was gone. There was no taunt to the words.

Yes, we *should* be perfect together, he thought.

And yet…

What was missing? Whatever it was, he had come to realize that Cassandra certainly deserved far more than what he could give, something that had nothing to do with lands or riches.

"That's all, Laird Haggerty," Red said.

"Pardon?"

"That's all. You may leave."

He bowed and exited the cabin. As he closed the door, he felt the further drop in temperature and realized with a certainty that a storm was coming.

In the distance, he could see a sheet of rain across the eastern sky. He didn't know how many miles off the storm was, but it was going to be severe when it arrived.

Brendan was striding toward him with a frown furrowing his brow.

He nodded curtly to Logan; he was anxious to reach the captain's cabin.

"A storm is coming," Logan said.

"Aye."

"We need to lower the sails."

"Aye."

Red had sensed the change from inside her cabin; she emerged now and stood by the door, as if smelling the air and feeling the direction of the breeze, which seemed to have gone suddenly still.

"It's coming from the east," Logan said.

"I'll order the sails brought down," Brendan said.

"No, not yet. Catch what wind we have. Isla Blanca is not far," Red said. "If we can make her cove, it will be a safer place than we might find here or by pushing out to the open sea."

"You can't outrun what's coming," Logan warned.

She gazed at him, aggravated. "I don't intend to attempt to outrun the storm, merely bring the ship into more protected waters. Brendan, take the helm and cut a hard course."

He nodded.

"And call the hands," Red said quietly.

"All hands on deck!" Brendan shouted.

There was a scurrying sound, footfalls upon the planks, as the crew gathered from their tasks.

"Batten her down!" Red ordered. "All cargo, no matter how small, goes below. Extra rigging, gear, anything that might blow or roll overboard…down below."

At that moment, an eerie silence fell over them, as if nature herself had stilled.

Logan knew that silence, just as the crew did, and knew it well. It was the calm that came just before the fury and tumult of a storm.

"See to the small rigging, Logan," Brendan ordered on his way to take the helm from Silent Sam.

"Check your setting. Hard west, northwest," Red ordered.

Amazingly, despite the deadened wind that was just a wicked tease before the gale, Red's orders brought them whipping hard toward the shallow waters. There were many islands here, Logan knew.

And treacherous sandbars as well.

At least they were far north of the reefs that might have torn apart the hull; if they could ride the waves without breaking up, they could weather the coming storm. As he wound and stored heavy ropes and canvas, he had to admire the seamanship of the pirate captain.

"Lower all sails!" Red called out when they reached the cove. Hagar took up her order, and it was roared about the ship.

Logan raced to join the men. Muscles bulged on massive, hardworking forearms as the crew set about the task. From the crow's nest, a crewman shouted down, "She's on us!"

Red stood at the stern then, her spyglass in her hands. Hagar was near, repeating her orders as she called them out.

"Down from the lookout, Davy!" the big man ordered.

And then the rain began.

It came with a sudden rage, along with the wind, which blew so hard it seemed the rain rose from the sea and tore at them horizontally. It stung like a swarm of bees. It was like being raked over and over again by massive talons.

"Lash yourselves to the mast!" Red yelled, but it was an unnecessary order, for the crew seemed to know by instinct that the time had come when the ship was at the mercy of the waves, and themselves with her.

Brendan tied himself to the wheel, doing his best to keep the ship perpendicular to the wind and avoid being hit broadside by the tremendous force of the sea and the storm. But despite their best efforts, a rope broke from the mainmast and came flying down toward Brendan, the large and lethal steel grommet at the end heading straight for his head.

Red saw what was happening. She hadn't tied herself to the ship yet, and she went running.

As Logan and Hagar did.

Logan launched himself at the rope, catching it just seconds before it could complete its downward arc. He flew with it and crashed into Brendan himself. The breath was knocked from them both, but the disaster had been averted.

Hagar, however, had been pitched, helpless, to the side of the ship just as she had taken a hard roll.

"No!" Logan heard Red's roar of denial, and saw her go flying after the man as he threatened to roll off the starboard side. She caught hold of him by the belt, and as the ship rose again and pitched in the opposite direction, she and Hagar rolled back to safety.

But the wind was wicked and ruthless.

It shrieked like a banshee, tearing around the naked masts, swirling the sea to further violence. The ship rolled hard again, and this time it was Red who was helpless as she was picked up by the storm and flung straight over the side.

Logan let out a shrill scream of anger, fear and fury that rose even above the howling of the wind.

He had to move in split seconds, even knowing that in this sea, with these waves, he was surely committing suicide with no chance of finding, much less saving, her.

But he had no choice.

He stripped off his coat as he raced across the deck, leapt to the rail and plunged into the vortex below.

PERHAPS IT WOULD be a welcome grave, Red thought.

She could swim, could even buck strong waves, and she knew about currents and giving herself over to the power of the ocean, floating to save her strength, to save her breath....

But there seemed to be no top and no bottom to the water. There was no wave that offered the promise of carrying her to shore. There was no air, no sky, no *surface*. She was plunging down....

She was dead, or soon would be....

She could hear it all again. The screams of the children. She could see it all again. The endless spill of blood.

No, she told herself. The scream was the wind.

The blood was the sea.

Then there were arms around her. Surely they belonged to those who now were only vague memories, whispers of what love and family could be. There was a world beyond, and she had to make it through this maelstrom to reach them where they waited for her.

"Breathe!"

Something vised violently about her chest. She spat out seawater, and her lungs instinctively dragged in huge drafts of air, but even the air was wet, and she gasped and choked. The pain was so great that she longed to slip below the cold surface again and let the water cradle her and draw her under.

"Breathe, damn you! Live!"

She gulped in air again. She was being dragged. Dragged through the water and the waves. She tried to breathe, but the waves were sweeping over her again and again.

"Hold on!"

Hold on? To what?

Then she could feel something. Something solid. Wood. And it was holding her above the waves. She felt someone tugging at her feet, and suddenly she wasn't being pulled down so heavily. She felt...her toes. Her boots were gone. And she heard a voice. "The coat... dammit, it has to go. We need to lighten you up..."

She felt like laughing. She wasn't a ship! But something logical in the back of her mind fought against the shock that had seized her, and she knew the boots would have dragged her down, and she had to hold on and kick to stay afloat.

The ghosts of the dead had *not* come for her....

She was dimly aware of Logan Haggerty's face, his dark hair plastered to his forehead, his amber eyes like strange beacons of fire, anger and determination.

"Hold on," he commanded again.

So she did, managing to wrest herself half out of the water, clinging to what she saw now was a barrel. He was next to her, one arm around her, the other clinging to the barrel literally for dear life.

The world was dark, the sea a swirling vortex from which there could be no salvation. The rain lashed at them, so cold, until she felt as if her fingers could grip no more...

Then...

The banshee wail began to fade.

"Kick!" he ordered.

And she tried, oh, God, she tried....

And after that...

What seemed hours later, she felt her feet scrape against sand. Then she was standing, struggling, the waves lapping around her feet....

She staggered forward. The world was still wet and dark and cold.

She fell.

But she fell on solid ground.

CHAPTER SIX

LOGAN REGAINED CONSCIOUSNESS SLOWLY.

First he heard the waves, gentle now, easing up on the shore. There was a cadence to them, a rhythm. It was pleasant, inducing him to close his eyes again and sleep....

But then he felt the sand, gritty beneath his cheek and in his clothing, caked along his jaw.

And there was a breeze. Something balmy, such a pleasant touch, inducing him to forget everything else, to fall asleep and dream.

There was the sun. Growing warm overhead...

Suddenly his eyes flew open, and all the force and fury and desperation of the storm returned to him. He remembered.

Red going over the side.

Brendan screaming.

And himself...

Following her into that storm-tossed hell.

There had never been a question. He remembered diving over the rail, praying that a sudden wave wouldn't tilt the ship over on top of him, that he wouldn't crack his head wide open before he had a chance to save her.

And then...

The water. Deep and churning. Violent. He had dived deep, terrified that he would never find her. But he had, and then he had surfaced and found the barrel, and somehow they had both ridden it as the storm raged and finally passed. He had talked to her throughout, but she hadn't heard him. And he could remember seeing land at last, and kicking for it with the tail end of his strength...

Well, he had evidently made it. He was alive, judging by the sunshine, the breeze and the gritty sand.

He sat up.

His shirt was sodden, molded to his body. His boots were gone. He had one stocking left. He vaguely remembered struggling out of his coat and vest. And Red... He had gotten rid of her boots, as well, tried to rid her of what weight he could. And she...

Panic suddenly locked his throat and soul.

Where was she?

He struggled up, looking around.

Where the hell was she?

He looked down the beach and saw the broken barrel that had been their salvation. There was other flotsam and jetsam on the shore, as well.

But he didn't see Red.

He started running barefoot down the beach, his heart pounding furiously as he raced past the barrel and skidded to a stop.

He exhaled, shaking and falling to his knees at her side. She lay there, clad much as he was himself, torn white shirt, ripped breeches and, amazingly, both stockings. With the wig gone, her eyes closed, her features pale, perfect and fragile, and the radiant color of her hair, she appeared as delicate as a kitten.

His throat seemed to close again.

Was she alive?

He reached out and touched her throat, seeking a pulse.

It was there.

As her eyelids began to flutter, he pulled back his trembling fingers.

Her eyes opened.

She stared at him in confusion. For a moment her gaze was innocent and questioning....

Then she bolted up, staring at him in horror, as her hand flew to her head.

She was looking for that stupid wig.

He could see in her eyes as it all came back to her.

The storm...

Going overboard...

Then...

"You!" she gasped.

He didn't know what to say. He hadn't expected her to fall all over him with gratitude for saving her life, but he hadn't expected such pure horror, either.

"Me," he said, crossing his arms over his chest. "The storm, the ship...remember? Then there was me—jumping overboard to save you."

"You...you know who I am."

She backed away from him.

"Don't be ridiculous," he snapped. "Of course I know who you are. Did you hear what I said? Yes, it's me. The man who jumped overboard to save your hide!"

She backed away again.

"I...I am a pirate. I am Red Robert!"

"Fine, you're Red Robert. Now stop worrying about the fact that you've lost your wig and you've very evidently a woman. This may shock you, but I was too busy being concerned about whether you *lived or died* to care much one way or the other!"

She stood very tall and wary, and clutched her arms around herself, as if that would somehow disguise her again.

"Where are we?" she asked suspiciously.

"On a beach."

"The ship?"

"I don't know—I dived in after you."

"You didn't have to," she informed him.

"Yes, I did."

"The others?" she asked, her eyes downcast with fear for her crew.

"She's a good ship. They probably rode it out."

"They'll come back for us."

"We can hope. We can also hope they'll figure out where we washed ashore."

"And now you know," she said miserably.

He couldn't help but laugh.

"*Now* I know?"

She stared at him, stunned.

"Of course I know. I knew all along."

"You did?" she demanded.

He stared back at her, irritated. His heart had practically broken when he had thought she'd died, and now this.

"Excuse me," he said. "I'm going to take a walk. I'm going to try to figure out if there's any water on this island."

He turned, heading into the tangle of palms and brush that grew not far from the shore. Hopefully that abundance of growth meant there was fresh water somewhere.

His back was to her, but he could feel her staring after him as he walked. The sand was still cool from the night before and the battering of the storm. He saw that the trees were coconut palms, so at the least they could drink coconut milk and eat the coconut meat.

He heard her when she came racing up behind him.

"You *knew?*" she repeated furiously.

"Of course," he said, moving into the shade of the palm trees.

"From the beginning?" she demanded.

"Yes," he said. It wasn't a complete lie.

She caught hold of his shirt, spinning him around. "That first day on the ship. The first day. When you fought me and slashed my cheek. You knew *then?*"

"Yes." Well, he'd known *something* wasn't quite right.

"Bastard!"

The word stunned him. He stood dead still and stared at her coldly.

"You chose to fight, and you fought like a hellion," he reminded her.

It didn't help the situation.

"Bastard," she repeated.

He shrugged, walked on, then turned back. "Look, we need to find water and—"

To his amazement, she charged him. And to his deep humiliation, he wasn't prepared. He went over backward, with her on top of him, her fists pummeling wildly. Luckily for him, she was so furious that she wasn't being her usual cool and calculating self, and her energy was quickly spent as he went for her flailing arms, trying to avert serious physical harm.

"Of all the despicable, horrid, obnoxious, wretched men in the universe…!"

She stopped raging at him only because she ran out of breath. He took advantage of the moment to gain the edge, clutching her arms and rolling her over so that he was on top, straddling her and pinning her to the sand.

She never stopped thinking, planning, conniving. He could see it in her eyes. Knowing she was wasting her efforts, she went dead still and stared up at him with twin blue beacons of blazing fury. She seemed beaten, but he knew her better.

She was just waiting for a hint of weakness, of vulnerability, on his part. He wasn't going to give it.

"I'm despicable? Because you're playing such a dangerous game?"

Her eyes narrowed with an ever greater anger. "This is no game," she assured him.

"You are no pirate."

To his amazement, her anger seemed to fade, but her demeanor was still icy. "I'm afraid that I am very much a pirate."

"The great and fearsome Red Robert?" he mocked.

"I took down Black Luke," she reminded him.

"I heard about that—*all* about that."

Her eyes widened then, and she cursed.

Like a pirate.

"Which one of those demented idiots told you... anything?" she demanded.

He had to hand it to her. One would have thought she was the one wielding the power.

"The cat sang," he told her.

She cursed again and struggled then.

"Stop it!" he told her. "Stop fighting and listen to me. You are amazing and incredible. What you did...it was foolhardy, but it was also brilliant and valiant, and you saved yourself and a lot of men. But...do you know what will happen eventually?" he asked softly.

"I cannot come to a worse end than what was intended for me."

He couldn't help but grin, and he relaxed back on his haunches, still wary that she might fly into another rage and attack, and then grew serious. "But you can stop now," he assured her. "The wretched woman who held your indenture papers is dead."

She stared back at him without comment.

"You can live an...an honest life."

She shook her head. "It's too late. I can't turn back."

"You could work for me," he said.

"As what? Your scullery maid?" she asked, and her fists started flying again.

"I didn't say that," he told her.

"Oh, I should perhaps be your mistress? Or merely your whore?"

"Never. I intend to honor the woman I marry."

She went still, staring at him. For a moment he thought there was a sheen of dampness—maybe even tears?—in her eyes.

Then she struck out at him again, and it was all he could do to stop her.

"Bobbie!" he said. The name he'd heard Brendan use with such affection came easily to his lips. "For the love of God, I don't want to see you at the end of a hangman's noose. Or at the mercy of such a man as Blair Colm."

She went dead still.

What was it about Blair Colm that upset her so? he wondered.

Had she already been at his mercy?

But she was alive….

"I am what I am," she said primly. "And that is a pirate. And now, if you would get off me, I would greatly appreciate it."

He slowly relaxed, but he didn't let go of her wrists. "I don't know."

"What do you mean, you don't know?"

"Are you going to hit me again?"

"You're worried that I'm going to hit you again? You sound like a little girl," she snapped.

He laughed.

"So *are* you going to hit me again?"

She let out an exasperated sigh. "No."

"Promise?"

"Pirate's honor," she said with aggravation.

"Then…" He leapt up, then reached down for her hand. She eyed his offering suspiciously, then accepted and let him help her to her feet. They were both still damp and sand-encrusted, but she was definitely different from the Captain Red Robert he had come to know. It was easy to see why she had come by the name. With the black wig gone, her own hair—even sea-tossed and salt-covered—was beautiful. It was a rich color, not as dark as Brendan's, but red and gold and still somehow deep and lustrous. Definitely unusual. He found himself imagining it clean and dry and cascading softly down her back in sunlight—or the moon's glow.

She cleared her throat.

"Water," she said. "We need to find water."

"Yes. Have you been shipwrecked before?" he asked.

"No. Have you?"

"No."

She smiled suddenly. "I *have* careened my ship in places similar to this, though."

"That's good. You won't be afraid."

"Afraid? Why would *I* be afraid?"

"Everyone is afraid of something."

"And what are you afraid of?" she asked him.

"Oh, I'm not so brave, really. I'm afraid of shot, swords, cannons…and of dying before making my mark on the world."

He had spoken lightly, but with the last words he had taken on an air of gravity. She studied him, frowning with concern.

"What?" he asked.

"I guess that's what I'm afraid of, too," she said.

"Cannon, shot and steel blades?" he queried.

"No. Well, I'd rather not be injured or lose a limb," she agreed. "But…it was the other. I just don't want to die before I've…"

"Really lived?"

"Well, that all depends on what you mean by 'living.'"

"Let's get on with this search for water, then we can discuss philosophy," he said. "Come on."

He led the way through the thick underbrush. If there were any trails through it, they were overgrown and long unused.

"What makes you think you can find water?" she called after him.

"Look around you."

"It does rain in the Caribbean," she reminded him.

"Do you have something better to do?"

"Maybe?"

"And that would be…?"

"We could build a fire on the beach, so my crew can find us," she said.

He was silent. Despite what he'd said earlier, there was no guarantee her crew had survived, and they both knew it.

"Okay, another ship," she said.

The idea made him uneasy. He wasn't sure why. Even if a merchantman were to find them, he wasn't a pirate, and with her red hair and bedraggled beauty, she would never be taken for the infamous Red Robert. Still, he was uneasy about the possibility of rescue.

Maybe it was because they were almost certainly in a pirate alley. Any ship that came upon them would probably be a pirate ship. And most pirate captains would either think his plight was amusing and leave him stranded or put him to work on their own ship. Or maybe just decide he should be slain on the spot.

The pirate code stated that no decent woman should be taken against her will. Female captives were usually ransomed. But the rules were not hard and fast. Red could be in serious trouble if they were discovered by the wrong ship.

And building a fire might bring the wrong kind of rescue.

And yet, what other option was there?

As they headed deeper into the brush, the going became harder. There were roots to trip over, and pebbles and rocks to cut their feet. The palm fronds grew low and thick. There were several varieties of palms, sea grape trees, fruit trees bearing what looked like little green limes and others apparently bearing figs, and more. The limes were a blessing, he thought. And there had to be a fresh water spring somewhere on the island.

"There!" he said suddenly, pointing.

He had broken through a grove of tall palms at the top of a small hill. And as he peered between the trunks, he could see a waterfall.

She crashed into his back, stumbling over one of the roots breaking through the thin layer of soil.

"It's…it's beautiful," she said.

Logan calculated they had come about half a mile from the beach. He didn't see any signs that the island was inhabited, but he had to wonder why. It offered the most important element of life—water. And there was enough real soil for vegetation to grow.

She pushed by him, eager to reach the water.

"Wait!"

She had fallen to her knees at the water's edge, but now she hesitated, water dripping from her cupped hands.

"Allow me," he said, walking up beside her. "The official taster, you know."

Despite his thirst, he only dabbed the water to his lips at first. It was sweet and clear. He sipped.

She was staring at him. He smiled. "Seems safe."

She drank. Then she sluiced water over her face, relishing the clean feel, before she drank again. He found himself watching her, relishing the delight she found in the fresh, cool sensation and the way she cast her head back to delight in the water pouring over her.

"It's a taste of heaven," she said.

Aye, a taste of heaven, he thought. Stranded he might be, but with clean, clear drinking water—and with her.

He rose and looked around.

"We should head back to the beach," he said.

"What? We just got here."

"And now that we've found water, we need to build a shelter."

She stared at him blankly for a moment, as if finally comprehending for the first time that they could be on this island for weeks, even months.

Or more.

Without a word, she turned around and started walking ahead of him toward the shore. He could hear her suck in her breath now and then, when she stepped on something hard or sharp.

Shoes would be nice, he thought. And a good strong knife or sword would be even better. He reached toward his calf, but in vain; he had lost his knife when he had cast off his boots.

Despite the pain to her delicate soles, she moved quickly. He kept close behind her.

She passed by a palm and held the branch out of her way; then it smacked him squarely in the face as he passed.

"Hey!" he yelled.

"Sorry," she said quickly.

But he could tell from her tone that she wasn't sorry at all. He wondered if she had let the branch snap back on purpose.

She reached the shore first and stood there, staring out at the waves. Just as there was often a calm before a storm, there was often one afterward, as well.

The world seemed to have been swept clean. The sea was like liquid glass, reflecting the glory of the sun. The sky was a soft blue, not a cloud to be seen. The roll of the surf against the sand was still like a sweet and pleasant whisper.

"I'll retrieve the barrel," he said. "The wood will be useful, and there might be something edible inside."

She followed more slowly as he strode down the beach toward the barrel that had saved their lives, then cried out suddenly, stumbling to her knees.

He turned back.

"What?" he asked in concern.

"Nothing!"

He walked back toward her anyway. She was sitting on the sand, holding her foot.

"Did you cut it?"

"I stepped on a shell."

"Let me see."

"No."

"Don't be such a...girl," he told her.

She cast him a dangerous glare, but she didn't say anything.

Hunkering down before her, he caught her wrist and moved her hand out of the way. Her foot was bleeding, but there was so much sand caked to her skin that he couldn't see how bad the gash might be.

"I'm all right," she said stiffly, pushing him away and starting to rise. Then she staggered slightly, and he rose quickly and lifted her into his arms, much to her indignation.

"Put me down!" she demanded.

He ignored her.

"Do what I tell you," she insisted. "I am the captain."

"You *were* a captain. So was I."

"I was captain last," she said irritably.

He ignored her, striding toward the water. She was an easy burden, despite the fact that she was stiff and totally uncooperative.

She slammed a fist against his chest.

"Hey! You promised not to hit me."

"I told you to put me down."

He had reached the water, and he was tempted.

"Damn you, Logan!"

He dropped her.

She went under, then came up quickly, sputtering and furious. She slapped at the hand he offered her. But when she staggered again, he caught hold of her anyway, to keep her from falling.

"We had to wash your foot," he explained.

Half standing, accepting his support to remain upright, she gave him her evil stare once again. "I'm soaked."

"You're the one who believes in bathing," he pointed out dryly.

"I thought you were concerned about my *foot?*"

"Actually, I am. An infection here could be serious. And saltwater will clean it and help heal it."

"So I needed an entire bath in saltwater…for my foot?"

He shrugged, picked her up again and headed the few feet to the beach. She swore, but he ignored her as he set her down easily and knelt at her side, taking her foot in his hand again. There was a slash right across her instep. He was grateful to notice that it didn't appear to be deep.

"Just a lot of blood, I think," he said lightly.

"It hurts," she admitted.

"Just sit here and let it soak in the waves for a few minutes," he told her as he ripped off a long strip of his bedraggled shirt. "Then we can wrap it up." His voice had grown husky. It was touching her that did it, he thought. Maybe he shouldn't have dropped her in the water. Her clothing was plastered to her body again, hugging her in a way that emphasized every perfect curve. The white cotton seemed to do more enhancing than concealing.

He stood quickly. He needed to get some distance from her.

"Where are you going?" she asked, frowning.

"Down the beach to get the barrel and do some exploring," he said lightly. "Who knows what treasures may lurk just around the bend? I'm sure we weren't the only ship caught up in that storm."

He left her, curious to see what might be in the barrel that had saved their lives.

Reaching it didn't help much. He had nothing with which to lever it open. The ship's cooper did an excellent job of sealing his creations, which helped preserve necessities on the ship. But now…

He managed to read the letters that had been burned into the side and realized that they had a barrel of rum—about a third full, judging by the weight, which had left enough room for the air that had made the barrel float and ensured their salvation.

Now he just needed tools to open it.

He looked back down the beach. Red was staring out at the sea. Her foot was in the water, though. The waves were inching up and crashing gently against the length of her slightly bent legs, and she'd folded her arms atop them. She looked like a mermaid cast up from the sea, not a far cry from the truth.

He stepped away from the annoying puzzle of the barrel and looked farther down the beach, where he saw numerous pieces of broken plank.

He hoped they weren't from the *Eagle,* and that Brendan, Peg-leg, Silent Sam, Hagar, Jimmy O'Hara and the rest were safe and figuring out how to rescue Red.

He started piling up the wood, mentally assembling the pieces into a shelter. His heart sank as he moved along; it was becoming obvious that at least one poor ship had broken up in the heavy winds and lashing waves of the storm.

He was definitely acquiring enough lumber.

After about a hundred yards, he came upon a large cargo chest. He stooped to examine it, then swore when he discovered that it was locked.

He found a thick rock and began slamming away at the padlock. When it was clear that he would never break the lock, he changed tactics and smashed in the lid of the chest, instead, then looked inside.

The chest had been well-built, with a strong seal that had kept out the ocean. The chest was filled with clothing, not the tools he would have preferred, and he saw breeches, bodices, skirts, dresses, silks, satins and lace. There were shoes and stockings, even jeweled brooches and collar pins.

He sat back on his heels, feeling relieved. He was certain that this haul had not come from their ship.

He was sorry, though, because he was certain an innocent merchantman had been destroyed in the storm, and the owners of the finery before him were now resting somewhere at the bottom of the sea, food for the fish.

He stood and looked out to sea. More and more

refuse was bobbing on the waves, washing up toward the shore. He ventured out to see what was coming his way.

Lots and lots of timbers, some with swatches of canvas sail and rigging caught around them. The rigging would be helpful in building, he thought.

And more barrels. He waded out deeper to retrieve the one floating closest. It had been staved in, he quickly realized, and was worthless.

He looked back toward Red again. She was up, a hand shielding her eyes from the sun as she, too, looked out to the deeper water. As he watched, she began to wade out, as he had been doing.

He didn't know what she had seen that had so drawn her attention. He started sloshing through the water to reach her position.

She stood stock-still. And then a cry escaped her, a cry so startled and shrill that his heart thundered.

"Red!"

He raced to reach her.

As he ran, he saw what had drawn her attention.

A man.

A man floating facedown in the water.

His sea-darkened hair was red, and he wore a coat similar to the one Brendan usually wore.

She was standing frozen in horror, so he stepped forward and, his heart in his throat, turned the body over.

CHAPTER SEVEN

THERE WAS A new ship in the harbor.

Using her spyglass, Sonya could see that it had taken some weather damage; men were even now busy repairing the mast.

There had been a storm; they'd seen it out at sea. But it hadn't taken a swipe at New Providence, and she was glad. It seemed to have taken a northeasterly path, perhaps cutting across Cuba and following the North American coast. She hoped it hadn't sunk Red Robert's *Eagle*.

All right, so she had taken some coins to betray Red Robert. This was a pirate island, after all, and in her own way, she was a pirate, too. It hadn't been personal. She had needed the money. And it had ended well, in any case.

But since the *Eagle* had sailed, she had been worried. She liked Red Robert, effeminate fop though he might be, but she had long had an ache in her heart for Haggerty. He lived within the law, but he seemed to understand those who were often forced to live on the other side of it. He was a man who abhorred violence, but he wasn't afraid of a fight. And when his eyes flashed with humor, she melted.

Even if he never wanted one of her girls. Or her.

She was jolted out of her thoughts when Blair Colm walked into the tavern.

It had been a slow morning. Though the storm had sent many a ship to this safe harbor for repair, the men had no time to go drinking. The able-bodied were busy at their work, sewing canvas, obeying the commands of the carpenters. The injured would be nursing their wounds, with the ships' physicians and even barbers sewing up flesh wounds and setting smashed limbs, or removing those that couldn't be saved.

Colm stared at her for a long while before speaking. He had been in before, and she took his money. After all, it spent just the same as anyone else's. But she had always hated the man, who was considered a monster by some and a hero by others.

She, for one, found it all too easy to believe the rumors that swirled about the man.

Rumors such as the one that said he had killed children by swinging them around by their heels and cracking their skulls open on rocks.

She felt a sudden wave of guilt. Red Robert might be effeminate, but the pirate had never been anything but decent to her. And she had betrayed him, knowing all the while that it was in the service of Blair Colm. True, the bald man had offered her a fine sum of money just to discover that Robert had left, and in what direction.

She had to survive, didn't she?

But she had known, deep down inside, that something evil was afoot, with a monster like Blair Colm seeking out Red Robert.

And she had taken the coins anyway.

"Sonya!"

She looked up.

"Captain Blair."

"Sir Captain Blair," he reminded her.

"Sir Captain Blair," she parroted.

"I'll have the private room, and your finest wench. No one old or worn out." He looked her up and down, to be sure she didn't miss the point that his insult had been directed specifically to her.

She only smiled and said, "As you wish."

"And your best rum. None of that rotgut you serve the drunkards."

"As you wish," she said again.

He still didn't move. She was dimly aware that the bar boys in the back had suddenly developed loose fingers and were dropping things. Blair Colm created such an atmosphere. He'd been known to backhand a lad or two for spilling a drop of rum.

"The room is yours, Sir Captain Blair," she said, hoping he would wait there for whatever poor girl she chose for him.

"You will join me."

She started. She was glad to be older and *worn out* when he was about.

"Aye?"

He let out something like a sniff. "I need information."

"I have no information."

"I believe you do."

He departed for the room. She rose slowly, afraid

not to follow. He'd not been kind to women who dissented, either.

She followed him in. "I can't see to your rum and services if I'm here," she said.

He took a seat against the wall. "Sit," he ordered her.

She sat with alacrity.

"Where did they go?" he demanded.

She stared at him, her mind genuinely blank. He was a big man. Muscular. But his features were sharp and vulpine. His hair and eyes were dark. He was English, but he had the look of a Spaniard. There was a sense of cruelty about the man, maybe in the very narrowness of his features, maybe in the way he moved, and maybe in those hellish dark eyes.

"They?"

"Red Robert and his crew."

"Oh. Yes, they were here, just before the storm," she said.

Blair Colm suddenly moved forward. It was the striking motion of a snake.

"Red Robert is coming after me, but that storm will hold him up."

"You tried to have him killed. Here," she said softly, guilt settling over her like a dark cloud.

He waved a hand dismissively. "I didn't try to have anyone killed. That wouldn't be honorable, now would it?" he asked quietly.

He was lying through his teeth, and they both knew it. She hated the man. All she wanted was to get away.

"They sailed out. They didn't say where they were heading."

Before she knew it, he was on his feet, holding her by the hair in front of him. "Red Robert took a ship before he got here and is traveling with a captive."

"Yes!" she cried out. He had her dead against him. She could feel strands of hair tearing from her scalp. Her heart was thundering.

She could scream, but she knew no one would come.

"The captive is Lord Haggerty," he said.

"Yes," she said again, and this time the word was a whimper. She had always thought herself hardened, inside and out. She had seen so much. She had slept with more men than most women ever knew. She despised them, as they despised her.

But now she was afraid.

He stared at her hard. "They are coming after me. Together. They are hunting me."

"I know nothing of that!" she insisted, frantic. "Think! Would they discuss their business with the likes of me?"

He leaned closer, eyes peering into hers. "Many men speak to you, wench."

What the hell did he want her to say?

"Perhaps they *are* seeking you out. I don't know. They sailed into the storm—they're probably all dead. Let me go!"

"Not yet. Now, the real question. *Who* is Red Robert?"

"What?"

Another jerk on her hair. Pain shot through her skull. Tears pooled in her eyes.

"Red Robert is…Red Robert," she said, tears of fear and pain springing to her eyes.

"Liar!"

She found herself flung onto the table. He was quickly on top of her. "The truth! I'll have the truth."

"I don't know! I swear to God, I don't know!" He was straddling her, and she knew fighting back was foolish, but she couldn't help herself.

She spat at him.

She should have expected it. He slapped her with a vengeance that knocked her unconscious, though for far too short a time.

She vaguely felt him rise, felt him shuffle her skirt out of his way. Too weak to fight, too groggy even to protest, she simply turned away. She never said a word.

And when he was done, he dropped a coin on the table as he casually straightened his breeches. "Who does know?"

"Bend down, kiss your arse and die," she managed to respond.

She was ready for the next blow. It was worth it.

"I'll find Teach and ask *him*," he said.

She laughed, not bothering to rise. "By all means, find him," she suggested. "He'll help you bend over, kiss your arse and die."

One last blow and he was gone.

Not even then did she burst into tears.

She told herself that she was too hard, but in reality she was simply too numb.

When she finally rose, she went to talk with her girls, and she told them that he had the littlest penis she'd ever seen and couldn't keep hard long enough to finish.

The girls would talk. It would be all over the island.

She began praying that Red Robert *would* find him on the high seas.

And that Robert did indeed intend to kill him.

LOGAN HESITATED, but they had to know the truth, one way or the other.

The dead man was floating facedown.

Red stared at the corpse, stricken, as he had never imagined she might be. Brave pirate, brave *actress*. She loved her cousin. She looked unbelievably fragile and vulnerable now, and he was afraid himself. He didn't want to turn the body over, because he felt helpless in the face of her obvious distress.

He swallowed hard. One lesson life had taught him: face all demons. Nothing could change what was, and acceptance allowed you to move on.

He turned the body over.

She gasped, and stepped back shaking.

It wasn't Brendan but some other poor soul. The fish had already been nibbling at his nose, and he was a pathetic and dreadful sight.

But he wasn't Brendan.

Logan reached out to Red to steady her. And for a moment, she leaned on his strength. Then she pulled away, as if furious with him. But she wasn't angry with him, and he knew it. She was angry with herself. Red Robert, who had mastered her act so long ago, was ruing her own show of weakness.

But the sight of the corpse was a horrible one. The

corpse had bloated in the water, and now he had the macabre appearance of something unreal, something that had never been human.

"I'll bury him," he said curtly.

"He—he isn't one of ours," she whispered.

"Whoever he is, he deserves a decent burial." He didn't add that a rotting corpse on the beach would create a horrible miasma. He turned, pulling the corpse through the shallows as he paralleled the beach. She was still for a moment; then he heard a splashing behind him as she followed to help.

He dragged the body up to a cluster of palm trees far above the water.

He didn't want high tide undoing his work.

He still hadn't found any tools, but a broken coconut made a crude scoop. Fifteen minutes later, when he was already dripping with sweat from the effort of working with so small a tool, he looked over and saw that she had gone back down the beach to discover a large silver soup tureen, which made a much better scoop, and had started digging alongside him.

"Let me," he said.

She was working vigorously and didn't even look up at him. She shook her head, intent on her task. She worked almost as if she were in a frenzy, burning her strength. He let her, certain she was trying to allay her fear that although the body they had found was not Brendan, the crew of her ship might have met a similar fate. When he was certain she had burned away most of her emotion, he stepped forward again, reaching for the silver tureen, forcing her to look at him. "You've done more in a matter of minutes than I did in twenty. Let me finish," he said gently.

She stared at him, blinked, lowered her head and nodded at last.

The tureen was a big help. His shoulders and back ached, but in the end, he managed a deep-enough grave. He pulled the man in and was ready to drop the sand back over him when she stopped him.

"Wait."

"Yes?" he said, and eyed her expectantly.

"Don't you…know a few words to say?"

"Don't you?"

"You're a captain."

"So are you."

"I've never lost a crew member," she said proudly.

"Neither have I," he informed her.

"But you—"

"I what?"

"You still believe in God," she said flatly.

He looked at her for a moment. *So do you,* he wanted to tell her, but something in her eyes told him to keep the words inside.

"Father, accept the soul of this, thy servant," he said instead, and crossed himself.

"And may ye be in heaven an hour before the devil knows ye're dead!" she said, and did likewise.

Strange prayer for a man who was already dead.

"Amen," he said, and she turned away.

Scooping the sand back on wasn't half as hard as digging it out. He was done in a matter of minutes. To his surprise, she had fashioned a cross out of palm fronds, and when he had finished, she set it into the sand covering the body.

"It won't stay, you know," he said gently.

"Ah, but it's there for the journey," she replied.

She turned away and started walking back down the beach. As she left, he felt his stomach rumble. Without the labor to take his mind off things, his body was reminding him that they hadn't eaten.

Well, if nothing else, there were coconuts. And rum.

But hunger didn't seem to be plaguing Red yet, as she examined the flotsam that continued to wash up on the beach. He followed her, collecting timber, then shouted out with triumph, seeing what appeared to be a chest of carpenter's tools next to a broken crate.

"Aha!"

"What?" she cried, startled and clearly afraid of what he might have found.

He was already down on his knees beside the chest, pounding at the lock with a sharp stone. When it split apart in his hand, he didn't care, he just picked up another one and resumed his efforts.

Finally the ring holding the lock in place gave, and he looked up at her, smiling in triumph, feeling as if he had just stumbled on a cache of gold doubloons.

"Nails! We have nails. And a hammer, a lathe...and a leather needle...!"

She didn't respond with the same enthusiasm.

"What?" he asked her.

"It's not...ours, is it?" she whispered.

He sat back on his haunches. "There are no markings," he told her.

She let out a sigh. "Ours had initials. It isn't ours."

"There's been nothing on this beach to suggest that the *Eagle* broke up," he assured her.

She looked reassured, at least for the moment.

"All right, take the chest," he said.

"Me?"

"Unless you want to carry the lumber?"

"And where are we going?" she demanded.

He rose and looked around, then pointed out a place a good twenty yards farther inland and a good hundred yards to the east of their hasty cemetery. Palm trees surrounded a glade where their shade had kept the earth barren of brush and scrub.

"Come on, let's go," he said.

"I'm the captain here," she insisted.

"Fine. You build the shelter."

"I am willing for you to be the carpenter."

"Ah. And were you going to sit somewhere on your arse while I worked?" he demanded. "That's no captain's privilege, not on a pirate ship."

"No, I was simply...setting the record straight."

"Let's move."

"You are still my prisoner."

"Indeed? Well, I'm a hungry prisoner who knows that night will come. And that it may rain again. And I'd like to get a shelter rigged up. So I hope you'll excuse me if I don't pretend I'm in chains and you're wearing a brace of pistols."

She picked up the chest of tools and started ahead of him, then stepped back and watched while he plotted the strength of the trees and their position. He quickly set forth flattening his chosen ground and mentally drawing the dimensions of the abode he intended to erect, and then got started with timber and nails, creating a frame. He couldn't have been happier with his find.

He realized she was missing at one point and began cursing beneath his breath. Had she gone from being a pirate to a princess?

But as he turned to head back to the beach to look for her, he heard the sound of something being dragged along the sand.

She was bringing back a huge mass of canvas.

A sail from the broken ship that had given them both the cargo and the corpse.

Tugging the canvas, she looked slim and frail. And yet he realized that though she *was* slim, she was well-muscled, and that all her pretending and parading as a pirate had certainly given her an excellent physique. But she was tiring, so he hurried forward to help.

"I thought we might be in need of a roof," she said dryly.

"I had certainly planned on one," he said. "But palm fronds would have sufficed."

"Canvas will be better."

"I agree."

She actually smiled.

"So you admit I've been helpful," she said.

The canvas was heavy. He had to admit it: he was impressed that she had lugged it so far. "I'm going to take part of it up that tree to get leverage, then drag it over the frame. I'll need your help, handing it up to me."

"Aye, aye," she said, but she looked irritated.

"What?"

She didn't say anything, just pushed the canvas toward him. With the first side done, he had to climb down, then shimmy up a farther tree, so he could lean out across the frame and pull the canvas over and down. He just managed not to let her see that he nearly fell during the effort. The near miss sobered him. It was one thing to be stranded on the island. It would be quite another to be stranded there with a broken leg.

When he came down from the second tree, he was sweating and exhausted. Red must have been tired, as well, but she didn't complain, and she looked at their pathetic little structure without criticism.

"Well?" he said.

"Bugs," she said.

"Bugs?"

"Bugs come out at night."

"The mosquitoes will no doubt make a meal of us— unless the poor souls on that ship carried netting."

"What about food?"

"We can start here," he told her, catching hold of a coconut, a chisel and a hammer. He could break a coconut with the best of them. He offered her a half, sloshing with coconut milk.

"Drink up."

Thirst won out over manners. She slurped at the milk and started to gnaw at the meat. He tossed her a knife from the chest. She caught it deftly and dug into the meat. He turned his attention to his own half, realizing he was ravenous.

"Back down the beach?" she asked, when they were done with their impromptu meal.

"Back down the beach," he agreed.

He brought the hammer and chisel. This time, he made quick work of the barrels.

They had a lot of rum.

And rancid water.

But finally the fifth barrel yielded dried biscuit.

They both dug in. It didn't have any taste whatsoever, but at least it was free of weevils, and Logan knew that it would, at least, sustain them. But after a few bites, Red was on her feet again.

"Done already?"

She graced him with a smile. They were both sweaty and dirty, but there was something appealing about the streaks on her face.

"I haven't begun, but we need to build a fire."

He looked out at the sea. They needed to be rescued, but he was still afraid of the wrong ship coming upon them.

He stood, still chewing. The biscuit was...hard.

"All right," he said, after he managed to swallow. "You want to boil water and soften this?"

She flashed him another surprise smile. "And improve it," she assured him.

She grabbed the tools and started searching through the rest of the barrels. She seemed to be looking for something specific, and when she found it, she cried out with pleasure as she opened it. "Logan! We've got sugar!" she cried happily. "And it's well bagged in burlap and...where's the fire?" she inquired sweetly.

He turned with a rueful shrug and started searching for something with which to spark a flame.

"No flint?" she asked him hopefully.

He glared at her. "My pockets, madam, are empty."

As he began hiking wearily toward the trees in search of rocks and twigs for fire-starting, he heard her cry out with pleasure once again.

"What, you've found a lit candle?" he called to her.

But she hadn't found a candle. Instead—and even better—she had found a magnifying glass. She raced toward the trees, seeking the driest tinder she could find. Dead fronds would easily catch fire.

But they would need branches to keep it going.

There were plenty of the latter near their hut, and he went that way. A minute later, she brought her collection of dry vegetation to the spot where he was arranging their firewood. The sun was already beginning to set, he realized, and he longed to take the glass from her hand to speed the task, but she was determined. At last the tinder lit. He blew on it gently, and the flame grew. In moments the branches were burning and they had a real fire, although a rather smokey one, since apparently not all the wood was as dry as it had appeared.

"It's a dreadful fire," she said.

"It's a fire."

She rose. "Where is that soup tureen?" She went for it, then ran back for the sugar and biscuit. "Water!" she called to him. "We need fresh water."

He muttered beneath his breath and followed her. Rummaging again, he found a pitcher and a silver teapot, and went off to fill them both. When he returned, he found that she had come up with a skillet and was already carefully warming it at the fire. She took the teapot from him and poured a small amount into the pan, then added the biscuit and sugar.

Then she looked at the pitcher.

He handed it to her. "Drink slowly."

She didn't. She finished every drop. Then she looked at him guiltily.

"It's all right. I did the same thing at the spring."

She flushed.

"I'll go see if we have plates," he offered.

They did. He was frankly surprised more bodies hadn't washed up on the shore, given how much cargo had appeared. One trunk contained service for twenty in fine Chinese porcelain. There was silver, as well. He decided to drag the whole trunk back to their shelter, on the theory that it was better to have more than they needed than nothing at all.

He brought over silverware and two plates, and sat cross-legged before the fire. He started to fork out a piece of the biscuit turned to sugar cakes, but she spoke while he was in midmotion.

"Actually, it would be good to have a grog now," she said, looking at him.

He looked back at her, ready to remind her that she was constantly striving to prove her self-sufficiency, but instead he rose and headed down the beach. He dragged back the sugar barrel first, then went back for the partially filled barrel of rum that had brought them to the island. When he returned, he saw that she had gotten up, as well, and came back dragging another of the trunks.

"Teacups," she told him.

"Ah."

Then, smiling, she mixed them each a grog of sugar, water and rum.

At last they were seated at the fire again. The biscuit was far better now that it had been soaked with sugar, and he had to admit the grog was smooth, seeming to heat and ease his muscles all at once. They ate in silence, still ravenous, and he knew they made a ridiculous picture, seated with their fine china before a crude fire and their palm tree, broken lumber and canvas shelter.

Maybe it was exhaustion.

Maybe it was the rum.

Maybe it was the setting sun painting the sky with streaks of orange and pink. The colored sky kissed the water, and the waves washed with a gentle and soothing rhythm onto the beach.

Whatever the cause, it was an oddly peaceful moment.

He realized his shirt was torn and ragged, his breeches frayed, and they were both streaked with dirt. Red's hair was wild and as wickedly colored as the sunset. Her clothing, as tattered as his own, still seemed to hug her body. And she had never appeared more alluring to him.

He finished his grog, made himself another.

She arched a brow but said nothing.

"What, Captain?" he muttered, fighting to keep his distance from her. "You had wanted me to take the helm?"

"We're not done," she told him.

"Oh?"

"We need blankets."

"I could sleep here and now."

"But...you won't."

He grinned slowly, relaxing after the hard work of the day. "Blankets. Should I find a mattress, as well?"

"You are not amusing, you know."

"Ah, but you...it's so hard to decide just what you are—Captain Robert."

"There is nothing to decide. I am exactly what you see."

"Really? That from someone who dresses up like a man and pretends to be the terror of the sea?"

"I *am* the terror of the sea," she informed him coldly.

"And after just one man."

She stared at him. "You are more complex."

"Me? I am an open book."

"Ah, yes. *Laird* Haggerty. Maybe now. But I sense it was not always so."

"No," he admitted. "I came from war, treachery, murder, betrayal..."

"And ended up with a good life."

"I was taken in by a good man."

"Taken in?" she asked softly.

"I served him, and served him well. But he was a kind man, and had no son of his own, and I grew to love him like a son. And then came the Act of Union, and I was a laird again. A letter from the old country made it so."

"You are a lucky man."

"I let myself be lucky."

She started to laugh. "You think a person chooses to have good luck or bad?"

"I think a person can choose to let the past take control and simmer until there is nothing left in their heart except hatred."

"Hatred can keep a person alive," she said.

"And hatred can consume a person from within," he warned.

"And you hate no one?"

"Aye, Captain. I know how to hate. But I wanted to find life, as well."

She shook her head, looking away. "You fell in love," she told him.

He hesitated. "I fell into good company," he said.

"What about your dear Cassandra?"

"She is...proper."

"She must love you very much."

"She is a loving person."

She rose. "Well, fear not, Laird Haggerty. There's every hope that we shall get off this island, and, as I told you, there is no need for ransom. You are a free man."

She spoke strangely. He didn't remind her that he was a free man already. They were both free.

And they were both prisoners. Of an island.

She walked off down the beach. He rose and joined her. As the sun set, it was growing cool, and he saw that she was shivering.

He strode past her, searching again. There were broken barrels littering the beach, those they had split, and still more to be opened. The refuse covered half a mile, he thought. There was a great deal still to be explored and discovered.

He found more fine china, crystal glassware, pewter steins, leather skins and a trunk of fine woolen cloaks. He chose a few to bring back, should they not find blankets. It was almost absurd. They had more to choose from marooned on this island than had they been given access to a king's wardrobe.

"Bed linens!" she called out to him.

"Good," he returned.

At last he happened upon a trunk that held several woolen blankets, and even a goose down pillow. He took all that he could carry and headed back toward the shelter. She had arrived before him and laid out the linens.

One bed on one side of the shelter.

The other as far on the opposite side as possible.

Naturally.

He spread out the blankets and handed her the pillow. She stared at him, her eyes widening. "A pillow," she marveled.

He shrugged. "Enjoy."

"But it was your discovery," she said politely.

"My pleasure that it should be yours," he said gallantly.

He returned to the fire, feeling a chill himself. He made a third grog and turned to her. "May I serve you, my captain?"

"I...yes," she said. To his surprise, she gulped it down quickly, then shuddered.

"Thank you," she said.

"Come, enjoy the fire."

"I'm so tired," she admitted.

"So sit." He patted the sand. "You know my story. I want to know the rest of yours."

"There is…just what you see."

Darkness had now fallen all around them. The moon rose above, not full, but still helping to light the scene. The stars were out. And the fire burned low and pleasantly.

The breeze moved softly.

She stood there, so defiant, both fragile and strong. He wanted to reach out to her so badly, wanted to hold her, take care of her.

In all honesty, he wanted much, much more. He could almost feel her. Feel her heart beat, feel her breathe, even at a distance. He felt himself harden and quicken within, and he knew what he wanted was simple and basic and instinctive….

But there was more. Much more.

She fascinated him.

He winced, looking downward and thinking of Cassandra. He loved her. She deserved love, by God.

And yet…

He realized then that something he felt for Red was what he had been missing with Cassandra. Something that wasn't *proper.* Something that was fine and noble, but also carnal and base. Fascination, liking, admiration…passion.

He almost groaned aloud.

They were alone on an island. She had been fascinating him for days, and now…they were alone.

"There's more. I know there is. If you just told me…" He let his voice trail off in expectation.

"You really are a strangely…noble man, in your own rather odd way," she said softly.

"Odd?" he inquired.

"Well, you're noble, you have a title, and yet you are friends with the likes of Sonya and Edward."

"Blackbeard?"

"Aye."

He shrugged, grinning. "In the right circumstances, a decent enough fellow."

She nodded. "Quite decent."

"He knows of your deception?"

She nodded again.

"How?"

She hesitated, then shrugged. "He'd heard about me. That I'd met Black Luke upon the seas, slain him and taken his ship. When he saw me in port, he started laughing and asked me into his cabin for rum, then demanded to know my story. I told him."

"But you won't tell me."

"You already know most of it. I am going to sleep. On my new pillow. Thank you, and good night."

"Good night," he said, and reached for the grog.

He drank it while the dark waves washed the shore and sky stretched above him like black velvet dotted with diamonds.

The breeze whispered, and he drank more.

The very word mocked him.

Noble.

It was going to be very hard to behave so.

CHAPTER EIGHT

LOGAN WOKE BUT didn't rise, letting his circumstances and surroundings sink home to him once again. There was the cool breeze of morning in the islands, the soft feel of the sun as it rose gently against the mists and mauve of the receding night. There was the hard bedding of sand and linen beneath him, and the wool around him.

Then there was…

The woman lying across the meager expanse of the shelter. So near…

So far.

She was still asleep, her hair radiant against the poor plaid of the blanket.

He wondered what played through her dreams.

He left her sleeping and wandered down the beach to the trunk with the clothing. He rummaged through it, found breeches and a shirt, and decided to opt for no more, as it was undoubtedly going to get very hot during the day. He stretched, unkinking muscles that were unused to a night on the ground. Not too bad. He'd slept in far more uncomfortable situations in his time. He had lain awake late, though. Knowing she was there. Listening to the sound of her breathing.

He should go through the rest of the refuse. He should start collecting the crates and barrels that held things they could use and then drag them up to their shelter.

But that would wait. They didn't have a schedule to keep.

He found several linen towels, which would definitely be useful. He found perfumed soap and winced, then decided it was better than none.

Red was still asleep when he passed by the shelter again on his way to the waterfall, so he didn't disturb her.

As he stripped and dove into the freshwater spring, he wondered that no one had yet settled this place. It was a natural haven. There were hills, but not really mountains. There were trees, and the soft white sandy beach. Someone could create a paradise here.

The water was crisp and cool. He savored the slide of it against his flesh. They had slept last night crusted in salt from the ocean, and though he loved the sea, the fresh water on his naked skin was a sweet relief.

He dove down several times, exploring the watery haven. He found strange rock formations beneath the surface and made a mental note of the geography as he tested the pool's depth. Fifteen to thirty feet, he judged....

He was still deep beneath the surface when he literally bumped into her. Even in the water, he heard the little cry that escaped her.

And there, beneath the surface and the sun, in the cool, aqua shelter of the pool, he turned to see Red in all her glory.

Her eyes were saucer-sized, the alarm on her face evident. But despite himself, his gaze dropped. She was sleek and tightly muscled and beautiful, and very much a natural redhead. Her waist was minuscule, her breasts perfect.

He shot back from her as she shot back from him.

They surfaced a good fifteen feet apart, but the water, which had seemed to hide so much before, seemed only to magnify his view now.

"How dare you?" she accused him.

"Me! How dare *you?*" he returned.

"You sneaked up on me!" she accused him.

"My dear girl, I have been in this water for some time now," he returned, then muttered, "Pirate, my arse."

"What?"

"The usual pirate captain doesn't become outraged when he comes upon his men in a pool."

"I am not the usual captain."

"No, that you're not." He grinned.

"Get out of the water," she demanded.

"You get out," he suggested.

"No!" she exclaimed, still facing him, but paddling desperately backward to put more distance between them. "I'm not decent."

"Nor am I—and I was here first."

She stared at him, chagrined, and shook her head; then her eyes narrowed. "And I called you noble! You are just like every other man, interested in a woman for nothing but…but entertainment."

That was a blow beneath the waist. "How do I know you weren't perfectly aware that I was already in the pool, and that you didn't come here hoping to catch a glimpse of…of my family's future and honor?"

"I would never," she assured him, her face as red as her hair.

"And I would never."

"Ah, that's right. You have Cassandra."

Her tone surprised him. There was that note of disdain he'd heard before, but there was something else, as well. Just a trace, perhaps, of jealousy.

"Actually, at this moment, neither of us has anything but this island," he told her.

And then he was done. The crystalline pool seemed suddenly chilly. He turned and swam away from her. He didn't tell her to turn away as he walked back through the shallows to the shore, his back to her, heedless of whether she did or didn't watch. He picked up the towel he had brought, dried himself quickly, then stepped into clean breeches. Only then did he notice the soap, which he had tossed down by his clean clothing.

He turned back to her and saw that she was still floating far from shore. "Hey!"

"What?"

"Soap," he said, and held it up to show her.

She wanted it. She definitely wanted it.

But she didn't swim any closer.

"Hey, I can only it throw so far."

She came closer at last.

He tossed the soap to her.

It landed closer still to the shore, where it floated on the surface.

She cast him an evil glare. "Thank you."

"It's nothing."

"Perhaps you should go back and work on finding breakfast," she suggested.

"Aye, Captain, I'll do that."

But he remained right where he was.

She stared back at him and swore beneath her breath, then apparently decided to call his bluff and swam for the soap.

Still looking at him. Still cursing him. And she could indeed curse like a pirate.

Ah, well. He took another long look and wondered how such a woman had ever managed to pass herself off to anyone as a man.

Then he turned, grinning, and headed back for the beach.

"BRENDAN?"

Brendan barely turned as Silent Sam walked up to him at the helm; his eyes were on the horizon.

"Aye?"

"Let me take the wheel."

"I'm fine."

"No, you're not. Everyone must sleep at some point."

"They're out there. Somewhere," Brendan said vehemently.

Silent Sam was silent.

"They're out there," Brendan insisted.

"They might be. And if they are, we'll find them. Have faith in the man in the crow's nest. We'll sail to every island off the coast, sail until we drop dead of old age. But you'll be worthless if you don't get some rest."

It was the longest speech Brendan had ever heard Silent Sam give. He looked at the man, and saw that his devotion to the cause—to Red—was real. At last he nodded wearily and stepped away from the wheel so Silent Sam could take his place.

"Who's in the crow's nest?" he asked.

"Hagar."

Brendan nodded. "I'll be in her cabin," he said.

Silent Sam nodded.

In the cabin, Brendan realized that he and Red weren't just cousins, or even the brother and sister they more often felt like, after everything they'd been through together. They were survivors. Her quest was his quest. And he couldn't believe, with all that life had already dealt them, that he could lose her, too.

He *wouldn't* believe it.

He had to believe she was alive. Logan had gone after her, and he was a survivor, too. Logan would have kept her safe.

If he had been able to find her in the churning dark waters.

If they had found a way to shore.

If...

They were out there somewhere together. They had to be. And they had to be...

Alive.

And he was going to find them. Or, as Silent Sam had said, die in the trying.

Be steadfast. Hold to the wind. It was the motto she survived by.

SHE HAD BEEN STILL for so long that the water felt cool, even chilly. She had watched him go, but even now, long minutes later, she was still staring at the shore.

Really, what does any of it matter? she asked herself mockingly. They could rot here for years. They could die here.

Another thought trickled through her mind.

Would it matter so much?

Most of her life had offered little but misery. She had learned about swords and pistols and sailing not for the pure joy of the thing but because it had been a welcome diversion from scrubbing floors and had offered her a better life, even if not an ideal one. She had stood up to a man and killed him because life had been preferable to death.

No way out of it. All roads led back to a slaughtered family, a massacre in a village and the end of the promise of a decent life. She knew that sorrow, even terror, visited every life. Death was no stranger to the rich, but it was harder on the poor, and often came on the order of the wealthy and the royal. Because kings could send soulless men to achieve their goals, with no thought to how it was done, commanding them only to leave no survivors, so there would be none left to tell the tale.

But Blair Colm was greedy as well as cruel. A healthy child who could work in the colonies would fetch a nice price. He had made one mistake, though. Blair Colm had never realized just how long hatred could simmer in the human heart.

That day on the pirate ship...

It had been her salvation. It had given her life, where

she might have had none. And knowing he was out on the seas had given her a reason to go on. She had won her own freedom, and with it a chance to fulfill her burning desire to live, to avenge all the vicious brutality he had done to others.

And then…

Like a fool, she had taken a prisoner.

A man of reason. And charm. Intelligence and courage.

And he was beautiful.

Built rock-solid, smooth and sleek. She had thought herself immune. But as he had walked away, his muscles rippling, his skin gleaming with the droplets of water touched by the sun, he'd been enticing. Captivating. *Seductive.*

What she knew about sex wasn't particularly appealing; she'd seen enough rutting right in the taverns she frequented to consider it all a rather nasty and grunting affair. What she'd seen of most men had not been attractive. Hairy, ugly…

But Logan…

She closed her eyes. The water seemed cold, but she was glad of it, because she felt flushed, burning from within.

She forced her thoughts onto a different path, remembering that awful moment when she'd seen the body and thought it was Brendan. It had been worse than death itself to think he might have died….

What of that poor fellow's life? Had it been good? Had he been married? If his wife had been on the ship with him, had she survived the tempest? Were they good people, or had they been wealthy and titled and cruel? She found herself praying that he had lived a good life, that he had known pleasure, that he had been kind and decent.

It was no use.

No matter how hard she tried to think of something else, her thoughts kept returning to Logan. She despised herself for caring about him, for being so fascinated by him, his glorious body as well as his mind. He could tease, he could taunt, and he could challenge her, but he was never cruel. She wondered not so much about sex, to what she had seen in taverns and dark alleys, but about what it would be like to feel a gentle touch. To be held by him. To have him there to defend her, as he had done when she was set upon by the men in the alley.

She wondered what it would be like to feel the palm of his hand on her face, the soft pressure of his lips on hers, to hear his whisper, gentle and sweet...to let go of everything else, if only for a brief moment in time, even though it would not be...

Proper.

She wasn't at all proper. She was the child of an Irishman slain at the command of William of Orange. She had grown up upon her hands and knees, scrubbing. And when she had turned out to be presentable, she had suddenly become the possession of a woman who had eventually seen fit to sell her once again. And then...she had become a pirate.

No, not a *proper* life at all.

She didn't think she would ever be invited into any of the fashionable parlors in Charleston or Savannah.

But what did that matter, if she was seeking only a moment?

But there was more.

There was Cassandra.

Another mystery. If she was as beautiful and sweet and intelligent as he said, what was his hesitation? Why were they not affianced? He obviously knew her well and cared about her, as she did him. So why...?

She would be a frozen prune in another minute, despite the fact that the sun was rising high enough to heat the air. She scrubbed herself thoroughly with the soap she had been holding for too long, then hurried to the shore, wincing slightly as she stepped on a jagged outcrop of rock. On shore, she hurried for the towel and the clothing she had chosen, cursing the fact that she hadn't noticed Logan had done the same before her.

She dressed quickly in a man's breeches and shirt, then happily slipped into a pair of hose and shoes.

She paused then, her thoughts inevitably returning to Logan.

He was a decent man.

Another man in such a situation might have raped her already. After all, she had captained a pirate ship. She was one of the brethren. She would have been seen as fair game.

Not by Logan.

In his way...

In his way, he seemed to know her. To understand her. Maybe, perhaps, admire her.

She had met men—even some, such as Teach, who

were reputed to be animals—who were decent. Many who were kind. Who had standards and ethics.

But she had never met anyone who made her pause, who had given her a glimmer of an idea that she might like to truly live rather than merely live for vengeance. Not until she met Logan.

And that was both ridiculous and dangerous. She did not dare care for him. She could bear no more pain in her life.

But what if Brendan and all her crew were...lost?

They couldn't be. The *Eagle* needed cleaning, but she was a beautiful, well-built ship. She would have made it through the storm.

And her men would come for her. She had to believe it, she thought as she started walking again.

She *would* believe it.

She stopped.

Her heart was beating too hard. She was trembling. She had to pray that they came soon...very soon.

THE SECOND BODY washed up on the shore while Red was still at the spring.

Grimly, Logan pulled the corpse ashore and dragged him to the place where they had begun their graveyard. He didn't know how Red was going to react to a second dead man.

Well, he thought grimly, she wanted to be such a tough pirate. She must have dealt with dead men before. Yesterday's reaction had been due to her fear that the ship that had broken up was her own and that the dead man was her cousin.

Still…

There was a vulnerable core beneath her facade, one he might never have discovered had they not landed upon this isle.

He walked down the beach, hoping to find something better to dig with than yesterday's soup tureen. As he walked, he discovered a broken timber that had been painted with the ship's name. D-E-S-T-I was what he read. Destiny? Probably. An ironic—indeed, sad—name, given its end. She must have been a merchantman, and she seemed to have been carrying personal belongings as well as cargo. Perhaps she had been bringing a bride to meet her groom in the colonies. Or perhaps the owner had been taking his wife on an extended stay to visit relatives in the new country. Or the old country, he thought. There was…no way to know in which direction the ship had been traveling. The man they had buried yesterday had appeared to be a gentleman, in any case.

Destiny.

It found them all.

A long box, partially battered in, offered him what he was looking for.

A shovel.

A most useful tool, since he was very afraid the day would bring more inhabitants for the graveyard.

He was on his way back to the cemetery when he saw Red walking toward him and stopped. She was dressed simply in men's breeches and a shirt again. He had wondered if she might choose something from the costly feminine apparel they had found, but apparently she felt the facade must be maintained even here, in isolation.

Whatever helps her survive, he decided. But he wondered if she knew that, minus the coat and other accessories, the clothing she had chosen hugged her tightly and only enhanced the curves of her form rather than hiding them.

Not that it really mattered, given that he could picture her as she had been in the pool, minus any clothes whatsoever.

He gave himself a mental shake; they had a dead man to deal with, and then there was going to be the business of finding more food.

"My dear Laird Prisoner Haggerty," she greeted him, her tone light, as if they had never met at the spring that morning. "I had thought breakfast would be prepared by now."

He held still, wishing he could speak lightly in return, that he could challenge her to be the one to create their breakfast.

She saw his face and paused, concern rather than a frown coming to her features.

"Has...it's not...?"

"I'm afraid another poor fellow has arrived, but *not* a man from your ship, Captain," he reassured her quickly.

Still, she paled. "My God," she murmured. "I wonder how many were lost."

Not at all a real pirate, he thought. The salvage would have been uppermost in a real pirate's mind.

"The sea can be a cruel mistress to any who risk her

waves," he replied. "Why don't you look and see if we've anything other than biscuit? I shall tend to the man."

She straightened her shoulders, stiffened her spine. "No," she said softly.

He gazed at her quizzically.

"Someone must mourn the dead," she said.

"As you wish," he told her. "But I found only one shovel."

She swallowed. "One is enough."

He dug, and when she offered to take over, he shook his head and told her he could manage, so she stood by his side and watched.

She didn't look at the dead man's face, for which Logan was glad. This fellow was in even worse shape from the fish and the bloating than the first man had been.

Logan dug deep, then piled the soil high.

Once again, Red fashioned a cross, and they said the same prayers as they had before.

Logan realized he was drenched and winded, and his arms ached from digging through the hard-packed sandy soil. He leaned on the shovel, looking down.

When he looked up again, she had moved down the beach.

He put his shovel in the shelter, safe from the rain that was sure to come, and thought about building some shelves, and raising their beds above the ground, away from whatever rodents and crabs might wander in.

He heard her cry out with a note of triumph in her

voice just as his stomach rumbled, and he hoped she had found food.

Leaving the shelter, he ran down the beach toward her. "What?"

"Fishing poles," she said.

He stared at her.

"Fishing poles. We can catch fresh fish," she told him.

"I see."

She smiled slowly. "You've never fished?"

"Of course I've fished," he assured her. Then he blushed and admitted, "Um, no, not really."

"Never?"

"I was the captain of my ship," he told her.

"And I was the captain of mine," she reminded him, then gazed at him curiously. "What of your life...off the sea, *Laird* Haggerty?"

"Let us just say that fishing was not among my duties. However, I do believe I shall figure out the basics."

She was still smiling. He let out a groan of aggravation and stepped forward to take a fishing pole. It seemed a simple enough device.

He took the pole from her and started toward the beach. Behind him, she cleared her throat.

"What?" he returned, more sharply than he had intended.

It only increased her smile. Perhaps he should be glad he could afford her such amusement.

"We should find some mangroves...that way. The

fish will be there. And…a dead crab will make good bait. Or a live crab, if we can catch one."

They walked on together, and he saw a crab shell on the beach, but on examination, the body within had long ago been nibbled away to nothing by other creatures.

"We could eat these guys, but they're not the tastiest. If we can catch a red snapper in the mangroves…that will be very good."

Logan managed to snare a live crab quickly, when it scurried up onto one of the trunks. He managed to keep away from the snapping claws, and then, irritated that she found his lack of expertise so amusing, he made quick work of sectioning the crab. If crabs suffered, that one did not do so for long.

She kept walking, then turned inland, where the ocean washed between the trees.

The area was sheltered and cool, and he could see that she had chosen well; the fish were actually visible in the shallows. Perhaps because he was once again determined to prove himself, he snared the first fish. And it was a snapper. A big one.

She watched him silently as he brought it in.

"Well?"

"Good prisoner," she commended.

He swore and, turning with his catch, headed back for the shelter.

She followed, but paused on the way by their cache of treasures, searching until she found something that gave her pleasure. He tried not to watch as he started building a fire, but when she returned, she seemed so pleased that he had to ask, "Well? What did you find?"

"Tea. And that's a lovely fire," she said.

They set about their tasks; he prepared the fish, while she brewed the tea.

It was almost domestic.

The fresh fish was delicious, and the hot tea, mixed with sugar, made the perfect complement. They both relished their food in silence, but as he savored his last bite, he realized she was looking at him.

"Have I failed you in some way, Captain?" he asked her.

She shook her head. "Just how and where did you grow up?" she asked him.

"I think your past is the greater mystery."

"Not a mystery. Just drudgery. But you...?"

"Your drudgery being a mystery, it seems my story should be the same."

She shook her head, watching him still. "But it isn't the same. I mean, it's evident that you are loved and highly esteemed by many."

"As are you."

She waved a hand in the air. "I know of no one willing to pay a fortune on my behalf."

"No?" he inquired curtly. "There are more than a dozen men willing to give their lives for you. I would consider that everything."

She lowered her head. He had touched a nerve.

"We weren't talking about me."

"I was."

"Well, we're not going to talk about me," she said,

looking up. "Your life is the far sweeter story, a way to pass the time until my men find us and you are given your freedom."

"I already have my freedom." he said, and when she didn't object, he went on.

"It is possible," he suggested, "that another ship will come upon us. Possibly a *legitimate* ship. In which case, I, of course, will do the right thing and introduce you as a poor maiden, lost in the storm. I'll not mention that you're Red Robert, since I would prefer not to see you charged with piracy and hanged until dead."

"You're too kind," she said dryly. "So what would happen to me, pray tell?"

"Well, then the legend of Red Robert would end in mystery, and you could begin to live a proper life."

"A proper life," she repeated.

"Aye," he said softly.

She shook her head. "It would be kind enough for you to help me to arrive at some congenial port. But I am not seeking a proper life. You are Laird Haggerty. You have Cassandra, your land, your title."

"So. Poor little Red. She has nothing, so she must remain a pirate."

She stared at him fiercely. "I have something to live for. It is just not to be found in Savannah or Williamsburg or elsewhere in 'society.'"

"Aye, you're living for vengeance. Against Blair Colm."

She shrugged and rose. "I'm weary of conversation," she told him.

"There is more to life than death."

"Not always," she assured him. And then she turned and headed back down the beach.

THERE WERE BOOKS.

Books!

There were so many containers still to be opened, but when Red came upon the books, she was simply delighted. They were beautiful, leather-bound, the pages gilded. But it wasn't the craftsmanship that so thrilled her, it was the fact that now she would be able to read. There were books on astrology and astronomy, sailing, ships, the exploration of the Caribbean, flora and fauna, and there were fictional works, as well. Chaucer and Shakespeare, and even a translation of Cervantes. She was on her knees in the sand, hugging one to her chest, when Logan made an appearance at her side.

"So, you do have love in your soul," he said lightly.

She flushed. "Look! Books!"

"So you read."

"Of course I read."

He hunkered down beside her, a small smile playing at his lips. "Many a pirate captain does not," he reminded her.

She waved a hand in the air. "Teach reads. Many of the brotherhood do."

True enough. While the majority of seamen did not read, those pirates who had chosen the life after making a living at privateering were educated in some fashion and could read well enough.

But he'd never seen a pirate look so rapturous at the mere sight of a book, no matter how beautifully bound.

"Cervantes. In English," he noted, smiling.

"You've read it?" she asked him.

"Indeed," he assured her gravely. "The travails of Don Quixote de la Mancha. The story of a man whose fancy touched the lives of those around him."

"I know."

She stood abruptly. "Cervantes was captured by Barbary pirates."

Logan's smile deepened. "His dreams and idealism kept him alive, perhaps."

SHE HELD THE BOOK to her chest and walked away, heading toward their shelter. She looked back once, quickly, and saw that he was following her. But he was hauling the broken trunk of books.

She sat in the shade of a palm and started to read, then realized unhappily that she was more aware of his movements, as he worked with hammer, nails and timber, constructing low bases for their beds, than she was of the words on the page. Only when the hammering stopped and he walked away was she able to become engrossed in her book.

A little while later she realized that he was back, had been back for a while, because there was a delightful scent coming from the pan he had set on the fire. She put the book down and went to stand by him.

He had just finished preparing their plates. Wedges of lime sat next to the biscuit, which had sliced mango atop it. Steaming snapper steaks continued to tantalize her nose. He added the last wedge of lime to a plate, then rose to hand it to her.

"Captain," he said politely.

"Thank you," she said.

"Grog seemed fitting for the evening libation," he said, handing her a cup.

"Again, thank you."

She sat, taking a place in front of the fire.

"Are you enjoying your book?" he inquired.

She lowered her head, not at all certain whether to laugh or cry. They might have been a married couple sitting down to dinner, she the cherished and coddled wife, he the husband who worked as a man of business and looked forward to some educated conversation at the end of the day.

"I'm enjoying my book, yes, thank you. And you? What have you been doing?"

She was surprised when he hesitated before saying, "I found a cave near the spring. I spent some time exploring it and camouflaging it."

"Why?" she asked.

"If and when a ship comes...well, we'll need to see the flag to decide if we wish to be found or not."

She shook her head. "But...if we are discovered by pirates, the worst they will do is rob the island of the salvage and leave us marooned. Most likely, though, they would take us aboard, perhaps even return us to New Providence."

"Maybe. Maybe not."

"But—"

"Red, many men think a woman upon a pirate ship is bad luck. And many pirates may live by a code, but there are those who would rather just kill us and be done with any argument over salvage. And..."

He fell silent.

"What?"

"Many would consider you to be fair game."

She hadn't thought she could blush so easily.

"It's wise to have a hiding place," he told her. "And wise to hide some of what we'll need to survive. Though I truly mourn the loss of lives upon that ship, its demise provided us with the wherewithal to make survival here far easier than it might have been."

She looked away, wondering why everything in life seemed to come with a touch of anguish. Suddenly feeling as if she were dangerously close to tears, she rose.

"Thank you for the excellent meal, Laird Haggerty," she said.

She left her plate on the sand and headed for their shelter, hoping he would not insist she wash her own dishes.

He did not.

She lay down, feeling hollow. And when night came, sleep followed.

CHAPTER NINE

LOGAN HAD ROUSED the minute she made a sound, but at first he kept his distance.

She talked in her sleep. She fought in her sleep. She muttered the same words over and over.

He moved to her side and sat. He wanted to touch her, to awaken her. Beneath their lids, her eyes moved erratically. A slim trickle of tears seeped out and ran down her cheeks.

And then she screamed, and he could bear it no more.

He drew her gently into his arms and held her tight, whispering to her. "It's all right, it's all right. It's over. You're safe."

It took him long moments to soothe her, time in which she struggled to awake, then finally did so with a start. And then she was cradled against him, looking up at him. For a moment there was something so naked and pained in her eyes that he longed to throw away the world, and promise her that everything would be right and safe for her in the future, vowing it on his life and soul. But then the ever-present shield dropped into place over her eyes, changing the very color of them.

She stiffened, as if she had been slapped, but she didn't pull free of his arms.

"I woke you," she said. "I apologize."

He shook his head, his arms still strong as he stared at her. Something about her drifted into him like the cool ocean air they breathed. He kept his hold gentle but firm.

"What horror do you chase in your dreams?" he asked. "Or does it chase you?"

She set a hand on his. She was still trembling, but her body heat seemed to light a fire inside him.

"I apologize," she said again with dignity, avoiding his question.

He didn't move.

"I'm all right now," she insisted. "The dreams don't come all the time. I hope not to wake you again."

She was still trembling, seemingly unable to stop, her voice tremulous.

He eased her back down on her pillow, but he didn't leave her. Instead, he stretched out at her side, leaning on an elbow, making it clear he wasn't going away.

"What demons do you fight in your sleep?" he asked.

She only stared at him. They were so alone. The sky was star-studded velvet above them, and the breeze was as gentle as her dream had been violent. Palms rustled quietly, and the waves rolled ashore in a lulling whisper.

"What do you want of me?" she groaned.

"The truth. The past."

"Why the past, when there is no future?" she asked dully.

Her words, spoken in a tone of such misery, surprised him.

"There is a future."

He watched her. She wasn't going to speak, so he went on. "I can try to put together your past," he said. "Blair Colm was one of William the Third's key men in Ireland. He murdered your family. He killed women and children indiscriminately, but he took you and Brendan and maybe others, because he could sell you into indentured servitude in the colonies."

She rolled onto her back. "You've been speaking to Brendan."

"If I have or haven't, it doesn't matter. I know the story."

"How can you?"

"Blair Colm was in the business of selling children for years," he told her.

She stared at him. "He...destroyed your family, as well?"

Logan sat up, watching her, his arms locked around his knees. "My father went into battle. Hopeless battle. He thought he'd left an escape route open for myself and my mother, but Blair had killed his man and taken his place. I don't know if he would have killed my mother or not, but she tried to fight him, so she died. And I was taken to America."

She got up on her knees and inched away from him, staring at him as if he had suddenly become the enemy.

"He killed your mother—in front of you—and you haven't spent your life, prestige and resources to hunt him down?" she asked and accused, all in one.

"I grew up in the house of a good man. I didn't see or hear of Blair Colm for years. I spent several years in the militia, and learned only recently that he was welcomed in drawing rooms in Savannah and Charleston, that he made port as far north as Boston, then set out to sea again. He was never in any port while I was there."

"I would have taken a dagger to him in the streets!" she charged.

"You're not listening. I never came upon the man."

"You should have made sure you did so."

"Frankly, I would prefer to see him shown to the world as the monster he is, stripped of his knighthood, proven guilty of his crimes and hanged by legal authority."

"Did he kill with legal authority?" she asked, then answered herself. "Aye, in a way. He was told to subdue the Irish, no matter how. So his brutal murder of children was condoned, and in his wake, children are now sentenced to death for stealing bread. To survive. Because their land was stolen, their families murdered—by Blair Colm. So what justice would it take to execute him, when he acts at the will of the king?"

He let out a sigh. "Why do you think I made friends with pirates and did business in such places as New Providence?"

"You hoped to find him?" she asked skeptically.

"Of course I hoped to find him. You, with your quest and your passion...you *would* have taken a dagger to him in the streets," he admonished. "You wouldn't have gotten near him. He takes great care when he enters into society. He has a guard around him that is carefully chosen from those who helped him commit his atrocious crimes. You would have been apprehended and hanged, with nothing accomplished."

She sat back, studying him, perplexed. "Then I have been right all along," she said. "Being Red Robert *is* my only hope."

"You're *not* right. It *isn't* your only hope."

"Oh, but it is. I'm not wrong."

"You're Irish and stubborn, and you apparently like the idea of being a martyr."

"I am not determined on being a martyr."

He leveled a finger at her. "Then believe in a future."

He went to her, gripping her by the shoulders. "Lady Fotherington is dead, as is the man she sold you to. I admit, you can't go home—I would never suggest you return to Ireland. It would bring you nothing but pain and bitterness. But you *can* make a life for yourself."

"Where would home be, then?" she demanded. "A house where I can once again be a scullery maid?"

"Life offers more than that," he told her. "Far more."

"For you," she said bleakly.

"For anyone. This is a new world we live in," he told her.

"A new world with all the old masters," she said.

He shook his head firmly. "A new world where the king's edicts come across the sea slowly. A king who is a foreigner, feeling his way through English law."

"I cannot forget. I will not forget."

"Do you think I have ever forgotten?" he demanded. "I have learned to bide my time. As you must," he added dryly. "All your anger and hatred, no matter how righteous, cannot be avenged as we sit upon this isle and await…fate." He almost said "destiny," but he thought of the lost ship and refrained.

She didn't answer him.

"You do realize you are allowing him to steal from you every day of your life, not just for the slaughter of your family?"

She frowned at him. Fiercely.

"He has taken your life, as well," he said, his vehemence soft.

She shrugged. "I died on that field that day. I have been in purgatory ever since."

"What if I were to swear to you that I would hunt him down and kill him?"

She stared at him with disdain. "When I came upon you," she reminded him, "you were busy transporting treasure—quite stupidly—for the gain it would bring you."

"Aye, that I was," he agreed. "But that doesn't mean I wasn't on the lookout for Blair Colm, as well. I don't only want him to die. I want him to die while I survive and flourish. I see that as the greater vengeance."

"We are different people," she said very softly.

"Yes—you wish to be a martyr."

"But I don't!"

"Think about what you're doing, then," he told her.

She stood, slipped an arm around their palm tree support beam and looked out at the moonlit darkness. "All else dims when I think about him," she said.

"Then your nightmares will continue until you die

for your charade, and vengeance will be left to someone else," he warned. "Tell me, is Brendan as obsessed with revenge as you are?"

She turned to him angrily. "Of course."

"Does he not desire to taste a life of freedom?"

"He was sold into servitude with me. He is equally bent on vengeance."

"I think he would prefer vengeance with a chance of survival."

She glared at him. "Laird Haggerty, I am ever so sorry for having disturbed your sleep. You have been of tremendous…"

"Help?"

"And aggravation. Please, leave me in peace, and I will do the same for you."

"How on earth can I leave you in *peace* when you are forever fighting?"

"Then let me wage my own battles in my own life and my own mind," she said sharply. "Please, go dream of your riches and your Cassandra."

"Why do you continually bring her up?" he inquired, steadfast in his intent not to grow angry, to remain rational.

"Because you…have made it clear that you value a…a *proper* life above all else."

"God in heaven, help me against fools and women!" So much for maintaining his temper.

"Oh! There we have it! If *you* were the one bent on vengeance, it would be a man's just fury. But when I see what must be done, I'm a fool and a woman!"

"You are a woman who is acting like a fool, that is all. You are Don Quixote, battling windmills, playing at being a pirate while you seek out Blair Colm. Why is it nobler for you to sail the seas attacking innocent ships while you hunt for the man than it is for me to seek a respectable life while doing the same?"

"Because you have a choice!" she cried angrily.

He inhaled, and in the shadows, with the world shrunk down to just the two of them, he knew she was right.

"Forgive me," he said simply, then walked over to her and took her hands. "You did what needed to be done when it needed to be done. But I can change what will come, don't you understand?"

"No," she said bluntly.

"You...have taken a good haul from the sea. And I will be, if not rich, comfortable, with a title and holdings, and I can start you on a good life."

"A path to righteousness?" she mocked.

"Bobbie," he began, the name a caress, "there are many ways to live."

She smiled. "No. There are but two in our world. The earth and the sea. I live a life free of pretenses. Your world is full of charades."

"That—coming from you?"

"My charade is no worse than those played out daily in your world."

He shook his head. "You are the most stubborn, mulish woman I have ever met."

"A far cry from sweet Cassandra," she agreed.

His temper soared suddenly. "Will you cease with that?" he demanded.

"Why?"

"Because as much as I admire her, I have told you—
I am not marrying *sweet* Cassandra!"

"Why not?" she asked. "The letter written promis-
ing ransom…it was written with love and admiration."

"She deserves far better than anything I can offer. It
would not be fair."

"Because you are not as rich as some men?
Logan…you would bring many fine qualities to a
marriage."

"It would not be fair to her because I do not love her.
I mean, I do love her, but I have realized I am not *in*
love with her."

He sighed. "My dear, you can take two perfectly
proper people, and they may like and admire and
respect one another very much—the very feelings most
people believe are exactly what is needed for a
marriage—and perhaps they may even believe that they
love each other, until…something shows them otherwise. Cassandra and I are those two people. Should I
have my own pocket again, there will be a coin or two
in it, and certainly we do care for one another. We could
well grow to old age together as friends, but she
deserves much more."

She was staring at him, stunned.

"But…"

"But what?" he demanded irritably.

"My God, you are a romantic!" she exclaimed.

"No. I intend only to be a…a *noble* man."

Noble? Not really. Why didn't he want to marry
Cassandra now? Because she deserved the best, a man
who prized her above all else.

Not a man who looked at another woman and burned.

Who longed to be a bad man, indeed, and drag her passionately into his arms with no room for quarter.

Holding on to the palm tree, she turned to stare again at the spot where the ocean met the sky, where the shadows caught the night and the white foam of the waves caught the light of the moon.

"Look," she said, after a moment. "The sun is just starting to rise."

And it was. He could see a tiny line where the day struggled to be born. It was soft yellow with a streak of pink. Even as he watched, the line broadened, a riot of maroon and gold. And slowly the yellow streaks of the sun began to dispel the darkness.

"What a beautiful day," she said, and walked toward the shore. He was tempted to follow her.

But she made such a strong and solitary figure, silhouetted against the colors of the dawn, that he let her be.

"LAND HO!"

The cry came from the crow's nest, and the minute he heard the words, Brendan jumped up from the bed in the captain's quarters.

Racing out, he saw Silent Sam in the crow's nest and Peg-leg at the wheel.

"Island?" he called.

Silent Sam looked down at him with a nod.

Twenty minutes later, their sails were furled and they were at anchor. A crew of six took the small boats in to the beach.

Brendan stood on the sand. There was some flotsam and jetsam on the beach, but not much, and it had all been there for a long time. He didn't need to wait for the others to return from farther inland to know they had not found Red and Logan. He felt his heart sinking, yet, he could not allow himself to give up.

Peg-leg came over to him a few minutes later and said, "I'm sorry, Brendan."

"I believe we're searching in the wrong direction," Brendan said, refusing to let the man see his fears. "We need to recalculate the wind from the storm and its effect on the tides. I believe we need to sail in a more westerly direction."

Peg-leg was silent for a moment. Then he said, "Aye, Brendan. Westerly. And good that it was not this sad shoal. Not a drop of water did we find."

Water. Brendan prayed there was fresh water wherever they had washed ashore.

Washed ashore *alive.*

"My friends," he said to the assembled crew. "We sail again."

As soon as they returned to the ship, he cried out the order to raise anchor and sail. As he stood near the helm, staring out bleakly at the expanse of the ocean, Jimmy O'Hara joined him.

"Brendan," he said hesitantly.

"Aye?"

The skinny little man whose life they had spared looked at him with frightened eyes.

"I believe he's out there."

For a moment, Brendan was confused.

"Who?"

"Blair. Blair Colm."

"What?"

"I was in the crow's nest, on guard, as ye' checked out the isle. There was a ship in the distance. My eyes are good. I could have sworn I saw the British flag—with his beneath it—on a ship headed west."

Brendan looked at him, his heart turning to lead.

"Then we must sail with all speed," he said.

ANOTHER DAY. Another bout of exploring their surprise bounty of resources. Red had been quite pleased to brew tea and nibble on plain, unadorned biscuit that morning, and it seemed that, after talking—arguing—through the night, they were both content to avoid conversation.

Midday, Red disappeared, heading inland with her book and towel. She said nothing as she left; her destination was obvious.

By mid-afternoon he had finished creating platforms to lift their beds off the ground, built up walls to meet the canvas roof of their shelter and, he thought, performed a fine feat of engineering, remaking their home so that it would both protect them and allow for the passage of the cooling sea breezes. He had rolling sheets of canvas to act as doors, because it was inevitable that they would find themselves beset by storms.

Then he went fishing and was once again successful, though he didn't think it had much to do with his prowess as a fisherman but more to do with the fact that fish were plentiful in the mangrove shallows.

By late afternoon he was weary, dirty and tired. Taking one of the linen towels, he headed inland.

As he neared the pool, he saw her clothing strewn on the embankment.

She was standing with her back to him on one of the rocky outcroppings in the middle of the spring, sluicing water from her hair. The sun glistened on the droplets that beaded her back. The sleek skin of her back alone was enough to remind him in painfully physical ways that he was a man who had been at sea a long time.

He was also a man who had built a shelter for them and patiently fished to provide for their well-being.

He was not going to allow her, or any form of wicked temptation, to steer him from the fresh pleasure of the bath he so richly deserved.

She heard him as he was shedding his clothing and turned.

"Pardon, Laird Haggerty. I am here now," she informed him.

He ignored her but kept his back to her as he folded his clothing.

"If my presence is objectionable, you will have to leave."

"Excuse me?"

"You are not hard of hearing. *I* have worked all afternoon for the betterment of our survival, Captain Robert, while you have played. This is my time."

"Did I ask you to become a master builder?"

"Out or not, I'm coming in."

She had turned away. He was glad. He hadn't felt like entering the water with his arousal so obvious to her eyes. He hurried in. Surely the cool spring water would help.

Damn, it did not.

And still he ignored her, swimming out, thinking exertion could be of some assistance.

It was not.

He swam harder, to no avail. Diving deep beneath the surface, he felt his muscles plow through the water. At last he headed to sure footing and hoped she had thought to bring soap.

"Captain Robert?" he called.

Now just her head was showing above water.

"Laird Haggerty?" she returned.

"Soap?"

"Catch!"

She threw it. He caught it deftly and nodded his thanks. Once again, sadly, he would smell faintly like a harem girl.

Better that than...

She was coming toward him.

Stunned, he spun around. She was only steps away. Perhaps she had intended to pass him and head for shore.

Then she stopped. He turned and met her eyes. Where they had wandered before, he did not know.

"You say you are a free man," she whispered.

He frowned. She was far too close. Within arm's reach. The sun dappled the water, and she was like elegance made flesh, fire so tempting as to be unbearable. She stood tall and without apology. Her skin was as sleek as the finest porcelain, the fullness of her breasts tapering to the hand span of her waist.

"A free man?" he echoed, frozen to his spot, afraid to move lest madness consume him. "You have made me so," he reminded her softly.

"No," she replied, her voice but a whisper. "I do not speak of that kind of freedom. I mean free as…in you are not…committed to another." He barely heard the last; he read the words in the movement of her lips.

It is madness, but I am committed to you, he thought.

He longed to speak the words, but they would not come, so he merely kept his eyes upon hers and shook his head.

She stepped closer then, and he cared not what was said or not said, because all the necessary information had been exchanged between them.

Life was a facade…

But she had stripped away that facade, and now they stood before each other naked not only in body, but in soul. He didn't know if she took the last step, or if he was the one who closed the last inches between them, but she was suddenly in his arms. The cool water should have turned to steam, he thought, given the fire that erupted within him. She was there, a tease, a touch, that satin flesh pressing against his own. And then his arms tightened, forcing her against him, muscle vibrant against muscle, her breasts crushed against his chest, sex to sex. His lips met hers like a whisper at first, savoring the feel of her mouth, and then with the kiss deepened, the pressure of his tongue insistent and thrusting deeply.

Wet and hot, she echoed the foreplay of his tongue, lips parting, tongue taking part in the same slow and then fevered duel. Unbearable heat seemed to sweep through him as surely as if he were standing too close to a forge, and carnal need became his driving force. Somewhere in the far regions of his mind, a voice of sanity spoke, then grew faint. His hands explored the length of her body. She was perfection, every sleek inch pure seduction.

Her fingers brushed over his shoulders, and yet each feathered touch was like lightning within. Madness seized him. It had been so long. And it had never been like this, such a desperate desire, such all-consuming need. Hunger. He lifted her high, then drove her hard down upon him. The air was cool, the water rushing deliciously around their naked flesh.

In seconds he realized he was the first lover of the fabled pirate queen. He froze in stunned surprise, and it was only her whisper that brought him back to life.

"Please…"

Not a protest.

A plea.

At first he was careful, but then the thirst, the hunger, raced out of control. It had been so long. He had lusted after her since he had first known what she was, he had craved her for long days and longer nights.…

Somewhere along the way, he lost his soul. Lost the slim thread of sanity. It was gone, all gone, and they were moving like the wind, like the storm that had marooned them there together, like the crashing waves that beat against the shore when the elements raged. He heard her breathing, short and rapid, felt her fingers, hard and strong now, as they dug into his shoulders, felt the fine muscle of her thighs, wrapped around him. And most of all he felt the tightness of her flesh sheathing him as he thrust feverishly within her, felt an agony so sweet that he trembled in its thrall.

He climaxed with a violence as strong as any storm he had ever weathered, his arms still tight around her, her thighs still locked around his hips. Her cry had been as desperate as his, and now she continued to hold him tightly, the warmth of their passion just beginning to fade. Her face was wedged into the junction of his neck and shoulder, and as he stood there, holding her, he could feel the massive pounding of his own heart, the echo of hers. He smoothed her hair back and whispered softly, "I didn't know."

He felt her. Warily, he allowed her to straighten, to disentangle herself, to stand on her own. She ran a hand through the wet strands of her hair and gave herself away, for her fingers trembled.

She shrugged. "What is there to know? I make my own choices."

He was staring at her hard, he realized, searching for something in her eyes, though he didn't know what.

But apparently whatever she saw in *his* eyes disarmed her, for she continued. "Good God, Laird Haggerty, I am a pirate. I have killed men. I am… ruthless. This…this is…of no great concern."

He tried very hard to keep a smile from his features. He didn't intend to force her to reveal any further weakness, for she had trusted him with her greatest vulnerability already.

"Bobbie," he said very softly, "you have killed men in self-defense and you have stood strong against injustice. That hardly makes you ruthless."

She tossed her head. "I make my own choices, and unlike most women, who are seeking a future, I live in the present." For a moment confusion was visible in the beautiful blue eternity of her eyes. Then her lashes fell, quickly shielding her thoughts. "You are well-built, you bathe…and I did not want to die without… knowing… We may perish on this island, and I would not want to die knowing only blood and death…and what I've seen of life as a servant and in taverns…"

He could not help himself. He laughed aloud.

"I pray I was a far better candidate than those men you have met in the taverns of New Providence and elsewhere."

Her face suffused with color. She was angry.

"I beg pardon. I am simply glad that I was found… appropriate to serve my captain in all ways," he assured her.

She turned away, her anger growing.

He reached out and caught her by the arm. "Don't deceive yourself, Red. Never deceive yourself. We are all, by nature, animals, and what you have seen in taverns is merely the result of a man's physical need and usually a woman's financial one. What you were seeking was much more. What I pray I can give soars far higher. I care about you. It should be most obvious that I care about you deeply."

"Well, don't," she snapped. "You are Laird Haggerty. There is a union between Scotland and England, but there is no such thing where Ireland is concerned. You are, in fact, as much my enemy as any Englishman."

He took her by the shoulders, as stiff as she was, and

drew her back into his arms, amazed that her show of temper could arouse him again with such a vengeance so quickly. He tilted her chin, forcing her eyes to his. "We are in a new world. And I am not your enemy."

This time, he did not hesitate, did not offer gentleness. He set his mouth on hers with sheer demand, giving no hint of quarter. He lifted her from the water, his mouth on hers the entire time. He laid her down in the shallows, with the cool water just rushing over them, and she curved against him and gave way to the depth of his kiss, then began to respond with a greater urgency. And it seemed, he thought, that she'd learned the pleasures of lovemaking swiftly, for it was as if her every twist and turn was calculated to drive him to madness. And so they made love.

Slowly.

Excruciatingly slowly.

Taking their time…

Tortured and torturing. His fingers tracked the silken curves of her breasts, his lips following with feathery caresses. He explored her flesh with the touch of his hands and the wet caress of his tongue, savoring, tasting…dying…

She moved with fluid beauty, and her hands grew bolder upon him, knuckles against the taut muscle of his chest, arms, back, thighs…and then her fingers, so light at first, grew bold upon his sex, as well. He neared total insanity, explosive, volatile insanity. But he relished the agony, the sweet feeling of desperation, the end no longer a whisper but a shriek in his mind that led him ever onward….

No quarter asked.

No quarter given.

The scent of her was something he knew would be emblazoned forever in his mind. The feel of her flesh. The look in her eyes. If he lived to be a hundred, he would never forget. He would never cease to cherish this time. Because suddenly, the taunting was gone, pride was lost, and it was simply the two of them, no longer driven by curiosity or raw hunger, but by something more.

Something deeper.

She felt it, too. He could see it in her eyes...

And therein lay the difference between needing a woman—and needing a woman to live, to breathe, to go on....

He continued to kiss and caress. He made love to her with his tongue, intimately, desperate that she should know the excruciating pleasure. His own pleasure did not even matter. The whispers and cries that escaped her were like the music of paradise, a match for the beat that pulsed in his body and mind. Her hands on him...that alone was worth dying for.

And finally, when the passion in him threatened to explode, they came together, and again he was sheathed inside her in a way that seemed more thrilling than anything he had ever known before, more than any promise, any dream.

He tried, oh, God, he tried, for something slower and gentler....

But it wasn't to be. They were frenzied, clinging, thrusting, arching, slick, the slap of flesh against flesh faintly audible beneath the incoherent sounds they made. He relished her cry of wonder and the earth-shattering climax that seized him, ripped through him. His eyes wide, he stared at the trees, the sky…and her.

Afterward they lay together, soaked and spent, gasping, for long moments. The sun dappled them as its rays passed through the trees. The sounds of the waterfall and the rustling palm fronds made themselves evident once again. The world returned.

Holding her was so sweet that he didn't speak. Couldn't speak. He idly moved his fingers gently over her flesh while they regained their breath….

As time passed, the breeze grew chill upon their naked, cooling flesh.

At last, her sense of self returning, she drew away from him, no false modesty now, but proud in her naked glory. She got nimbly to her feet and looked down on him with a knowing smile.

"Actually," she said, "I do believe that was quite a bit…nicer than anything I've ever seen in a tavern."

And with that she returned to the water to rinse. And, in time, without looking at him again, she found her clothing and dressed, then walked away.

CHAPTER TEN

CASSANDRA STOOD ON deck, staring out at the beauty of the water. The day was sunny, and yet the breeze was enough to keep the air cool, making it far more pleasant outside than in her cabin. She only wished the breeze could blow away the worry that tore at her heart.

A little while ago they had passed a merchantman and learned of the storm that had demolished many a vessel. And there had been no word from the feared pirate Red Robert, so many assumed he had gone down to the bottom, as well.

She winced. She was and always had been a child of privilege. But a responsible one, she thought. Now the lesson that her father had always tried so hard to teach her came home with a vengeance.

Money could not buy everything. It couldn't stop the wind, and it couldn't control the seas. It couldn't defeat death.

She sensed her father coming to stand by her. "We will find him," he consoled her gently.

She hesitated, unsure what to say. She loved Logan. He was her best friend. But she didn't dare tell her father that she wasn't sure she wanted to spend a lifetime with him. She didn't want to explain that she didn't want to be there, where they were, sailing the dangerous seas that Logan loved so much. She liked dry land. She loved tea parties and balls. And books. Logan was handsome and strong and exciting, and she loved his stories of adventure. Loved the passion and excitement in his eyes when he talked of his life on the waves. But…she wasn't sure she wanted to share that life.

There were times when she was afraid she wouldn't be able to survive the mad combination of passion and fire that made up his life.

But that was something she certainly wasn't about to attempt to explain now. Now when her father was risking life and limb and fortune on Logan's behalf, first to find him and ransom him from pirates, and then now…hoping against hope he was alive. Somewhere. In a sea that somehow seemed larger than the whole of the universe.

"Of course we will find him, Father," she said now, then smiled and hugged him tightly. He was such a fine man. He always stood up for his beliefs, even when it meant disagreeing with the governor, and even if his opinions were not always popular. But he was above reproach. Quietly firm, never violent. His mind and his eloquence were his weapons. He had funded homes for orphans, the aging and the dying. He had told her once that God had been so kind to him that he would surely rot in hell if he didn't match God's heavenly kindness here on earth.

She pulled away and studied him. He had a fine and firm physique for a man of such peaceful conviction. He was tall and sturdy. His snow-white hair was abundant, so he was never in need of a wig. His cheekbones were high, his brows were bushy and slightly darker than his hair. He was always dressed impeccably, and stood ramrod-straight, except when he paused to offer a hug to a friend, a child or his own beloved daughter.

"We will find him, Father," she said again. "I have no fear," she assured him, though inwardly, she winced, for was it not her fault Logan was here, at best a prisoner, and at worst...

For Logan had set out to sea at least in part to earn enough money to be worthy of her hand.

But there were darker reasons, as well, she knew and had always known. She had tried to dissuade him from his search for vengeance, even though she had known that should she succeed, she would surely change the man she so admired.

Her best friend.

No, as dear and fine and reasonable as her father was, this was not the time to explain that when she saw Logan again, she would have to tell him that they were not meant to be man and wife, partners for life.

"Logan is a survivor, child. He is out there. The ship might have been damaged. They may even now be lying low in an inlet somewhere, making repairs. Whatever has happened, child, we shall find him."

"Ahoy!"

The call came from above. Shading her eyes against the sun, Cassandra looked up as the sailor in the crow's nest shouted out, "Ship on the horizon!"

Her father fumbled for his spyglass. She heard the

captain running forward, and she hurried with her father to join him at the bow.

"Well?" her father demanded.

"Looks like…someone just took down the Union Jack."

"So…it's a British ship?"

"I don't know," Captain Reynolds said. He was heavy in physique, still hinting of a once powerful body, and his bandy little sea legs were strong. His face was a mask of worried wrinkles.

"A British ship, changing its flag?" Cassandra said.

"It's a pirate ship," the captain said.

"A pirate? It might be…Red Robert!" Cassandra said, hope flooding through her. The pirate would keep their bargain; she was certain of that with all her heart.

But the captain shook his head slowly. "I know the flag beneath which Red Robert sails." He was frowning.

As they watched, they saw the other ship raise a skull and crossbones.

The gun hatches opened.

The captain turned in a rush and shouted,

"Man the guns! Steer hard to the east, and pray God we can outrun her!"

JIMMY O'HARA found Brendan at the captain's desk, his expression dismal as he studied charts. So many islands. So many inlets…

Were Red and Logan even alive?

They had to be. Red's quest had been his quest. Life was…the fight, the chance, the hope, that she had given him. Given all of them. She was out there, she was alive, and he was going to find her. That was that.

He had bidden the man to enter but been so intent on his maps that he hadn't even looked up. When O'Hara cleared his throat, Brendan shifted his attention to his visitor at last.

"Aye, O'Hara?"

"I thought I might be of service."

Brendan was skeptical. The man was a damned good cook, but he was also a coward, and he had accepted money to attack Red when she had done him no ill. That was hardly laudable, especially in the pirate world.

"You wish to be of service?" Brendan asked skeptically.

O'Hara nodded.

"In what way?"

O'Hara walked forward and picked up Brendan's compass, setting the point upon a spot on the chart. It appeared to be water, surrounded by tiny islands.

Brendan arched a brow to him.

"Me brother was a mapmaker, and he told me a secret of the mapmakers' brotherhood, the existence of Isla de Muerta. Those who have happened upon her do not chart her. A silent agreement."

"Isle of death?" Brendan asked, confused.

O'Hara shrugged. "She is an oasis many a captain does not care to share, and so the name. Volcanic formation, a fresh water spring, rich with mangoes and fish. If you look at our position before the storm, think of the wind and currents…" He drew an invisible line.

Brendan nodded, feeling a surge of hope.

And a sense of wariness.

He had no problem believing that the men who had chanced upon the island and partaken of its resources might not want its presence known, but...

He stared hard at O'Hara.

Was the man offering this information in honest friendship and good faith?

Or was it a trap?

AH, YES, SLAKE THE THIRST, and then it will go away.

No. It would not.

Red wished Logan were cruel. That he was foolish, unaware of books or the world. That he had the usual sense of superiority possessed by titled men. She wished she could find one thing about him that was loathsome.

She wished...

She wished with all her heart that she had never set eyes on him. And she wished most desperately that she had never touched him, never let him touch her, for now she knew a passion that was far sweeter than any revenge.

She felt the heat of the sun and wondered just how long she had been staring at the waves, her mind in constant turmoil.

She knew she must make a small and pathetic figure against the vastness of the sea and sky. Insignificant. The Old World was far, far away, and even the New World seemed to be distant here. All her rage and hatred were nothing against the scope of the ocean, and yet the ocean itself was as nothing to the hurt in her heart and soul.

Because sooner or later they would be found.

And then...

Whatever bond they had created here would be nothing once they were back in the world, just as she was nothing against the enormity of the sea.

She was so deep in her thoughts that she was startled when his hands fell on her shoulders. She spun around to look at him, then quickly stepped back, afraid now of closeness as she had not been before.

"Tea is served, Captain," he said.

She blinked. "What?"

"Tea. Also, a delicious menu of softened biscuit and sugar, with tidbits of coconut."

"Lovely."

"Not to mention the not-so-delicately seasoned salt beef I just uncovered. I'm afraid I've been soaking it for a bit now, but it's still a challenge to the teeth."

She lowered her head, smiling. "My God. I had no idea how long I'd been standing here. You've...prepared a veritable feast."

"Feast? You are too kind, dear Captain."

"Ah, well, these days, one's definition of a feast can be quite...fluid."

"Come, then, if you will?" He offered her an elaborate bow. "This is the kind of feast much better enjoyed hot, before the true taste makes itself known."

She lowered her head, smiling, and preceded him back to their living area.

"Shall I pour?" she asked politely.

"Indeed," he said, and she made a play of preparing

their tea, her mannerisms a perfect mockery of afternoon tea at the finest mansion in the colonies.

"You're very good," he said.

She shrugged. "Brendan said I could have been an
actress."

"A better choice than pirating."

"I didn't choose pirating, it chose me." She kept her
attention on the food he prepared.

"Pirating *chose* you?"

She stared at him then, her expression a mixture of
defiance and matter-of-factness.

"It did."

"Many a pirate has found a way to make a living
on dry land."

"Some have," she admitted. "But usually they find
their end in the embrace of a noose."

"Because they didn't change their ways before they
were caught by those who give orders to the hangman,"
he said, his tone hard and aggravated.

She looked up at him, refraining from returning his
anger. "Laird Haggerty, you will not change me, nor
will you deter me from my purpose."

Stubborn woman, he thought angrily. Couldn't she
see that his intent was to help her? He had to make her
see the error of her ways, no matter how passionately
she loathed Blair Colm. He could, and would—somewhere, somehow, some way—deal with the man himself. He had as much right or more.

"You must realize—"

"I realize a great deal, Laird Haggerty. And it
changes nothing."

"You are a stubborn mule, and a foolhardy one."

"Foolhardy was taking you prisoner," she returned, and he saw that her temper was rising to meet his own.

"It makes no sense for you to continue pursuing the man so feverishly."

"I'm stranded on an island," she reminded him. "I'm not pursuing anyone."

He moved closer and leaned over her, his face so close to hers that she couldn't possibly ignore him. "I will find him. We will both be avenged."

Her eyes narrowed. "Ah, yes, the laird will go after him, the all-powerful laird."

"I have power you don't."

She stared at him for a long while, not flinching away. And then she smiled again. "Who was the prisoner, *Laird* Haggerty? And who had the power?"

He swore, moving away from her, his patience tested by the fact that he had no good answer to her question.

He wished he could walk out on her.

That there was a door to slam.

Since there wasn't, he swore beneath his breath again, then strode away to stare out across the water.

A few moments later, he heard her come up behind him.

"What?" he snapped.

"You really should partake of the food you prepared," she said.

He turned and stared at her.

"I can go elsewhere, if you wish, and leave you in peace while you eat," she offered.

"I don't think that's possible. I've met you and now

I shall have no peace," he muttered. But then he started back toward the fire, food and his tea. He was hungry, damn it, and he had prepared the meal, after all. He winced. Was there something of male pride in all this? God help him. Was it instinctual? They'd made love. Made love, dammit. For what they had shared was no simple act of desperate sex.

Why couldn't she see that he was trying as hard as he could to protect her?

She followed him back. "You are attacking me, bear in mind. I've not said a word against you or your way of life. However *stupid* it might have been."

"I beg your pardon."

"You knew the sea was full of pirates when you decided to make your riches-laden journey across the Caribbean."

That she was right didn't help matters in the least. He knew he shouldn't have risked the voyage. Knew it. But he had gambled. He had the right to gamble—and the need. How else could he find the where-withal to make his way in society and rebuild the home that had been so brutally taken? Those were things he needed to do in his father's name. And yes, once Cassandra had seemed to be part of that dream. But he had always intended revenge, as well.

"I knew what I was doing."

She simply stared at him cuttingly.

"It was a calculated risk."

"Your calculations were off."

He smiled politely. "I am alive," he told her.

"Because I'm merciful."

"And you're alive right now because of *me,*" he reminded her pleasantly.

"I didn't ask you to save my life," she said.

"No. Sorry, it was just an instinctive thing to do."

She spoke slowly. "You saved my life, and I am grateful. But it is still *my* life."

"Actually, in certain cultures, you would now be my slave."

"But you're my prisoner."

"Hardly. I think we've established that."

A flash of anger touched her features. "Nothing has been *established.* Out of human decency, I decided to let you go free. Meanwhile, we don't know who will come upon this island first, do we? I know my men will be looking for us. Tonight we must raise our fire, so that they will find us."

"I'm not so sure we should do any such thing."

"Why not?"

"Do you know how many pirate ships are out there?"

"Exactly? No," she said with aggravation. "But it doesn't matter. Pirates do have honor."

"Among pirates. And then only some pirates," he said.

"They will honor the name of Red Robert."

He looked her slowly up and down. Then he started to laugh.

"What the hell is the matter with you?" she demanded.

"Let's see, the wig is gone. And though you have donned men's attire, I cannot say you look the least bit like a man. Pirate's honor? What pirate will believe you are the notorious Red Robert?"

"But I *am* Red Robert."

"Nonsense. Red Robert is merely a myth."

"I am very real."

He shrugged.

"So what do you suggest we do?" she asked.

"Lie low. Brendan will check every island until he finds you."

"Assuming…"

"The ship survived," Logan said flatly. "I'm certain of it."

"How do you know?" she asked, a note of anguish entering her voice.

"Because she was weathering the storm fine when… when we went swimming."

She shook her head. "You can't know."

He shrugged. "But I do."

"And if it doesn't come?"

He shook his head, looking off at the horizon. "Whether you like it or not, you'd best pray for a merchantman. I like to think of myself as adept with a sword—as I know are you," he added quickly. "But there is no way either of us could stave off a full crew. They would most likely just *kill* me."

What might happen to her lingered unspoken on the air.

She shook her head. "Pirates don't…harm unwilling women. It's the code."

"And every man out there follows the code?"

She turned away. "Brendan will come. You said so yourself."

"But we don't need to tempt fate by making a huge fire at night."

"I'll think about it," she said. "For tonight we'll do things your way."

He smiled grimly. Tonight and every night. He would see to it.

But he kept his own council. His food had grown cold, but he forced himself to eat anyway. She walked to their shelter where she found her book. As the daylight was dying, she came back to the fire and sat and read in silence. He finished eating, then took his utensils to the water to rinse them.

There, at the water's edge, he sat. The light was fading, and the sea met the sky unbroken by any sail.

The sun dropped lower. Blue melted to deep purple. The purple turned the aqua sea to black. The sun's rays burst out in a farewell whisper to the day. And then all color was gone and the night had come.

He rose and walked back to the fire. She was gone.

He heard a slight movement and looked into the shelter. She was there, in bed, but she had dragged her bed and its small platform toward the middle of the small space.

He stood there watching her for a while, but in the shadows he couldn't tell if she was awake or if she slept.

And then she spoke softly.

"Are you sorry?"

"Sorry? For sailing the seas?" he asked. "For diving off the ship after you? Or for this afternoon?"

"Any or all."

Smiling, he pulled his bed over and stretched out beside her. "For sailing the seas—stupidly, as you pointed out... No, oddly enough, I'm not. For diving after you? I could never be sorry, never, not even if I had all the time in the universe. And this afternoon... my dear Red...might have been the highlight of my life."

She gazed at him in the shadows, and her lips curved into a smile that seemed to send rays of liquid fire through his limbs and straight to his soul.

"So nobly spoken," she said.

"I spoke nothing but truth," he said. Mere inches lay between them, and in an instant, those inches evaporated, like dew touched by the sun. She was in his arms, sweet and vibrant, a creature of extraordinary life and sensuality. Supple and vulnerable, soft and giving. And he discovered that touching her lips was both new and yet intoxicating in its familiarity. She was as addictive as fine wine, he thought, for he ached to know her again, to be within her, part of her, and yet he was equally hungry merely to touch her, taste her satin flesh, close his eyes and explore the shape of her body, then open his eyes and enjoy the sculpted beauty of her face and form. The night was theirs. The *world* was theirs. And if they stayed thus, abandoned and together, for an eternity, he didn't think he could tire of being with her. Each stroke of her fingers was like a new awakening, her whisper stirred his body and mind, and when he thrust into her, it was as if he had discovered all the riches of the seven seas.

Was he sorry?

A groan escaped him.

Never.

In his life, he had never spoken a more truer word.

RED WOKE TO FIND Logan propped upon an elbow, watching her. He smiled.

She smiled back.

And the next thing she knew, she was in his arms again.

The sun had risen, and the day was gently coming into being. It wasn't yet hot, nor was it too cool. A golden glow seemed to waft lightly on the breeze that moved around them.

They were naked to the elements and to the light, and it didn't matter in the least. They were alone, and they were with each other, and only the sun and sea gave witness. Their lovemaking was somehow pure, and yet deliciously sinful, as well. It was discovery and exploration. Eyes wide open, she learned his every muscle, the tiny freckle near his ear, the laughter in his eyes, the smoky color that touched them when his hunger grew and soared....

They made love, and then she rose, laughing, and raced ahead of him to the pool.

He followed.

And there, with the fronds so gently waving above them, the water alive with sound and movement, it was as if they found a piece of paradise. They played, carefree, running, teasing, swimming to one another and then away, before collapsing exhausted on the shore. Finally they rose, starving for breakfast now that a more crucial hunger had been satisfied.

She boiled the water and brewed the tea, while he dished out the biscuit and beef.

As she was chewing very hard on a piece of salted beef, Red found herself smiling.

"What? Is the meal displeasing?" he asked, affronted after his effort.

She laughed. "No, far better than what I've had aboard ship many a time. Pirating is hardly a profession in which one gets to satisfy the temptations of the palate."

His smile faded at the reminder of her profession, but he said nothing, only looked away.

She knew she had been a fool, reminding him of the gulf between their worlds.

He was still Laird Haggerty, a nobleman. His lands had been brutally seized from his father, and his mother had been murdered. She did not believe he had ever forgotten, and he had certainly spent long hours of his life dreaming of and planning vengeance.

A man such as Logan might spend an idyll on an island with such a woman as herself, but not a lifetime. He would never offer marriage.

And she would never be any man's mistress.

She could never be what he wanted, a governess, a maid, even a kept woman, set up with all the comforts of life around her. She had set out upon a road, and she would have to go on until she reached the end of it.

Was she so wrong, or simply being stubborn?

No. Blair Colm was still out there. And while he was, others might have their lives destroyed, just as she had.

She was about to say something light when she saw that he was no longer looking at her but staring down the beach.

She frowned and turned.

A large piece of a ship's hull had washed ashore.

And two bodies lay in view atop it.

He was already standing. She leapt to her feet, her heart thundering.

She started to run toward it, afraid it was a piece of her own ship and that one of the bodies was Brendan's.

He caught her arm and stopped her.

"For the love of God," he said intensely, "let *me* go."

She turned to him, torn.

"Stay here," he said.

He started striding down the beach, but when she moved to follow, he swung on her.

"Stay here," he commanded again.

She couldn't just stay; her heart was aching, and she had to know.

But he had massive strides, and he had reached the site before she had made up her mind what to do.

"Logan!" she cried.

He turned quickly to face her. "It's not Brendan or any of your crewmen. I fear these are more people from the ship that provided us with our supplies."

She stayed where she was. She'd seen enough death, and he clearly didn't want her to witness more.

But he looked so terribly sad, there by the bodies.

"Logan?" she called softly.

He rose, shaking his head.

"It's just…I think they survived a long time at sea. They…tried so hard to survive and almost made it."

She felt ridiculous then, just standing there, so she went to him.

"You spare yourself nothing, do you?" he asked in awe, turning her to face him, rather than the bodies.

"Life spares us nothing," she informed him.

Then she looked down at the bodies, and a soft "Oh" of pain escaped her.

They hadn't been young. That was the only saving grace. They were in their sixties, perhaps older. They were lashed together and to the boards that had carried them so far, and from the way they were wrapped in each other's arms, they had clearly enjoyed many years together.

They had lived longer than most, she told herself.

Tears, so unlikely for her, sprang to her eyes. There was so much tenderness in this pair, even in death. She had been wrinkling and graying, and he had been losing his hair. Time had stolen youth and beauty, but love had remained.

She felt an ache that was almost unbearable. She didn't want Logan to see her pain, so she turned toward the water.

"Why do I imagine they were kind?" she asked, staring into the distance.

"It is in their faces, even now," he said.

He began striding toward their shelter, and she knew he was going to get the shovel.

When he was gone, she fell to her knees beside the

pair. She touched the woman's cold face lightly. "I am so sorry. God grant you both a speedy trip into his arms." Was there a God? There had to be. If she didn't believe that there was, that justice wasn't meted out in the end, at least, she would have gone completely mad.

"At least you had one another, and you...you don't have to mourn each other now, because you're together."

She could see Logan digging and closed her eyes tightly for a moment, then opened them and looked again at the couple. They might have been asleep, he with his wig gone, his vest askew, she with her hair a tangle around her face, the salt and sand-crusted folds of her skirt crisp in the sunlight. Except they were not asleep, and that was evident, too.

"Thank you, and forgive us for using your belongings," she said.

It was then that she saw the locket around the woman's neck. She leaned over and opened it. There they were, smiling in a miniature that had been faded by contact with the sea. There were three handsome boys arrayed by them, tall, young adults. There was a little child, as well, seated on the woman's lap. A grandchild, certainly. A friendly-looking younger woman just peeked out from behind one of the young men. The wife. She held her husband's arm, as if for reassurance and security.

Theirs had been a good life....

She looked up and wondered how long she had been staring at the locket. Logan was there, sweating, his shirt sleeves rolled up, the buttons open, his chest damp and glittering in the sunlight. He was breathing heavily, and she was certain he had dug hard and deeply.

He began working at the knots, drawing a knife from his pocket and cutting the heavy rope that had bound the couple together and to their raft. The bodies were stiffening.

"Wait," Red told him as he reached for the woman.

He looked at her, surprised, when she gently removed the locket.

"At some time we may be able to find the family. At least…at least we can tell them that they were together. That…they died in one another's arms."

He nodded.

She took the locket and slipped it into the pocket of her trousers, then stood and accompanied Logan to the hole he had dug. He had worked hard. He might have dumped the corpses one atop the other, but he had made the grave wide enough that they could lie side by side.

In time, the man rested beside his wife.

They covered the grave with sand and palm fronds.

Red fashioned a cross.

Logan, glancing at her, managed a solemn prayer.

When they were done, she rose, went to their shelter and lay down. He followed and held her.

Simply held her.

They lay awake for a long time.

And when night came, they were still lying there together.

Even in the darkness, she knew he still lay awake when at last she closed her eyes and slept.

CHAPTER ELEVEN

DAY HAD TURNED to night, and the battle had finally ended.

But the darkness hid nothing.

In the light of the moon, there was blood everywhere.

Cassandra stood on deck, shaking, wide-eyed.

She was unhurt.

Her father was unhurt.

But the others…

Oh, God. There was so much blood everywhere. As she stood there, guarded at sword's point by a seaman who reeked to high heaven—even in her state of shock, she couldn't miss the smell of him—she watched as the pirate crew pawed through the massacred and wounded seamen of her father's ship, tossing each one overboard after removing whatever he had of value.

There were no survivors, except for the two of them.

It was horrible, too horrible. She had seen broken men, screaming, as they were thrown overboard. This wasn't the way it was supposed to be; even the wretched fellows she'd seen dangle at the end of the hangman's noose hadn't been accused of this kind of depravity.

They had killed, yes, but they had set the living adrift in longboats. They had not killed for the sheer pleasure of it.

"For the love of God," her father was pleading. "I'll give you anything, just don't hurt my daughter."

"Shut up, old man," someone said.

"Pirate scum," her father returned.

No, Father, no, she thought. Please don't antagonize them or they'll hurt you, they'll...kill you.

"Pirates?"

The question was spoken in a deep voice. One Cassandra was certain she had heard before.

He had spoken calmly, as if he were offering afternoon tea....

She spun around to face the man walking the few steps down from the deck. He was tall, and his height gave the impression that he was lean, but his shoulders were broad, and on closer examination, he was bulky with muscle.

His name was Sir Blair Colm, and she had met him at a summer night's barbecue in Charleston. He had just come ashore, with letters for the governor from King George. Some of the girls had giggled, then whispered of his dark and dangerous past.

But he had made her skin crawl even then.

There had been something about him. A coldness in his eyes. A viciousness beneath the veneer of civility.

"Sir Colm!" her father cried, shocked. "You...you are with these pirates?"

To her astonishment, the man shook his head, laughing. "Good God, man, do you think that I am deceived?

It is you who would run with pirates. You and that wretched captain of yours—attempting to rendezvous with the likes of Red Robert."

The man strode forward, his eyes filled with ice and his lips turned upward in a smile of grim amusement.

Death entertained him, Cassandra thought.

Her father was shaking, but not with fear. He was a brave man, and had fought with the crew until she had been threatened. He was shaking with anger and indignation. He had seen what this man had done.

The killing.

The blood...

Oh, God, the screams of the men as their broken bodies were tossed like refuse into the water.

Blair Colm pointed a finger at him. "You, Lord Bethany, were planning an assignation with one of the most foul and ruthless men sailing the sea, until the storm disrupted your plan. Do you think the governor does not know that you are a sly and cunning man, and that you planned all manner of havoc against the kingdom, the colonies and the king and all his faithful servants?"

Her father gaped with absolute amazement. Then his jaw snapped shut and he stopped shaking. He drew himself to his full height and stood with complete dignity. "I have never, in thought, word or deed, in any way or at any time betrayed my king, country or governor. You, sir, are making a complete mockery of law and justice."

"So sayeth the man as the noose tightens," Blair said, shaking his head, apparently undisturbed by her father's accusations.

"You are mistaken. 'Tis you who will meet the hangman's noose," her father responded.

"I don't believe so. I have subdued our country's enemies, in the name of both God and the king. I am a hero of many a battle, as surely you know," Blair said.

Her father's rage struck with such swiftness that even Cassandra was stunned.

"Hero? You are a murderer before God."

He did not shout, yet his scorn was as apparent in his tone as in the pulsing of the vein at his throat. "By the very God of whom you speak, you are bound for hell. I have heard the rumors of your deeds. You make the mistake of selling your prisoners in the colonies, and word of their fate travels. To my great shame, I refused to believe the words I heard about you. I believed they grew from the bitterness of a people who lost their loved ones and homes in battle. The broken and the subdued. May God forgive me and every man of stature in the colonies that we did not see you brought to justice and the scaffold."

Blair Colm smiled coolly as he stared at her father, but Cassandra knew her father's eloquence and justified fury had affected him.

That smile still upon his face, he bowed.

Then he struck with the speed and savagery of a viper, striking her father across the face and sending him to his knees. Cassandra screamed and burst free from those surrounding her, rushing to kneel at his side. "Father!"

"Take care, precious child," he said through bloodied lips, before she was wrenched from his side.

Then he glared up at Colm. "If you harm her, I swear, by God and all that is holy, her mother will rise from the grave to see that justice is done to you."

Cassandra prayed that his heart would not give out as she fought to return to his side. She was held by two of the crewmen, and her struggling did nothing to ease the hold of either man.

"Harm the girl? For fraternizing with a pirate?" Blair asked.

"Laird Haggerty is no pirate," Cassandra informed him.

"He joined with Red Robert. And for that he will dance the hempen jig," Blair informed her solemnly. "And as for you, girl, watch your tongue and I will consider mercy. Behave and I shall leave it to the courts to decide your fates." He turned to his men. "Take them below!"

Her father tried to stand, but he was dizzy from the blow, so the crewmen simply dragged him to his feet.

Their hands were bound, and then they were thrust forward to the steps that led below and dragged down into the bowels of the ship.

And *bowels* was clearly the appropriate word.

She had thought that Blair Colm's crewmen had stunk, but the smell in the decks below was even more rancid.

As they went down, and then farther down still, she prayed she would not be sick....

"Breathe through your mouth, daughter," her father said weakly.

She couldn't see. It was pitch-black and stifling so far down, and no sea breeze alleviated the pent-up heat and stale air in the small hold where they were shoved at last.

"Breathe, Cassie, and try to save your strength," her father said. He was trying to sound brave and assured for her benefit, she knew.

Breathe…?

Or jump overboard at the first opportunity?

Was there any help for them?

Oh, God…

She touched his shoulder in the darkness. At least she and her father were alive.

And life was always worth fighting for.

"I am fine, Father. And you are innocent, and the finest man alive. You will never be convicted. He is a madman," she said, and she, too, tried to keep her voice strong and brave and filled with conviction.

"Dear child," he said.

And that time she heard his fear.

RED AWOKE and realized she felt at peace for the first time she could remember. She felt Logan's arm around her and knew that he was watching her.

He smoothed back her hair. "Good morning."

"Is it?"

"There was a time when I knew that any morning when I awoke to live, breathe and fight, was a good day," he told her, and smiled ruefully.

She found herself smiling gravely in return.

"Indeed."

He disentangled himself then. And she was suddenly afraid of the solemnity between them.

She slipped free from his hold and rose, then stepped outside to greet the day, ignoring the distant mounds of sand that were a haunting reminder of those the sea had taken.

"Last one to the spring cooks breakfast," she said as soon as she heard him come outside behind her, and then she ran.

He caught up with her at the water's edge, swept her off her feet, spun her about so she couldn't help but laugh, then continued into the water, both of them fully clothed and gasping for breath.

They splashed and played, and Red wondered if she'd ever really played before she met him.

She wasn't certain, but it felt wonderful.

When she closed her eyes, she could see his face so clearly in her mind.

And even beyond death itself, she thought, she would remember his touch....

And all the emotions it evoked.

They made love in the water, and again on the bank, then just lay there together, their bodies entangled, drifting into dreams. The feel of his arms around her was so sweetly gentle and protective.

The sun rose higher overhead, and all the world seemed kissed by it.

"I do believe we've quite missed breakfast, my love," he told her lightly.

My love.

He didn't mean it, of course, she told herself. It was just a turn of phrase. It went with the abandon and even the laughter of the morning. It went with the fact they were together as if they were playing house, marooned on this island haven.

"Oh, dear," she replied lightly. "I suppose we must have an early supper, then. I imagine the servants, lazy rascals, are all lying about somewhere. I'll have to see to the water for the tea myself."

"Lovely idea. I'll see to the fire, and dig about for sustenance," he returned.

And then, reluctantly, they got up and set about the domestic duties of the day.

BRENDAN EXTENDED his spyglass, looking out across the water. There was a ship in view, but she was but a dot on the horizon, and he could not tell if she was a fine ship or a leaking barge, much less what flag she flew.

"Englishman? Spanish? Dutch...what is she?" Peg-leg demanded on his right.

Brendan shook his head.

Silent Sam was at his left shoulder. "Pirate," he said with assurance.

Sam had eyesight like an eagle, Brendan thought. If he said it was a pirate ship, then a pirate ship it no doubt was.

"What pirate?" he asked.

"Blackbeard," Silent Sam said.

They held their course, as did the other ship, and in a little while, he knew Silent Sam was right.

Both crews maneuvered their ships until they were lying broadside to each other, close enough for conversation.

There was never any mistaking Blackbeard. Even when he wasn't dressed for battle with his beard afire, he was imposing. He was a huge man, and he always wore several braces of pistols, his cutlass at his belt, and knives sheathed strategically about his body.

"Where be Red?" he called out now.

Brendan shouted in return, "We're searching for Red and the colonist. They went overboard in the storm."

"Red? Overboard?" Blackbeard was skeptical. Brendan thanked God the man knew the truth between them, that he was Red's cousin, and the two of them were all that each other had in the world. If Blackbeard thought he'd done any harm to Red...

"Red fell over trying to save a man, and Laird Haggerty went after to save her. We're searching for them," Brendan explained.

Blackbeard stared at him. "Aye? I'll be searching myself, then. But you must be warned. Blair Colm was in New Providence. He was indeed the one to set up the attack."

"You are certain?"

"Sonya told me, and she is equally certain he is hunting Red in these waters now."

Sonya? Sonya had abetted the attack, Brendan thought bitterly.

Was she feeding them false information now?

And yet, did it matter? They hunted Blair Colm, so what difference did it make if he hunted them in return?

Still...

They had to find Red.

Before Colm did.

A moment of doubt seized Brendan. Did he dare trust anyone? Especially Jimmy O'Hara, who had told him about the little island they now sought?

"I believe Blair Colm caught a merchantman," Blackbeard went on. "I saw the final firing of her mast just last night. Sail with care."

Blackbeard was silent for a moment. Brendan thought the man might even be grieving. "I'll leave you to these islands, then, and head north to the Carolinas and backtrack. If Red and Logan live, we'll find them between us."

"Aye, then, and thanks," Brendan said in return.

The two ships parted.

"Full sail!" Brendan commanded. "To the island with all speed!" It was all the more imperative that they find Red, and quickly.

Before Blair Colm could find her.

TIME WAS SUCH a strange concept, Red thought. It felt as if they had forever, and yet it all seemed to pass so quickly that she wondered if she would be able to remember it all—the pleasure, the laughter, the comfort and security and joy. And most of all, that ridiculously heady sensation of being cherished...

The nearly savage heat of his body against hers...

The conversations and the arguments, the moments when irritation turned to impatience, and impatience to passion. The times when they loved, and when they just lay together...

She knew his face was permanently ingrained in

her mind, as was her knowledge of his character. The way he valued logic and reason. His quiet determination, for he was just as stubborn as she, in his own way. For all those years she had thought she was alone in her frustration and fury, emotions so strong that even Brendan had been unable to fully share them. But now she knew that Logan, too, had been bent on finding the same man, albeit his aim had been justice rather than revenge.

Could this idyll go on forever?

Did he want it to?

Or was it only she who feared the passage of time, and even the possibility of rescue?

It was late that afternoon, when they were quietly sitting on the beach together, drinking grog, that Logan suddenly went very stiff.

"What is it?" she asked.

"A ship...I think."

Her heart should have soared. Instead, it seemed to sink like lead.

It could mean...

But she didn't want to be rescued. Not yet. Perhaps... one day.

People were sometimes marooned for years....

They'd shared just four days...five, counting the storm.

Logan was staring out at the horizon, and she followed his line of vision. At first she saw nothing.

Then...a speck. One that would disappear with the coming sunset, she was certain.

Logan rose, then ran hard back to their shelter.

When he returned, he had a spyglass he'd found in one of the trunks. He looked out through it for a long time, saying nothing.

"Should...I stoke the fire?" she asked at last.

"Not yet."

"But..."

"I don't know the ship. I can't see a flag."

"If you can see the ship, can the ship see us?" she asked.

He looked at her. "Two specks on the sand? I doubt it. But soon enough... We need to douse the fire."

"But...if we douse it..."

If it was Brendan out there, as well it might be, she couldn't let him search and not find her.

"We have to know who sails her first," he said, then went back to looking through his spyglass.

She tried to remain patient, but she was about to explode when he spoke at last.

"I don't trust it."

"Is it my ship?" she asked.

"No...the masts are wrong," he said.

"You can see the masts?"

He took the glass from his eye and handed it to her.

She wasn't pleased that it took her several seconds just to find the ship, and even then, she could see almost nothing, only that it *was* a ship. And he was right. She couldn't actually count the masts, not when it was still at such a distance, but the shape was wrong.

"We need to douse the fire now," he said. "We can prepare a few torches for ourselves for the night, though the moonlight will probably be enough. We'll bring essentials to the cave I found behind the spring—we must make sure we supply ourselves with plenty of drinking water. The pots and pans...rum, for medicinal use. And we'll take the surgeon's kit...some clothing, and then..."

"And then? It's obvious someone has been living here. Can we strip away all hint of habitation so quickly?" she asked.

He shook his head. "No. If you will begin to transport our belongings..." He paused, wincing, then looked at her. "I will prepare to dig."

"Dig?"

"The gentleman and his wife. I'm afraid I will have to dig them up and make it appear that they reached the shore, then...perished here days later."

She stared at him in horror. "But..."

"Their bodies are...they are not long dead."

"Still...wouldn't a physician know...?"

"I doubt that any ship's 'physician' is going to perform an autopsy," Logan said. "We will let it appear that the husband died holding the wife. That she perished first. The elements...the hardship...their age...all would have worked against them. I doubt any questions will be asked."

"Oh, dear God," she said. "After all they suffered... and all that we have taken from them."

"I hardly think they would begrudge us for saving our lives," Logan said gently.

She nodded.

"And yet..."

"Yet what? It isn't your ship."

"It might be Edward Teach. Or someone else I know."

"Who else knows that you are Red?"

"I could pass as your...cousin?" she suggested.

"We must see what ship this is, first. Thanks to the coming of night, they will not send boats ashore until dawn. Let's hurry."

She felt ill, and yet it was indeed time for action, which meant she couldn't allow herself to be weak in any way. She had come to depend upon him, and that was something she should not have done and which now must stop. She had taught herself once to be fair, merciful *and* as strong as steel, and now the time for steel had come again.

"If you wish, I can dig, as well," she offered.

"You're fast. You will be better at arranging a hideout deep in the cave. As the stronger, I can dig faster."

Red nodded and set to work.

As she began the task of going through all they had salvaged from the shore, she realized she could not leave her pillow. Some of the bedding, yes. It was necessary it be left behind, so that an enemy crew—should their visitors indeed be enemies—would believe that the old couple had lived there and made use of the flotsam and jetsam until they died.

But her pillow...

It went with her on one of her many treks to the cave.

As she worked, she thanked God they had been cast ashore upon an island with a spring and a deep cave. She explored their home-to-be a bit, intrigued when the deeper tunnels proved to be filled with bats.

After bringing in everything she thought they would need, she began to plan.

She found several little escape fissures in the rocks, and decided on the best place to set up their camp, a spot from which they could easily access the spring itself and where they would be well hidden. They could even eavesdrop upon any visitors to the spring, so they would know if their refuge had been discovered.

When she returned to the shore, the last golden light was playing across the beach, and she had to hold back the gasp that came to her lips.

Logan was standing just outside their little structure, as the fire burned low.

The waning flames gave just enough light for her to see the tableau he had arranged inside the shelter. He had painstakingly dusted the burial sand from the elderly couple. The man's body had been seated against one of the trees supporting the structure, and he appeared to be looking downward in dejection.

The woman was stretched across his lap, her face turned up to him.

His hand rested upon her graying hair, as if he were cradling her in a last embrace.

The stench of human decay suddenly hit her, and she turned away.

Logan saw her but didn't move to touch her, only doused the fire, then straightened.

"I have to…bathe," he rasped, then turned to head inland.

Red noticed he had left the spyglass near the fire.

Trying not to breathe, she picked it up and looked out to sea.

The ship was closer now. She could count two masts, but she still couldn't make out the flag. And the last light of the sun would soon be gone.

She set the spyglass down where she had found it, and as she did so, she became aware of the drone of flies.

They were going after the corpses.

There was no help for it.

She noticed crabs on the beach, and she knew that they, too, would soon be feasting upon human flesh, and her heart revolted in her chest. She was certain they had been good people, and they had deserved so much more.

But she wanted to survive. She still had so much to achieve, and now...

Now she had other dreams, as well.

She stiffened, turned and followed Logan back to the spring. He was in the water, the bar of soap in his hands, scrubbing himself furiously. As she watched, he dived down and came back up with a handful of sand, then scrubbed himself with that, as well, and she understood.

He could bathe all night, and he still wouldn't feel clean, not after he had dug up two people who should have been left to rest in peace.

She shed her clothing and walked out to him. As he stared at her, she took the soap from him and worked it into a lather against his back.

The day's colors changed.

Gold and pink became mustard and crimson.

He turned and locked his arms around her. She closed her eyes and rested her head against his chest.

Eventually he lifted her chin and very lightly kissed her lips.

"It may be our last night," she said, breaking from him.

He shook his head and smiled slightly. "No, Red. I'll not let it be our last night. Perhaps the last here in this paradise, but never our last night."

"Still…" she said.

"Still…" he agreed.

He turned and, taking her hand, led her from the water. He reached for their clothing, but she shook her head, and when he gazed at her, his head at an angle, a brow arching, she flushed.

"I should show you our new accommodations."

"I would dearly love to see them."

They left their things strewn on the shore. She led the way to the far bank of the spring, fringed to the shore with palms that hid the entrance to the cave. She didn't show him how she had strategically planned their new quarters, though.

She simply led him to the blanket and pillow.

When they lay down, darkness had come.

And in the darkness, they made love. She was wilder than she had ever been.

She clung harder.

He moved deeper.

Spent and gasping, hearts pounding, they lay still

afterward, holding one another. Then she moved, just slightly.

And they made love again.

Ever more desperately.

And so the night wore on, each bout of lovemaking more powerful than the one before.

They did not sleep. When it was still long before dawn, he rose reluctantly. She joined him. They retrieved their clothing, but Logan insisted she don one of the dresses that had been in the trunk; he didn't want anyone to suspect that she might be the notorious Captain Red Robert.

She went to the cave and changed, as he had suggested, then went to find him standing in the cover of the trees and staring across the beach.

The ship was anchored now out beyond the reefs. It was still quiet, but it would not be so for long.

He had the spyglass, and he was standing stiffly.

She did not need the glass to understand his tension.

She could see the ship's flags clearly.

The two flags that rose high on the pole. Just below the Union Jack was a personal flag.

And it belonged to Blair Colm.

CHAPTER TWELVE

"YOU'LL GET IN the next boat."

As near as Cassandra could tell, the man giving the order was Blair Colm's first mate. She had heard him called Nathan.

He wasn't particularly tall, and he was a far cry from Blair Colm, who could easily play the part of the great statesman, the soldier, the hero and the gentleman. This Nathan was a solid man, bulky with muscle and with no discernible neck. He was surprisingly agile, however, given that he was built like a squat tree with legs instead of roots.

She absolutely loathed the man. He was bald, and had a grin that made her uncomfortable every time he looked her way.

She had heard rumors about Blair Colm; she had simply never believed them. They were too terrible, and had come only from the underbelly of society-indentured servants who were most often alive only because they had been saved from the terrors of Newgate or the scaffold and sent to work in the colonies. She remembered those rumors now, though, and believed them, even—or possibly, especially—the one that said he sold women.

And that, she was convinced, was why Nathan undressed her with his eyes every time he saw her, but didn't touch her.

Help had to be out there somewhere.

Unfortunately, it did not seem to be coming today.

She and her father had been dragged from below at the crack of dawn, only a few hours after she'd managed to fall asleep. They were at anchor outside the reefs surrounding a small and quite beautiful little island. The white sand beach sparkled beneath the dawn. Hills rose behind a rich display of palm trees, sea grapes and other tropical growth.

"Someone is there," her father whispered.

"What?" she whispered in return.

He inclined his head toward a spot on the beach. She had to squint to see what he was indicating, but then she saw the small shelter he had spotted.

"And he's looking for someone," she said softly, indicating Blair with a quick nod.

He was on deck, his spyglass in hand, staring at the island. He had not gotten into the first tender.

He was probably waiting to make sure the first boatload of crewmen was not murdered by some native tribe—or whoever had been marooned there.

Even to go ashore, he was dressed impeccably. His white shirt was pristine, his vest richly embroidered, and his hat sported an impressive feather. He might have been dressed for dinner at the governor's mansion.

"He's looking for Red Robert. And Logan," her father said with a sigh.

"Father," she said quickly, "Logan would have died before causing you anguish."

"I know that, daughter," he said, and squeezed her hand. "I have never blamed a decent man for the evil in others. I blame myself for stupidity. I have attended social functions with the monster now labeling me traitor."

"Stay calm, Father, I beg of you. Where there is life, there is hope," she whispered.

He attempted a smile. "Where there is life, there is hope," he agreed.

"Lord Bethany, Lady Cassandra, if you will?" Blair Colm said. "I am ever so sorry to trouble you, but my prisoners remain within my reach at all times."

"Down the rope ladder," Nathan commanded.

Maybe he thought he was smiling pleasantly, Cassandra thought. Perhaps the man was simply incapable of a smile that did not look like a leer.

Her father went first, reaching up to help her once he reached the boat, but she needed no assistance. She was far more worried about her father than herself.

Horatio Bethany was no coward and no weakling. He rode his own estates, and he was not adverse to helping out when necessary. Cassandra was so proud of him. He would help a servant staggering under a heavy load, he would read to the children, and he had seen to it that those in his household learned about books and writing.

She hoped he would not do aught else to draw Blair Colm's wrath.

She took a seat as properly as she could. Her cotton

gown was stained with blood and dirt, and wrinkled from her confinement. Her hair was falling down in snarled tendrils.

Four of Blair's men were in the boat with them, another six already on the island, and as they moved away from the ship, she saw he was following them in a third tender. She had tried to assess the total number of men under his command. Twenty-five, she thought, and that count might have been a bit high. But certainly no more than that.

And were they all refuse, as he was himself? Killers who did not care who they killed, especially since it seemed their commander had the right to murder under the law?

She smiled as she stared at her father, but her thoughts were running in far less pleasant directions. They must all be monsters. They had taken no prisoners other than her father and herself. Because they had some value? Or because he needed a legal excuse—her father's supposedly traitorous activities—to justify taking and sinking the ship?

"I wish you had a parasol," her father said.

What a ridiculous comment, she thought.

But he was smiling at her, so she kept smiling in return. We must bend but not break, she thought. No matter what happens, we must remember who we are, and that we are decent, compassionate human beings.

They reached the beach. One strong fellow leapt out and dragged the boat high up on the sand, so it would not slip back out to sea.

He turned to give her a hand, but she was already ashore.

To one side, Blair Colm's boat was being run up on the beach, as well.

From the direction of the shelter she had seen earlier, she heard a cry. "Captain! Captain Colm! You must see this!"

Blair strode rapidly forward, while one of his men prodded Cassandra and her father to follow—at sword's point.

As they neared the crude shelter, Cassandra, who was in the lead, heard the buzzing of flies, and just as she realized what that meant, the odor of decay hit her.

And then she saw the couple.

Her stomach lurched as she fought to keep from being sick. She felt faint, and it was only the support of her father's arm that kept her from keeling over.

It wasn't so much that the couple was dead. It wasn't even the fact that they had apparently died in one another's arms.

It was the cruelty of what came after death.

The birds had fed upon the faces.

And the crabs had wrecked havoc on their flesh.

The odor, the flies, the birds, the crabs…

It was suddenly too much. She pitched forward onto her knees and started to scream, but it didn't help. She could still hear the flies droning….

And then she dropped unconscious to the ground.

RED AND LOGAN had watched the pirates arrive from the safety of a tall sea grape, midway between the shelter and the spring, one that afforded the cover of thick branches and fat green leaves, but still allowed them to see most of what was happening on the beach.

Red had seen his face when the boat carrying the young woman and the older man had come ashore. She had known she was seeing Cassandra and Lord Bethany even before he muttered the woman's name beneath his breath.

Time stood still.

Logan's original plan had entailed waiting until most of the crew was ashore, hopefully drunk on the barrel of rum he had left in an obvious spot by the shelter, then stealing one tender after destroying the others, and making their way out to the ship. Foolhardy? Maybe. But possible. A skeleton crew would have remained on board. A crew that might be taken stealthily by night.

But when she studied his face now, she knew everything had changed.

It had changed when Lord Bethany and Lady Cassandra had stepped ashore.

She knew they had only been in these waters because they were attempting Logan's rescue.

And if she knew it, then he had to be thinking the same thing. The woman he loved—even if she was not his fiancée—was in this horrible predicament because of him.

Red wasn't close enough to see the details of Lady Cassandra's features, and she knew that in such dire circumstances, she shouldn't be wasting time reflecting on the young woman's stature and beauty.

But her heart sank nonetheless.

He had not lied. Cassandra was beautiful. Her posture was regal, and despite the circumstances, her head was held high atop a neck that was long and slim.

Then she watched as Cassandra stopped walking, stared in horror at what Red knew waited inside the shelter, fell to her knees and screamed.

That scream tore through the air, and even Red, who knew its cause, winced at the sound.

Lord Bethany was quick to catch his daughter as she fell. Down on his knees himself, he cradled her body, putting his own bulk between her and the sight of the dead couple, despite the fact that Cassandra seemed to be unconscious.

A knife seemed to tear into Red's heart.

My father would have loved me like that, I know he would have, she thought, then stiffened. The world was what it was. Her father was long dead at the hands of the man who had now taken these two people prisoner. God only knew what Blair Colm had done to those with whom Lord Bethany and Lady Cassandra had sailed.

No.

She knew.

She had seen the man in action.

And she could see him now.

Everything in her cried out that she needed to jump from the tree and race forward and plunge her knife through his heart. If she were quick enough, perhaps she wouldn't be stopped, and once he was dead...

She started, feeling Logan's hand on her arm. His eyes carried both understanding and a warning.

"No," he whispered.

She indicated Cassandra.

"I know," he returned softly. "And I will find a way."

"But…"

"We watch," he said, his whisper soft.

And so Red turned her eyes back to the scene at the shelter. Blair was watching Cassandra, laughing softly. "Ah, the lady shows such sweet delicacy," he said.

"There's no sign of Red Robert's ship," a short, stocky man announced. "There was a wreck, whatever ship this man and his wife sailed. But there is no sign of any other."

"Is there salvage?" Blair asked.

"Some."

"Take the food, and then we'll see to water."

"What of those poor folk?" Lord Bethany demanded.

"What of them?" Blair asked. "They are dead."

"They must be buried."

"Must they?"

"I see a shovel. I will dig, if you've not the crew to manage such a simple task," Lord Bethany said.

Blair Colm shrugged. "My dear Lord Bethany, I'm afraid you might have a heart attack, attempting such labor. Billy, you and Victor dig. Nathan, take the others out to search through the salvage."

"I need water for my daughter," Lord Bethany said.

"You two," Blair said, nodding toward several crewmen. "Look for fresh water."

Logan's hand was still on Red's arm. Now he gave her a slight nod, indicating that he considered them well concealed, so they could continue to watch what was taking place from their perch.

Several of the pirates disappeared beneath the canopy of the trees as they started inland. They reappeared almost directly beneath Red and Logan as they headed toward the spring. One turned back a few moments later to report on the fresh water.

Red looked at Logan, who shook his head. She didn't know if he was opposed to killing the men because it would be murder in his eyes or only because he felt the time wasn't right.

Either way, he had judged correctly, for in minutes there were ten pirates at the spring, drinking and splashing, heedless of their clothing and even their boots.

Red began to wish they had left their vantage point when more and more of the ugly fellows began stripping off their clothes to bathe, but she knew they were there for the duration, so she listened and waited, barely breathing. She had mocked Logan for not seeking vengeance with enough passion, but she knew now that she had been wrong to doubt the strength of his intentions. There was something in his eyes today, something she hadn't seen before. And though it was obvious he was horrified that Lord Bethany and Cassandra were Colm's captives, she knew in her heart that his feelings went deeper.

He had learned patience, and he was calculating every possible strategy for taking down Blair Colm.

But whatever his previous thoughts might have been, the game had changed.

She knew he would die before harm came to Lord Bethany and Cassandra.

"First time I've really seen your ugly mug of a face, Nathan," one of the younger men said.

"And first time anyone could be downwind of ye, Billy Bones," the one called Nathan responded. Red looked at him more closely and realized that what he was washing off was blood. There was little doubt now as to what had happened to the crew of Lord Bethany's ship.

"It's a fine island," another man said.

"Not fine enough," Billy said. "The captain was hoping to find that Red Robert had gone down in the storm. Maybe even that the ship had broken up and his treasure had washed ashore. Instead, we have the finery of an old merchantman."

"We should stay on here a bit, explore the place," Nathan said, looking around. "It's a fine place for a hideout, eh?"

"Except we're not the only ones that know of her, eh?" Billy said.

"Aye, so they say. Some other bastard would be digging up what we buried," a man with one glass eye said.

"But we won't be stayin' anywhere," Billy said. "Cap'n knows Red Robert is after him, and he can't stand it. He wants to know who the fellow is and why he's after 'im. Become a bit of an obsession, it has. He wants Red Robert dead, so he does. Offered a fortune in New Providence to have the fellow killed."

"But the fools failed," the glass-eyed man said.

"We'll be finding him eventually," Nathan said with assurance. "And it will be a slow and painful end for Red Robert. Cap'n Colm says he'll cut the bastard's tongue out first, shoot him in the kneecaps and then the balls, and then watch him die."

Red felt ill. On the one hand, she longed to point out that there would be no shooting her in the balls.

On the other, she was suddenly afraid.

What if they found the *Eagle* and captured her?

What if they thought Brendan was Red Robert?

There was only one thing for it.

Blair Colm had to die before he could leave this island.

She didn't look at Logan, because she didn't want him reading her mind. She would let him think she was party to any plan he came up with, but if it didn't include the death of the man who had massacred so many, she would resort to her own strategy.

If nothing else, she would have the element of surprise in her favor. True, she would die on the spot if she killed him, with so many of his men about.

Even so, it would be worth it.

And such an attack *could* be carried out. She would have to bide her time. And wait.

"Do you believe Cap'n Colm will really see to it that old Lord Bethany hangs?" Billy Bones mused.

"Ye've seen the captain at work," Nathan said, then chuckled with pure pleasure and anticipation. "And as to the daughter…"

"She's worth a good fortune—he'll have that in mind," Billy warned.

"Perhaps. Then again, perhaps no one will know if she's not so pure on her return," Nathan said. "She'd be unlikely to say anything, wouldn't you agree?"

Red glanced at Logan and could see the pulse ticking at his throat. But he had the strength to remain dead still.

"Ah, well, it's a fine enough beach, offering fine enough beds," Nathan said.

"We'll be staying here?" another man asked.

"Oh, aye. Despite what Billy thinks, Cap'n said if Red didn't go down, he'd be looking for a place to careen his ship," Nathan said. "Might even give it a few nights to see if he shows."

Eventually Blair Colm's crew tired of their conversation, dressed and left the area.

Even then, Logan waited until he was certain no one was lurking beneath the trees before he slipped down, then reached up to help her follow.

"Back to the caves," he said. "We need to plan."

THE BODIES WERE GONE.

Blessed mercy.

Still, Cassandra didn't think she would be able to bear seeing a crab ever again.

She realized she was alone with her father in the small shelter and wished she could be somewhere— anywhere—else.

This was where the corpses of the couple had been. She kept envisioning the flies and the crabs. But if she intended to survive, and for her father's sake, she had to accept the comfort of the shade. She and her father had apparently been left to their own devices.

Why not? Where was there for them to go?

After reassuring her father that she was fine, she looked outside and saw that Blair Colm and several of his men were busying themselves with the barrels and trunks that lay strewn about the beach, having already laid claim to the booty that had been dragged up near the shelter. They had found porcelain, silver, pots and pans, ceramic pieces, dresses, breeches, fine shirts and jackets, lace undergarments, and even a few jewels, not to mention a carpenter's toolbox and a surgeon's kit. Not a bounty in gold, but the finery of a once substantial couple was not to be sneered at.

The men were clearly more interested, however, in the booty provided by some of the barrels.

Rum. Definitely rum.

But there was also salted meat, biscuit, sugar, salt and pepper, though it was clearly the rum that interested them most.

Though Cassandra's temptation was to scorn anything offered her by these men, she knew that she and her father needed to eat, so she accepted the horrible, tasteless rations one of them gave her when he saw her watching, and, later, the much more appealing coconut meat one of them brought.

As she watched the men throughout the day, she noticed that Blair Colm had a democratic manner with his men. Military men sailed under strict rules of discipline for set pay, but Colm's pirates—for however legal their charter, their behavior marked them as the worst pirates she'd ever heard of—had a certain degree of autonomy and clearly shared fully in whatever spoils they found.

How else did a man get others to commit murder and other atrocities, she wondered, if not for a rich reward?

The day seemed endless.

Yet did she want it to end? As long as they were all busy, she and her father were left alone.

She realized how much she loved him, and how sheltered her life had been, how she had been guarded and cared for, because he loved her so much in return. She had always known there was hardship in the world, and danger. She knew he was very worried for her now, and she wished he would believe her when she assured him that she was stronger than anyone might think.

She would live with courage.

And die the same, though she prayed it would not come to that.

And she could even believe it…so long as the sun rode high in the sky.

LOGAN PACED WHILE he ate, one eye on the entrance to their cave, so he could make sure no one was nearby and likely to discover them. He had feared his ruse might not work, that Colm and his men might search the island for further signs of habitation. But apparently Colm had been content to believe that the only tenants were dead.

"The plan is still good," he told Red. "I believe the men will drink themselves senseless as darkness comes. I believe Cassandra will be safe, as he feels she is a valuable asset. I fear for Lord Bethany if she is threatened, but I know how Blair's mind works, and he will not allow the urges of his drunken crew to ruin a fine profit." He paused and looked at Red, clearly worried as to how she would react to his words, for she knew far more than he did himself about the value placed on a woman's virtue.

But she was looking back at him, shoulders set, head high.

"I don't understand. You mean to go through with the plan to steal a tender and damage the rest, then seize Blair Colm's ship? How will that aid Cassandra and Lord Bethany?"

He let out a long breath.

"The catch…"

"Aye, the catch," she said.

"We must return and steal them out from under Blair's nose once we secure the ship." He took a deep breath and went on. "I believe you will be better remaining aboard ship while I accomplish the rescue."

She had been seated against the wall of the cave, gnawing with stoic determination on her biscuit. She stood then, and though her dress was somewhat stained from their adventure up the sea grape tree, she still wore it with elegance. Her hair streamed down her back, and stood out against the beige and blue linen and lace of the gown like a cascade of regal fire. Her eyes were bright and determined, and her chin was set.

"My dear laird, you know my abilities, as well as my desires and resolve. If you imagine that I will cower in a cabin while you fight alone, you are quite mistaken. In fact, you'll have another fight on your hands if you think you can order me about in such manner."

He smiled slowly, wondering if she had any idea what she had done to him, how she had changed him. If she knew that he felt he would have no world if she were not a part of it.

"My dear Red...Bobbie... I do not want to order you about. I ask only that you live, that is all."

She lowered her head quickly.

"If I am to live, I believe we will both have to fight."

He walked toward her, and she moved away, puzzling him. "Red...?"

"Logan, I would like to reflect upon the coming battle at the moment, if you do not mind."

He turned away, realizing he had forgotten to keep watch, a mistake he could not make again. "I prided myself on a plan that offered danger only when we scuttled the boats and might be caught. Once on board, I believed—and still believe—we could dispatch the remaining crew. But I could not live with myself if I didn't put every ounce of my will, my life and blood, into the effort to save those who found danger only in their attempt to rescue me."

"Of course," she said. "I would expect nothing less."

"I'm going out to see what they're about," he told her.

"No, I will do so. If I'm caught, I am no threat, merely a young woman who hid when she heard him coming, one he can use to increase his riches on his return to the colonies," she said.

"All right," he told her.

She started past him, clearly surprised by his easy acquiescence. He caught her by the shoulders, and she turned back to him. He smiled, then knocked her quickly in the jaw.

The surprise in her eyes was an agony to him.

But it was better this way. She wouldn't be unconscious long.

She slumped in his arms, and he laid her gently down, her head upon her pillow.

AS THE AFTERNOON waned, the pirates built a fire. They cooked, and they ate.

And they drank. A lot.

Cassandra saw Nathan watching her now and then. Saw the look in his eyes. And she was afraid. She stayed in their shelter, keeping as close to her father as she could, nestled almost into the trunk of a supporting palm tree.

Time passed. The sun dropped lower in the sky. The breeze grew cool. The waves lapping against the shore were a constant and almost soothing sound.

Earlier, she had discovered a book, an English translation of Cervantes. She picked it up now, feeling sad again. Someone had carefully set a tiny slip of canvas between the pages to mark their place.

The woman who had died? Or her husband? It didn't matter. In the end, both had been nothing but a feast for the flies, the birds and the crabs.

The pirates were growing rowdier. When the first barrel of rum was finished off, someone found another.

Blair Colm had not been drinking with the others. He had watched them—as a mother alligator might watch the follies of her vicious brood. Somehow she was certain that, drunk or not, his men paid him heed.

As the sun continued to fall, he walked out to the

water and looked across it with his spyglass, no doubt searching for ships on the horizon.

Finally he returned to the fire, where his men ate, drank and jested. One of them had donned woman's clothes and was pretending first to be a fine lass in a drawing room, and then a harlot on the streets of Jamaica. The others hooted and hollered, and cried out ribald comments.

Still, she was left alone.

But Blair Colm had started drinking.

And where, she wondered with a shudder, might that lead?

RED AWOKE WITH a sore jaw. But other than that…

She felt almost as if she'd had a lovely nap.

It was almost completely dark in the cave, and as she blinked, trying to adjust to the dimness, she remembered that Logan had struck her. Struck her!

And then apparently stretched her out comfortably, her head upon her pillow.

How long ago had he left her? How long had she been unconscious, and what had happened since he had gone?

She jumped up, terrified. What if he had been…

Caught. Tortured.

Killed.

There was enough light filtering in to tell her that it was coming on dusk.

Not yet full night.

Without thought, she started toward the mouth of the cave. Then she realized she could do nothing without some sort of weapon. She turned back quickly and grabbed a sword, then added an ankle sheath and a knife and headed for the exit again.

Her heart was pounding. She wasn't afraid for herself.

She was terrified that…

At the entrance to the cave, she went dead still, forcing herself to breathe slowly.

She had to take care. How sad it would be to fall prey to someone who simply took her unaware because her heart had overridden her logic. How sad if she caused Logan's death because she was a fool.

She heard the slightest rustle of a branch, caught the barest hint of movement, but it was enough to tell her that someone was out there. Someone in the trees, moving with silence and stealth…

She watched, eyes straining. Whatever she had seen, she knew it had not been a bird or a lizard, or any kind of an insect.

She flattened herself against the wall of the cave, just inside. From there, she could see. And from there, she could retreat.

She stood, and she watched, and she waited. Her eyes never left the entry.

Then a hand fell on her shoulder, but when she started to scream, to swing around, to bring her sword into a position…

A hand clamped over her mouth, stifling all sound.

And a strong arm knocked her sword from her grasp.

CHAPTER THIRTEEN

"PEG-LEG?"

"Aye, Brendan," Peg-leg replied.

"Anything?"

"We've another eight hours, I'd say. I know the spot O'Hara speaks of…at least, I've heard tell of the island. By my reckoning, and the wind…eight hours. Seven if we're lucky."

Brendan looked at Peg-leg, a sense of desperation growing within him. "You believe that it's true, then? That the island exists?"

"Aye."

Inwardly, Brendan damned himself. If O'Hara's coordinates were right, he had been sailing away from the island because he had misjudged the storm. If he had but thought out the wind and the currents and the positioning…

Hagar, eyeing the sails, said, "We're moving fast and night is coming, Brendan," he warned.

Peg-leg cleared his throat. "She may not be on the isle," he said softly.

"She must be," Brendan said quietly.

The others were silent.

"We may find more than what you're looking for," Silent Sam told him.

Brendan looked at him questioningly.

"O'Hara could be lying. He could be sending us into a trap," Silent Sam offered.

Strange, Brendan reflected. He was doing a lot of talking lately. They might have to change his name.

"I know that," he said.

They all looked at him. "I know, but there is nothing else I can do. I must believe that Red is alive, and that island, if it exists, is the most likely place. And I must find her." He hesitated and lowered his voice. "If any man chooses not to sail, I can arrange for his safety."

Silent Sam let out a loud sound of protest. "Are you mad, Brendan?"

"We just want you to be wary," Peg-leg said.

"We'd all die for her, Brendan, and you know it," Hagar said. "Each of our lives is owed to her. But we need to be ready to fight, and that's a fact."

Brendan nodded. It was true.

They should all be expecting a battle. Even...death.

For there was no telling who else might have found Isla de Muerta a safe port in the storm.

"We are heavily gunned, and we sail with the finest fighting crew on the seven seas," Brendan said. "Aye, we may well be sailing into a trap. But it can't truly be a trap if we're prepared to do battle. Tonight, we'll see to the fuses, ball and shot, grenades, swords, knives, pistols—all our weapons. Boarding axes are to be honed. We will be prepared for any eventuality when we arrive."

"Aye!" the men cried in unison.

As Brendan turned to head below and see to their supply of ammunition, he noticed Jimmy O'Hara standing by himself at the bow.

"O'Hara," Brendan hailed him.

"Aye, Captain?"

"I don't captain this ship—she is Red's," Brendan said.

"We will find the captain. I'm certain of it."

"Why didn't you speak of the island first thing?"

"You seemed to know our position."

"True, but the sea can be fickle. As can men."

O'Hara stared back at him and said, "I have sworn myself to Captain Red. I've proven myself a coward, aye, but I gave my oath when my life was spared in that alley. I cannot promise you that no danger awaits, but I *can* swear that I know nothing more than you do yourself. And that the island exists."

Brendan tried not to betray any emotion, and certainly no weakness. "We are prepared," he said, and turned away.

He was glad of their stop at New Providence, glad of the supplies they had purchased through the sale to Blackbeard of Logan's gold. They were heavily armed, carrying powder and shell, guns and swords.

The ship needed cleaning, but she had held fast during the storm, and the lower decks had kept the powder dry.

Now all they needed was speed. He didn't know why he felt such a pressing urgency to get there so quickly. Looking into Jimmy O'Hara's eyes, he hadn't believed they were being betrayed.

Not by man, anyway.

He could only pray they weren't being betrayed by fate.

DARKNESS WAS COMING, Cassandra thought as she stared out of the shelter at the beach. The day, the long day, was ending at last. She had learned how the sun set in the Caribbean. How at first the night seemed to come slowly, with brilliant colors that reflected over the water, then, almost imperceptibly, began to change. So bright…and then so subtle. Deepest purple. Darkest, bloodiest crimson, turning to shadow and blackness.

She felt her nerves growing raw. Fear was setting over her with the surety of the dying sun.

Her father…was sleeping.

The heat, the exhaustion of worry, had taken a toll on him.

She saw that Nathan was staring straight at the frail shelter where she huddled in the dark, and Billy Bones was doing the same. Those two were intent on rape, she knew. If Blair Colm became too drunk…

He wouldn't, though. She was sure of it. The man was watching, but watching for what, she didn't know.

Watching for…Logan and the pirates who held him?

Were they even still alive, after the storm?

With her father sleeping, she made up her mind to speak to Blair Colm. He watched her approach, eyes narrowed warily, but he let her take a seat next to him.

"To what do I owe this honor?" he asked, his tone deceptively mild.

She looked at him and fought hard to keep the rancor from her voice.

"You are the captain of your ship, the leader of your men. I have come to ask for your protection."

He smiled, pleased, and then he laughed aloud. "What makes you think you don't need protection from me?"

She lifted a hand in the air. "Women love power. I'm sure you have many women. The virtue of many a great lady is often freely given. Lonely widows, wives with husbands at sea or across the Atlantic, are often at the mercy of…need. You have no interest in me. Not for yourself. And I must assume you see my virtue as a valuable commodity."

He watched her for a long moment, sipping his rum.

"Clever girl." He held out his mug of rum, as if in toast.

She smiled and took the mug from him, then sipped herself. "I realize that I will most probably be for sale. You may try to see my father hanged, but I'm worth more alive. If I'm to be sold, I ask only this—that you find a buyer for me who is not only wealthy but so old that he cannot possibly survive long. Preferably someone without heirs."

He laughed, the sound genuine.

"And you think I can find such a buyer?"

"I'm certain that you can, perhaps even that you already have such a man in mind."

"I will need to offer him a maiden, of course."

"Of course. Therefore, I trust you will protect me from the sad, ugly sacks of flesh who are your crewmen."

He stared at her. "You may consider yourself protected...at this time."

"You cannot have my father hanged."

"Maybe they will grant him mercy."

"You know my father is no pirate!"

He leaned back, taking the mug of rum back from her. "I know a pirate called Red Robert is looking for me. If I find Red Robert, and kill him, then I will have the power to be merciful to your father."

He was a liar. He would hurt her father no matter what.

But she couldn't let that factor into her negotiations. She was trying to keep her father alive through the night. If she were attacked, he would try to stop that attack, but he was old and outnumbered. He would die, and she would be raped anyway.

She shook her head. "My father is not in league with Red Robert. He has never met the man. Laird Logan Haggerty was taken prisoner by Red Robert, and we were seeking his return and nothing more."

"You carried a ransom."

"No ransom was required."

"But you didn't know that when you set out," he said.

She realized that before killing all the crewmen on their ship, he had forced someone to reveal the location of the ransom money, and that the money was now in the hands of this man.

"Yes, we carried a ransom, which no doubt you now have." She looked at him. "Think! If we were in league with him in any way, would we have offered or brought such a ransom when we set out?"

"But you say Red Robert did not require a ransom," Blair Colm said calmly. "And why would that be, do you think, Lady Cassandra?"

"Because he is a fair and just man? His crewmen told me that Red Robert granted Laird Haggerty parley, and that there was a fair fight. Red Robert honored the agreement they had made, and Laird Haggerty, too, is a man of his word."

"A man of his word is still worth his ransom," Blair said sharply.

"A woman worth money is only worth her price if she arrives at the bargaining point intact," Cassandra snapped. "I trust you will see to it that my father and I sleep peacefully through the night. I will not have the least difficulty telling any man who offers to pay for me that I am only as pure as the men who raped me." She stared at him. "And you should take extreme care. My father has a reputation in the colonies that is not misted with rumor, and the governor is his friend. Try to malign my father and you may find that you are your own greatest enemy."

He stared back at her and smiled. "You don't understand, child. You would be surprised by how eager men are—especially when they have long lusted after a young woman they could not touch—to hear that she was really of easy virtue and offered herself to a man with power."

"You're trying to force *me* to question all that I know and trust. But you cannot do it with me. And you will not be able to do it with others."

"Nonsense. My word is always believed." He smiled coldly. "And now I must bid you good night, my dear. This conversation is at an end."

"You will rot in hell," she promised.

"Hell is what men create for themselves on earth," he told her.

"Yours is coming," she promised pleasantly, and managed to turn with dignity.

Then, shaking, she returned to the shelter.

She was grateful to see that her father still slept, and knew that she needed to do so, as well. She had to be ready.

Ready for what?

She didn't know, she realized with agony.

She lay down and prayed for sleep. She needed an escape, even if a false one.

Just a few dreams, at the least, to give her a reprieve from the nightmare she was living.

"RED, IT'S LOGAN. For the love of God, stop fighting me...."

She had never felt such a trembling before. She had been terrified for herself.

She had been terrified for him.

She had thought herself in the arms of the enemy.

He eased his hold, and she shoved a hand against his chest and pushed him backward, deeper into the cave.

"Red!" he protested.

She slapped him hard. He was stunned.

"You punched me," she accused him.

"All right, all right, we're even."

She moved to slap him again, but this time, he was ready and caught her arm.

"We're nowhere near even," she said. "You nearly scared me to death just now."

"I couldn't say anything. You were staring out, and I thought someone might have been out there."

"There was. *You.*"

To her astonishment, he was smiling.

She didn't care and held herself stiff as a board as he drew her to him. "Stop it, Logan. What in God's name is the matter with you? Cassandra is out there."

He sobered quickly but didn't release his hold. "And I intend to save her," he said grimly.

"So…"

"So…?"

"Let me go," she said very softly. "It's…over. Paradise or lust…it's over. We must return to the real world."

He inhaled, staring at her hard. His eyes were blue ice in the whisper of moonlight. "I told you that I love her, and I do. I also told you that a marriage will never take place between us."

She heard his words, but they meant nothing to her. Perhaps he wasn't madly, physically in love with Cassandra, but that didn't change the fact that she was still the right woman for him, as he would no doubt come to see once they were back in civilization. Cassandra had risked her life for him. They would wind up together. And she herself would be left even without what had sustained her all her life: her desperate desire for vengeance.

"Logan, please."

"Please what?"

"What did you see?"

"I believe the plan can work, and that I can alert Cassandra and Horatio."

"How?"

"The men are drinking heavily. Even Blair Colm is drinking. Cassandra and her father are sleeping in the shelter. I can reach them from the far side and tell them of our plan, and that we'll return for them. There's when we will face danger." He looked at her and inhaled deeply. "There's no help for it. Unless..."

"Unless?"

Again he inhaled. "I beg you once again to stay aboard the ship once we take her, and let me come back alone to deal with Colm and rescue the Bethanys."

"You know I will not."

"I've prayed that you would."

"I have a good sword arm. You will need me."

He pulled her into his arms, staring at her. "Red..."

She looked into his eyes, but as she did, she lifted her leg and took the knife from its sheath at her ankle, then brought it to his throat.

"Don't underestimate me, Laird Haggerty," she said very softly.

"I would *never* underestimate you," he told her.

The look in his eyes was more than she could bear. She started to turn away, but to her vast surprise, he moved swiftly, and it was her turn to be taken. Before she could escape his hold, he had wrested the knife from her grasp.

"You used my trust!" she accused him.

"As you used mine."

"But—"

She was taken by surprise once again when his mouth fell on hers with a searing force.

The knife dropped between them. He fell to his knees, drawing her down with him. For a moment she was stunned. For another moment she struggled. Then the realization that everything she had dreamed of for years was about to happen suddenly roused a passion in her that was beyond desperate.

They probably would die tonight.

And the taste of his mouth was something she needed to know one last time.

The feel of his hands on her flesh, the fevered pressure of his fingers, even the hasty, hurried, fumbling with their clothing, those were all things she couldn't die without experiencing again. His mouth fastened to her breast, his tongue bathing her torso. His hand slid between her thighs, and the pressure of his body forced them apart. He moved against her, making love intimately, so feverishly that she didn't feel the hardness of the earth but writhed in response to the liquid fire of his tongue, then arched into his thrust, urgently needing the madness, the frenzy, of both the sex and the sensuality between them. She fought to keep silent, to keep her cries from giving away their presence, but he kept them both silent with the power of his lips and the fury of their coupling. When it was over, they lay as they were, not far from the cavern opening, with the air growing cool around them, and the sanity and the pressure of the night and the reality of imminent death returning as if on the wings of eagles. But finally he stood and moved away, awkwardly straightening his clothing.

She caught his arm. "I need to put on breeches," she said simply, knowing she could never fight effectively in a dress. She rose and walked away from him, deeper into the cave where their store of clothes lay. Tears stung her eyes, tears she could never allow him to see. She thought their idyll should have ended far more sweetly. There should have been a bed of fragrant grass. There should have been time. They should have had long moments of lying tangled together, drifting in the pleasure of what had been. There should have been whispers, gentle touches...

But there had been none of that, and there never would be.

She hurriedly found a man's light shirt. But finding no clean breeches that would fit her, she figured she had to make do with what she wore, and thought she could cut a slit up the side if the skirt's fabric got in her way. She found a second knife and belted it around her other ankle. She would have only her knives and a sword, nothing more, though she was certain Logan planned to take guns off the crew when they boarded. They would have to do so carefully and stealthily, taking the remaining men off guard. It was a good plan.

They could prevail....

Or they could fail.

So many things could go wrong....

But it didn't matter. It was the best plan they'd been able to come up with. It had to work.

She slipped silently back to the front of the cave. It was time.

Logan was there, his shoulders broad and stiff as he stared out into the night.

"Logan," she said softly.

He turned. She saw the anguish in his eyes and realized that he, too, knew they could far too easily fail.

"Stay. I beg you," he said softly.

Without a word, she hurried past him, straight out into the night, moving quickly.

There was no turning back.

CASSANDRA CAME awake suddenly, startled but unsure why.

"Cassandra?"

It was barely a whisper, scarcely louder than the breeze, but someone had spoken her name.

She looked around as her eyes adjusted to the darkness and saw a face.

Her breath caught.

Logan!

He brought a finger to his lips.

He slipped closer to kneel beside her, and it was all she could do not to touch him.

"Am I dreaming?" she whispered.

"No, but I must speak quickly. You must stay here for now. I'm so sorry. We're taking his ship tonight.... But we'll be back for you and your father."

She felt like crying, but she forced herself to smile and then nodded to show she understood.

She could do anything now. Somehow, miraculously, Logan was there, and that meant there was hope.

"You must wake your father and tell him of our plan," he said.

She nodded again, not trusting herself to speak.

Then, just as silently as he had come, he was gone.

RED KNEW SHE HAD TO take great care creating the leaks. She couldn't make an obvious hole, which would be seen if someone decided to check on the boats in the night. She crouched flush with the side of the second tender, looking up frequently to make sure no member of the crew had moved. She was somewhat surprised that Blair Colm had not set out a guard, but perhaps, having searched the horizon for ships and seen none, he had decided himself safe for the night.

She was so attuned to the night that she wasn't taken by surprise when Logan came up to her. Hunching down, he whispered quickly, "It is time. Are you ready?"

She nodded, then saw him crouch low and push the third tender toward the water. In seconds he had disappeared into the darkness. She was about to wade out to join him when she realized she had dropped the knife. She hurried back for it—and was startled by a sudden commotion from the shelter.

Suddenly Cassandra burst out into the firelight, a man behind her, clutching his groin. Colm's crew were mumbling and starting to rise.

Torches were lit, and suddenly the whole area was aglow.

"What's going on?" Blair Colm raged.

Every one of them was awake now. Even Lord Bethany came stumbling from the shelter, crying out, "Cassandra! For the love of God, Cassandra!"

"Stop!" Blair Colm shouted.

Everyone froze, as if in a tableau, and Red knew she could make it to the tender, but something gave her pause.

Cassandra.

Red hid in the dark shadow of the tender and watched the drama unfold.

"You gave me your word!" Cassandra accused Blair Colm. "I was to sleep in peace. But instead this sack of pus came after me,"

"She stabbed me with my own knife and wounded me privates!" The man Red recognized as Billy Bones was the fellow who complained.

"I'll kill you!" Lord Bethany cried out, rushing forward with a poor weapon, a tree branch.

"Shoot him," Blair Colm snapped out, pointing at Bethany. "And do with her what you will."

She could have made it to the ship. Red knew it.

But instead she inhaled deeply as one of the pirates drunkenly reached for his pistol.

She stood from her position behind the boat and threw her knife as hard as she could at Blair Colm. The distance was too great; her chances of hitting him were one in a million, and she had never been lucky, she thought sadly. But the blade buried itself in a palm tree right behind him, which was enough to arrest his attention.

The sharp impact of the blade into the wood startled everyone.

She thought about running, but she would only be caught, and hurt. And she couldn't guarantee she would keep the attention of all the men away from Cassandra and her father.

So instead she prayed that Logan was even now crafting a plan to save them all and walked slowly into the light of the torches, knowing she had drawn every eye.

No ONE COULD HAVE appeared more surprised than Cassandra, though neither she nor her father seemed to have any idea of who they were looking at.

But Blair Colm did.

"By God! It's a ghost!" he said. He stared at her incredulously as she walked up to him. "The little Irish whelp I sold to Lady Fotherington. I had heard you died…hearsay, of course. Obviously. You should have died, wretched girl. I'd had my finger in what should have been your happy marriage, but…you…"

Everyone else was drunkenly silent, weaving, confused, watching.

"Where in hell did you come from?" he demanded.

She shrugged. "I've been living on this island for some time."

He frowned. "With corpses for company?"

"That poor couple…. I tried to help them, but I could not, and they died."

"Who is she?" someone whispered.

"An old friend," Blair Colm replied, staring at her, smiling slowly. A grim, vicious smile.

"An old enemy," she corrected. "I just tried to kill you."

"You missed. Pity for you."

"I won't miss next time."

"There won't be a next time."

For a minute she was afraid her sacrifice would be in vain. That he would simply shoot all of them.

But as he stared at her, she realized that he was seeing her as a woman—an attractive woman—and she could use that to her advantage.

Thank God he did not know she was Red Robert.

"You!" Blair said suddenly, spinning on Cassandra and her father. "Get back inside now," he growled.

"And you!" He turned to Billy Bones. "You disobeyed a direct command. You're the one I should be shooting."

"But you just said—"

"Speak again and I'll be deciding between the cat-o'-nine-tails and death," Blair told him. "The rest of you, go back to sleep. Except you, Nathan. You're on guard through the night. Through the entire night, do you understand? And sober up, you sots! Come the morning, we'll take the prisoners back on board ship. There will be no more of this."

"You must not hurt her," Cassandra began, but Colm cut her off.

"I can still shoot you both," he said, not glancing her way. "Get out of sight—now."

Lord Bethany reached for his daughter. He was shaking, looking old and frail beyond his years. Cassandra was obviously torn, but finally she grasped her father's outstretched arm and retreated.

And Red was left staring at Blair Colm, seeing the man who had destroyed her life so many years ago. Seeing blood.

Oh, yes, her vision was clouded with red.

His crew surrounded them.

There was another knife, sheathed at her other ankle. She could draw it and kill the man now where he stood.

But if she did...

If she did, the crew would not only kill her, they would certainly kill Lord Bethany and rape Cassandra, and probably kill her in the process.

So she just stood there as Blair Colm reached out to her, then bent in the mockery of a bow.

"Do come closer, child. We have a lot to talk about."

She stood her ground.

"Shall I have you dragged?" he inquired pleasantly.

And so she walked over to him. The man she despised more than the devil himself.

CHAPTER FOURTEEN

THE MINUTE HE HEARD the shouting, Logan turned and looked toward shore.

In a heartbeat, he took in everything that was happening and realized he was going to have to come up with a new plan to save Red, as well as Cassandra and her father, or die trying.

As he watched, he saw Red throw the knife, then stride up the sand to face the man she despised. He saw Cassandra take her father's arm and move toward the shelter. He saw the pirates, standing around almost stupidly, and he saw Red start to walk toward Blair Colm.

He swiftly pushed the boat back up on shore, then crouched beside it as he tried desperately to figure out what to do.

Red stopped in front of Blair, and then the bastard's arm shot out, and he hit her so hard that she fell down on her knees.

Everything in Logan quickened.

His heart was pounding, his muscles tensing, as he fought to keep himself from screaming in protest and racing toward certain death in a vain attempt to rescue her.

He watched with dread, telling himself that she was clever and could hold her own. He was glad that the dark wig she'd worn as Red Robert was at the bottom of the sea somewhere. There was no way Blair Colm could know she was his nemesis, the pirate everyone who sailed the Caribbean knew sought his death. She would think of something. She would be safe as Cassandra was safe. Colm would humiliate her, punish her, but not really harm her, because she was valuable. A beautiful young woman with such unusual red hair would be a valuable commodity in the whorehouses of the pirate ports—but only if both her body and her mind were whole.

He saw her rise and prayed she would not strike back.

She did not. Maybe she had learned that retreat could be the finest measure of courage; maybe he had even influenced her reckless desperation for vengeance.

As he watched, Blair Colm angrily threw out his arms, apparently ordering the others back to their drunken slumbers.

But he didn't touch Red again. He kept his distance. They spoke, and then, with regal dignity, Red headed for the shelter.

The men who had moved off seemed to be looking to their leader once again. Colm walked among them in a rage, then sat down against a palm, his sword out, his hand upon the hilt.

Then one man disengaged himself from the group and began walking toward the tenders, so Logan hurried back into the water and swam silently out of sight.

The ship, he thought. He had to get aboard the ship and take her. That would be the only hope for any of them.

IN ONE RESPECT, Red thought, she had certainly succeeded in her longtime plan. Blair Colm had been stunned that she was alive, not to mention that she was on the island. Stunned that *anyone* was on the island. She was certain he would question her with skill and rapacity, come the morning. But at least he hadn't trusted himself to deal with her that night and sent her away.

Which didn't mean she was safe.

Safe? Oh, God. He was truly the devil incarnate. And she was not safe, not so long as he still breathed upon this earth.

They hadn't spoken long, but she would never forget his words.

"They say that all babes should be killed. And most oft I do. For babes grow to be men and women with an unseemly lust to right the wrongs they think were done them. I see it in your eyes, girl. I see the hatred. I see your hunger to kill me. I should have killed you, as lucrative as you proved to be. And I still may. But there's something in me…that finds the hatred you bear me almost…delicious. What would hurt you more than anything in the world? Just my touch, perhaps. Hmm. I'll think on that tonight. You'll never know, will you, what to expect while you're in my power? One minute,

I let you live. The next, perhaps the cat. And the next...who knows? Maybe you're not worth selling again and I should just use you 'til I tire of you, then pass you to my men. You are an intriguing catch."

"Maybe you should kill me now," she had suggested.

"No need. Not yet. I decide, for I'm in power."

"Now."

"I'll always be in power."

And then he had smiled, and looked at her with such amusement and cruelty that it had made her skin crawl. He would never take her because he wanted her. He never gave in to mercy, thirst, hunger, exhaustion...or even his own lust—unless it suited his purpose. He would only touch her if he thought she would find it the worst form of torture imaginable.

"I believe I'll sleep on it, my dear. And I'll let you sleep on it, as well. Or maybe I'll drag you out in the middle of the night...if I get bored."

"You can't really touch me. It won't matter."

"Oh, yes, trust me. I can. And it *will* matter."

She'd forced a shrug. She didn't want him to know that watching him murder others would be a far worse agony than anything he could do to her directly.

He smiled, then looked at Billy Bones. "Search our dear friend for other weapons."

Red had tried to maintain a stoic expression as fear set in. He would find her second knife, and she would be left defenseless.

Billy Bones, with a lascivious grin on his face, had come forward and ordered her to lift her arms. Then he'd patted her down slowly, her breasts, her stomach.

He'd let his hands linger, grinning all the while. She had remained rigid, staring straight ahead. When he had allowed his hands to ride her thighs, she snapped out, not at him, but to Blair Colm, "As you can see, I'm hiding nothing," and stepped back.

And Billy, Bones, the rodent, had nodded with amusement, looking to Blair. "She's clean—but I'd be happy to keep checking."

"Calm yourself for now, Billy," Blair told him. "Maybe later…"

It had been a threat, but she hadn't cared. She'd been so afraid she would tremble and fall with relief at having kept her knife.

"Go inside," Blair had told her. "If you would have any reprieve."

She was smart enough to take whatever reprieve was offered.

Blair Colm had always had patience. She knew many of his political prisoners had thought themselves protected, thought he was handling them with decency, only to have him discover the one piece of information he'd wanted from them, then strike them down in cold blood in an instant.

For now, she had to control the fury within her, the urgency, the near madness. She had done what she'd had to do. In the split second in which she had made her choice, she had chosen well, for the man had lost his urge to shoot Lord Bethany, and Cassandra was not at the mercy of the crewmen.

In fact, the beautiful Cassandra and her esteemed father were on their knees, huddled together, when she entered their realm. The tight confines of the shelter didn't exactly offer privacy, for their voices would carry easily out to the crew, though some were so drunk that they had fallen back into their slumbers. But those who remained awake were now on guard as they had not been before the chaos.

Very little light filtered into the shelter, but there was enough so that after a moment Red could see the faces of Lord Bethany and his daughter. They were staring at her, still as stunned now when she had first made her appearance.

"I don't know who you are," Lord Bethany said, whispering, "but you saved my daughter from God knows what horror, and you saved my life. We are eternally in your debt."

"Truly we are," Cassandra said gravely, staring at her wide-eyed.

"We are not yet safe," Red told them.

"And you *know* this wretched man?" Lord Bethany asked.

Red inhaled. "A long story, and not for tonight."

"You were with Logan," Cassandra said, staring at her. "He said 'we.'"

"By God…" Lord Bethany said, his voice trailing off as he turned to his daughter. "Then…you were not dreaming. He is out there."

Red nodded.

"So…he has escaped? To take the ship?" Cassandra asked.

"So I pray," Red replied. "Though how he is to do that alone…"

She realized that Cassandra was looking at her strangely.

What was going on in her mind? Red wondered. Did she sense that the man she loved, the man she had risked life and limb to rescue, had betrayed her?

She didn't know the woman, Red thought. She owed her nothing.

But from what Red had seen—and though her heart and soul balked furiously against it—she admired Cassandra, Lady Bethany. She had acted with courage, fighting the filthy wretch who had attacked her. She would have fought for Red, if it had not been for her father. Even now, she was not cowed but looked expectantly at Red.

"You're Irish," Lord Bethany said suddenly.

Red frowned, certain she had long ago lost the accent.

But he was studying her gravely. "Ah, poor lass, I know your story now. He seized you from your parents and sold you in the colonies as an indentured servant."

She nodded. "But that is not all. Blair Colm makes his income not only by raiding the seas beneath the British flag and seeing there are no survivors. He has contacts in the highest levels of society, and he arranges the sale of women to wealthy, even titled, men in search of mistresses. I've heard he also makes great sums trading women in the Middle East, where the novelty of a light-haired or fair-skinned woman is an asset."

"The man is despicable," Lord Bethany breathed.

"But you escaped him," Cassandra noted.

"An accident at sea," Red explained.

Cassandra was still studying her intently.

"It's a long story," Red said again, since something more seemed to be called for.

"You were a prisoner of the pirates, too?" Cassandra asked.

"I was taken aboard their ship, yes."

"Poor dear. What a wretched time you've had of it," Cassandra said.

How ridiculous, Red thought. Nothing might matter to any of them in a matter of hours, yet she felt a gnawing of guilt in her soul.

"Please believe me, I learned to weather hardship very well," she said.

Cassandra nodded gravely. "It seems that at least some pirates indeed practice a code of ethics."

"Far better than at least one man decorated by the crown," her father added angrily.

Cassandra wasn't to be deterred. "Red Robert...we received the reply to our offer of ransom saying that none was needed, and that Lord Haggerty would be left at a safe port. You were treated as decently?"

"I was treated quite well," Red replied, wishing she could fight the temptation to look away. "And I believe we have much to live for, so we need to be very careful. I have every reason to believe that the ship sailed by Red Robert will come looking for us here. Soon, I fervently hope. Those on board will be searching for Lord Haggerty and myself for...for many reasons. Unfortunately, I'm equally certain that Blair Colm will return to his ship in the morning, though he will have to make more trips than he expects, and I also believe he will find a smaller crew aboard."

"How many of the boats did you fix to sink?" Lord Bethany asked.

"Just two. We had intended to use the third."

"He will know that you scuttled his boats," Cassandra pointed out.

"He already knows how much I hate him."

"He will hurt you," Cassandra whispered. Her concern was far more difficult to accept than Red had expected.

"What of this pirate seeking you?" Lord Bethany asked.

"If the ship comes…well, those pirates will not be against us."

Lord Bethany said, "We don't even know your name, child."

He spoke so gently, and it was far more painful than any blow Blair Colm could have struck her. Such a good man, with the tenderness of a father, extended now to her.

Why couldn't she at the very least dislike Cassandra? She had a wonderful father, and she had genuine strength, though she had no doubt been cosseted her whole life.

And Logan cared for her very deeply—more deeply, perhaps, than he even knew himself.

"My name is Roberta. Bobbie," she said.

Lord Bethany gripped her hand. "Lass, if by the grace of God we should survive this, I swear that I will spend my days seeing to your welfare."

The passionate tenderness and true gratitude in his voice hurt almost unbearably.

"Well," she whispered briskly, "first we must survive this. It's imperative that we be ready to assist Logan, come the morning. We must get some rest."

"Two at a time," Cassandra said. "I was resting when that vile pretense of a man made his way in here and..."

Lord Bethany groaned.

"I am fine, Father," Cassandra said quickly.

"I had some rest this afternoon," Red told them. She refrained from explaining that Logan had knocked her flat to keep her from walking into danger. "I will keep what watch a prisoner can." She hesitated. "I believe we're being watched too closely right now, but in case there is a chance at some point...there is something you must know. There is a cave behind a spring, which can be reached by walking straight inland. And there are fissures in the rear, not really entrances, but small enough to slip through. If there's ever an opportunity...you may have to run fast. You won't easily see the entrance, because it's shrouded with growth. But it's there, around the spring, to the east."

"If we escape, you will be with us," Lord Bethany said.

"I dearly hope so, but you must know where we are running, should we have an opportunity to run. Logan has a plan, however, so we will only go against it if it appears that we must," Red told him.

Lord Bethany nodded.

"Logan will know what he is doing," Cassandra said.

Logan is desperate, Red thought, and his options are few. We're all desperate.

But she smiled with encouragement.

Lord Bethany nodded and sat, leaning back against a palm. Cassandra sat at his side, resting her head on his shoulder.

Once more, Red couldn't help but feel a pang.

Once upon a time, I had a father who loved me, too, she thought. He was a noble man. He died trying to save my mother and myself, and the others in the village.

Cassandra did not rest long, though. She waited only long enough for her father's breathing to deepen as he slept, then moved toward Red. "I fear for him so greatly," she whispered.

"He seems a fine man."

Cassandra shook her head with worry. "Men…they feel they must be noble. That life is nothing if they are not. They don't know how to use guile and their wits. Women's weapons. If he thinks I am in danger…he acts rashly. A woman can wait. She knows patience. She knows that some battles are best lost so that a war may be won. It's something we are taught by the very society in which we live." Her last words sounded bitter, and Red wondered if there had been times when Cassandra longed for a different life than that dictated by her position.

Yet somehow the words seemed important to her, as well.

Had she forgotten there were weapons other than guns and blades?

Perhaps it was a lesson she should make a point of recalling.

LOGAN REACHED the ship. The waves slapped around him, washing him against the hull. He swam around it, seeking the trail of the hempen ladder he prayed was still hanging over the side. Had the remaining crew hoisted it?

The darkness wasn't to his advantage, but he looked up to find the davits that had held the tenders silhouetted against the sky and used their positions to orient himself, and there, at last, he found the ladder.

Carefully, he looked up. No one was in sight, so, grasping the ladder, he pulled his knife from the sheath at his ankle and slowly, carefully, made his way up.

When he had almost reached the level of the deck, he paused and looked back to shore.

All seemed quiet.

He could just see Blair Colm seated near the fire, his back against a palm. Did he sleep? Or had Red's appearance unnerved him enough to keep him awake?

Logan kept climbing and, as silently as possible, checked the immediate area, then eased himself over the rail. He looked toward the helm, but there was no one at the wheel. Since he had come this far undetected, he reasoned there was no man in the crow's nest, either.

He hunched low against the ship's rail and inched along, watching. Finally, as he neared the stairs to the deck, he saw a man on guard. The fellow was lax; he was armed, but his pistols were set in holsters that hung low on his hips, and his hands were on the rail.

Logan felt a moment's unease. He had killed in battle. He had never killed in cold blood.

He had to remind himself that these men had been part and party to the murders of dozens of men aboard various ships, even if they had not been with Blair Colm when he had massacred whole villages in the name of King William.

He *was* killing in self-defense.

With that, he moved as quietly as the air and came at the man from the back. He felt the hot blood spurt over his fingers as he slit the man's throat.

He was tempted to push the dying man overboard, but he didn't want any corpses washing up on shore with the dawn and warning Colm, and so he dragged the body back behind two supply barrels shoved against the rail, taking the man's two fine pistols and sword for his own.

One man down. How many more remained here on the ship?

He decided to explore the deck first.

He almost tripped over the man by the rail near the mainmast. He was sprawled against it, arms crossed over his chest, eyes closed.

The position was bad, but he had to remove each crew member as he came upon him. He held his breath for a moment, then struck, going swiftly, straight and hard for the jugular vein. The man's eyes opened. Too late. The blood gushed. Logan was covered in it this time. But slitting the throat ensured a quick death, and a silent one, severing the vocal cords. The man died in less than a minute.

A surprised minute, one that Logan thought might haunt him forever. Those eyes, just staring...

There would be no way, come the light, to hide the

pool of blood. But in the darkness it might look like shadow, should the rest of the crew rise. He laid the body against the rail and hid it with a pile of rigging.

He heard voices then; two men walking toward him from the captain's cabin.

"Did you not enjoy Lord Bethany's surprise when Captain Colm assured him that *he* would hang for a pirate?" one asked.

"Still and all, it gets a bit irksome, don't ye think?" asked the other. "We should have killed the old bastard with the others. And the daughter! A rare beauty. Why must we keep the girl all safe and pure? She should be booty to be shared, like everything else."

"Well, she will be booty. I heard he planned on offering her to a Moroccan prince—who will tire of her eventually, of course. Maybe we can make a deal to get the girl back...used," the first man said, clearly amused.

Logan felt his jaw lock, and any sickness he had felt at the thought of killing these men faded. But there were two now, and he dared not let them see him. This would demand finesse.

He let them walk by.

As they ambled along the portside rail, he moved. Silently, swiftly, he crept behind the rigging he had just used to cover the last corpse.

As they turned and walked back, musing on Cassandra's feminine assets, he spoke from the cover of the rigging.

"Mates!"

They turned.

"Over here."

He waved the arm of the dead man.

"It's Brewster," one of the men said.

"Get up, you drunkard," the second one ordered.

"I need your help…fer the love of God…please…" Logan said, slurring his words.

As the two came forward, Logan barely breathed, calculating the perfect moment to strike.

The first of the men was frowning; he had stepped in the pool of blood.

"What is this…?"

"Help!" Logan repeated.

Both men came closer and leaned down.

Logan shoved the corpse toward them. Before they could cry out, he attacked, with a sword to the neck of the first, his knife to the neck of the other.

His knife had severed the vocal cords of the second man.

The other, despite the gash to his throat, didn't die as quickly.

He staggered, falling against the rail, as Logan swung again.

The man's hands were at his throat as he stared accusingly at Logan. Then, after what seemed like an eternity, he fell to his knees, then slumped down. Dead.

Four.

Four were gone.

He closed his eyes. For a moment, just a moment, as the sea breeze failed to waft away the smell of blood on the air, he remembered the past.

Remembered it as if it had been just yesterday….

His father, riding away…

His mother, turning to fight...

Dying.

This was it. The smell of blood he could never forget....

He straightened, stepping away. Let them stay where they lay. Now he had to carefully calculate where he would find the rest of the ship's onboard crew.

The master's cabin, perhaps, where these two had come from. While Blair Colm was on shore, his men— who no doubt had their moments of envy—might well be enjoying his private quarters.

Silently, his blades in hand, he started toward the captain's door.

IN TIME, CASSANDRA, too, fell asleep. Red didn't mind being on guard; she couldn't have slept, anyway, so she was happy to stay awake, ready to do her best to divert any trouble that might appear.

It was amazing what hope could do for the human soul.

Allow it to rest.

She kept looking below the canvas cover, out to sea.

So far, nothing. No sign of trouble from the ship.

Had Logan made it out there? He was a good swimmer, so she had to believe he had the strength to reach the boat safely, but what if he had been brought down by some small danger he'd never imagined?

Red-legged Jeeves, a privateer during Queen Anne's war, had met many a Spanish ship and survived, then been killed when one of his own rigging lines had snapped.

What if Logan had met with a shark on the way to the ship?

No, she had seen sharks many times. They attacked only when there was blood, and Logan hadn't been bleeding.

What if he had scraped himself on the coral as he passed over the reef?

At the very least, she was certain he hadn't been caught aboard ship, for undoubtedly the alarm would have been sounded if an intruder had been found.

She looked around the beach, taking care to lie on the ground and look beneath the canvas, rather than through the open "doorway." Most of the pirates—that supposedly decent crew sailing under the Union Jack—were still sleeping off their rum, but she saw that the one called Nathan had taken his orders to heart. He was pacing the shore, occasionally stopping to look out to sea.

He kept his hands constantly on his gun belt, ready to draw at the slightest provocation.

And Blair Colm?

She couldn't see him and wondered if he slept. She doubted it. She had certainly taken him by surprise tonight, but even so, she would live—unless he decided she should die. He didn't consider her to be much of a danger. In his mind, she was just a slip of a girl.

No threat at all, and worth a fair sum.

Unless he figured out that she was Red Robert.

A chill swept through her. He didn't know, and she didn't want him to find out...until seconds before he died.

She closed her eyes tightly and prayed that there

was justice not only in the next world, but in this one, as well.

She heard a soft sound and surveyed the shelter.

Cassandra was awake again, and she was praying.

Red considered joining her.

Please God...

It was as far as she got.

If He was out there somewhere, He knew what she needed.

THERE WERE MULTIPANED windows on either side of the door to the captain's cabin, but to Logan's relief, the thick curtains within had them blocked.

He inched along the outer wall, then ducked low to try to see inside past the edges of the fabric.

As he had suspected, the crew were within, four of them, dicing. Luckily they seemed oblivious to anything going on outside.

He watched one man roll and the three others groan when he won. The money flew about the table.

"Double or nothing, winner take all," insisted one fellow, angered by his loss. He was about forty, perhaps older, and had long graying hair held back by a striped cotton band. His fingers were bejeweled. In the flickering lamplight within, Logan could see that one of the rings was an insignia with a family crest.

A Scottish coat of arms.

He couldn't help but wonder just how, when and where the man had acquired the ring. He knew that the scent of blood clinging to him wasn't imaginary, and once again it sent him careening into the past. The men's voices brought him back to the present.

"Double or nothing, when I'm already sitting on all the money?" asked the man who had just won. Slim and wiry, he sported two gold-capped teeth and a gold earring. His head was clean-shaven.

"Coward," the one with the rings accused.

"Nay, just smart," chortled the third crewman. This one was stout with deep jowls.

The fourth man, middle-aged, well-muscled, with wisps of dark hair and a heavy beard, offered his opinion. "Oh, don't leave a fellow cryin' in his grog. Once we've sold off the girl—and with that ransom intended for that Laird Haggerty, we'll all be sitting fine enough—while we watch old Horatio Bethany dance the hempen jig."

Logan felt his fingers twitching at his knife. But as he kept his eye on the foursome, he reminded himself that there were most likely more men belowdecks. He could create a minor disturbance that would draw these four out, but if he had to resort to pistols, he would certainly rouse any others on the ship.

What to do?

Go below first?

No, because he didn't want to take his eyes off this group. They were drinking, but not drunk. And they all appeared able-bodied and quick enough.

As he stood debating and the four argued about continuing the play, the man with the jowls suddenly rose. "S'cuse me, mates. I've a need for fresh air—and the slosh bucket."

"Piss over the side, you louse. Spare the man on loo duty," the man with the rings said.

"Fine, I'll piss in the night breeze."

Logan straightened against the cabin wall instantly, quickly shifting his plan of action, grateful for the man's call of nature.

He held still and silent while the door opened and the fellow walked out. He was tall, very tall. And big. Strong as an ox, Logan decided. He would have to be very sure and very quick.

The big fellow looked about, then ambled toward the rail. "Brewster?" he called out. He swore when he wasn't immediately answered.

He stopped on his way to the rail, and Logan swore silently to himself and hoped the fellow wasn't going to investigate.

He crept silently behind the big man, his knife at the ready. When his quarry stopped, Logan stopped.

"Brewster?" the sailor said again. "You sorry excuse for a man! You're supposed to be on guard duty. What if some ship happened upon us, eh?"

He walked forward.

In another moment he would stumble on the bodies.

There was no choice for it. Logan prepared to spring. As soon as the big man bent down to look closer at the bodies of his fallen comrades, Logan made his move. He landed on the man's back and drew the knife across his throat.

He didn't die easily.

Even with his life's blood gushing from him, he managed to stand and throw Logan from his back. But the element of surprise, and the man's own actions, had given Logan the advantage. No man, no matter how big or strong, could survive a severed jugular.

Logan, tossed down hard on the deck, remained still as the fellow staggered, tried to speak…and fell at last.

He would not be laughing at the hanging of Lord Bethany, that was a certainty.

Logan quickly gathered his wits and got back to his feet, careful to keep a distance from the slippery pools of blood the man had left behind. Looking past the dead man, he noticed the barrels set against the rail at the bow.

He looked toward the cabin. He could hear them arguing.

He strode to the first barrel and pried it open with the bloody blade of his knife.

The thing was filled with jewels and gold.

He looked back toward the cabin. There was no time. Still…

He moved swiftly. He didn't dump the entire barrel; he was afraid of the noise it would make. Instead he quickly tossed item after priceless item over the side. It took only moments. He opened the second barrel, and the third. In short order he took supreme pleasure in the fact that the treasure that would have allowed these men the luxury of watching a hanging from the best seats was now lying on the seabed.

Then he made a silent retreat back to the cabin.

"What the hell? Do you think the big oaf fell straight overboard, his thing a'flappin' in the breeze?" the beringed fellow asked.

"Go check on him," Gold-earring commanded.

"You go check on him," Rings replied.

"Want a chance to get your money back? He's the only one on your side, mate," Gold-earring pointed out.

Swearing, the loser with the rings rose and came outside. Leaving the door open behind him, he stepped forward and called, "Griffin, where ye be?"

Logan inched closer, gently pushing the door so that it would close slowly, as if from a shift in the ship.

When the man turned, Logan ducked.

"Griffin? Brewster?"

He would cause an alarm if he was left alone any longer, so Logan sprinted up behind him, clapped his hand over the man's mouth and slipped the blade of his knife between two ribs to pierce the heart.

For a moment, the man gurgled wetly and struggled.

Then his struggles weakened and he grew silent.

Logan eased him to the deck, then rolled him behind a water barrel.

Two more. He made his way back to his post outside the captain's cabin. Long minutes passed. The two remaining men discussed the lack of quality whores in both New Providence and Jamaica.

"Where are those two?" the bearded man finally asked.

The thin pirate rose. "We'll find 'em. Maybe they're out there hoarding the gold, eh? Well, I'll not be losing out on it!"

Both men were coming out at once.

Logan knew he had no choice.

The skinny man saw him, so he pulled one of the pistols and shot. The explosion seemed louder than a roll of thunder directly overhead.

. The other man was pulling his own pistol, so Logan let his knife fly. It caught the man straight in the heart.

But the shot had created a noise he hadn't needed.

And there were far more men still aboard the ship than he had imagined. They were suddenly streaming up from belowdecks, using ladders at both the stern and the bow.

He emptied his pistols, threw his last knife and drew out his sword.

There were dead men everywhere. His efforts were aided by the fact that Colm's crew was slipping and sliding in the blood; those who had pulled their pistols fired off shots that went wild and twice hit members of their own crew.

The remaining men dropped their pistols as spent or dangerous and drew their swords.

How many of them were there? Logan wondered.

No matter how many swords he parried, there was always another. He didn't know how long his senses would cue him in to a man at his back, or how long he could fend off a man in front and another at his side.

He was forced back, again and again.

He was nicked, and he knew that in time the blood loss would begin to sap his strength.

He leapt atop the rail, with them grouped around him. He had but one chance to survive and fight another day.

To leap into the water.

He never leapt.

And his opponents never forced him over.

Because suddenly, out of the darkness of the night, came an explosion.

Loud. Shattering. The ship itself trembled.

And then he *was* cast overboard, and as he fell into the dark, he was aware of the scent of burnt powder and the orange of flame.

As he struck the water and plunged hard and deep into the sea, he realized that Blair Colm's ship had been hit by cannon fire.

CHAPTER FIFTEEN

BRENDAN HAD NEVER intended to start a gun battle that night.

But Jimmy O'Hara had called down from the crow's nest as, under cover of darkness, they had reached the island.

As they rounded the shore, they had seen the ship anchored just outside the reef and recognized the flags it flew, then seen signs of activity on the island. If Red *was* there with Logan, they might have been captured by Blair Colm, Brendan thought in fear.

And if the man knew he was holding the notorious pirate who had been chasing him around the Caribbean…

He didn't want to think about that.

If she were aboard Blair Colm's ship, he didn't want to sink it. And yet he couldn't become a sitting duck himself.

Then Jimmy O'Hara had called down that a man who appeared to be Logan Haggerty was waging a savage and single-handed battle against nearly two score crewmen, and Brendan felt he had no choice.

So he had ordered cannon fire, a singe shot from the

thirty-two pounder. Blair Colm's ship was a merchant-man with a thick hull; it would take far more than a single round to sink such a ship. But something had to be done.

Strangely, the cannon fire seemed to coincide with the break of dawn. The shot exploded and a fire burst up from the deck—good God, they must have hit a powder reserve—and then the horizon seemed to stay alight, a yellow line sweeping across to separate sea from sky.

"The beach!" Jimmy cried.

Brendan drew out his spyglass and studied the shore. People were scurrying about the beach, looking almost like ants from this distance, trying to ascertain the source of the explosion and gauge the danger. Brendan had run the ship in the dark, and they might have stayed hidden if he hadn't fired off the shot.

Jimmy had been right about more than just the existence of the island. Logan Haggerty *had* been fighting for his life on Blair Colm's ship. Brendan had seen him just before the shot went off.

He focused the glass in that direction now, but there was no sign of Logan anymore. The men aboard Blair's ship were working frenziedly, hauling up the anchor and putting out fires.

He swung the glass back to the beach.

He didn't see Red. All he saw were men reaching for their weapons and running toward the boats.

Then he saw Blair Colm.

He was standing on the beach, in full view, as if he were convinced he was invincible. He was shouting orders, and the men were rushing to obey.

Brendan shouted to Peg-leg. "Turn the guns. I want one volley—straight on the beach. Aim forward, not into the trees."

Peg-leg turned, hurrying to deliver the order. Already gunners were taking their positions at the swivel guns on the deck.

Their aim was true. A shot exploded in the shallows, and men went flying.

And then Brendan saw her.

It was impossible to miss her. Her hair was like a beacon—and she was wearing a dress.

A dress? He could barely remember how she looked in such attire, which she had last worn the day the notorious Red Robert had been born. He thanked God. Perhaps that meant Blair Colm had never recognized her as the pirate captain.

She was with a woman and an elderly man. Lord Bethany and his daughter, perhaps? How the hell had they all come to be together?

He couldn't dwell on the question. He saw Red almost dancing with the fellow she was fighting.

The other woman was no silly fool. He watched her knee a man in the groin as he made a lunge for her.

"Fire again! One more volley, and take care—the captain is ashore!" he cried.

The beach and the water exploded once more.

"Man in the water!" Jimmy O'Hara shouted.

Brendan looked up toward the crow's nest.

Jimmy was waving wildly. "Man in the water!" he shouted again. "It's Laird Haggerty!"

TIMING WAS everything, Red thought, as she realized what ship had arrived.

Oh, God, if only Brendan and his crew had made it a day earlier...

But they had not, and now Brendan was doing the best he could, and making all the right moves under the circumstances.

A quick glance out to sea showed her that Blair's ship had been hit—and there were more than a dozen men racing about the deck.

Her heart sank.

What had happened to Logan?

Was he dead?

Or had he somehow escaped?

She wielded her second knife to keep Colm's men at a distance and managed to find the Bethanys and drag them along the path that led to the fresh water and the cave.

"What are we doing? Where are we going?" Cassandra gasped.

"To the cave. The entrance is behind those trees. Hurry, and don't stop, no matter what. You'll find more weapons there. Now run!"

But as they rounded a bend in the path and she pushed them ahead, she nearly went sprawling face-down on the embankment by the pool.

Someone had hold of her skirt.

She reassured herself that Cassandra and her father were racing ahead, as commanded, then turned, her knife ready, and the man who'd caught her—Billy

Bones—laughed and jumped back. "You want to fight me?" he asked, amused.

"You want to fight *me?*" she returned.

He laughed again. "Oh, little girl, don't be foolish."

He made a grab at her; she swiped with the knife.

"I like them feisty," he said with a nasty grin.

"I understand you're equally fond of livestock," she informed him. She had assessed him as the kind of man who was quick to anger, and like most men, he would make rash mistakes when he was angry. It would give her the advantage she needed.

"You *are* livestock, little girl," he countered.

He flew at her then, still laughing.

She was ready.

She never even had to stab him.

He impaled himself on her blade.

His weight and momentum knocked her to the ground under him, and he stared at her in disbelief. His laughter turned to a gasp, and then, his mouth and eyes still open, he died.

With a cry, she shoved him off her, wrenching her knife free.

But before she could rise, she was pinned to the ground by a boot on her chest. She moved to stab at her attacker's leg, but someone else stamped down so hard on her arm that she cried out. The knife slipped from her fingers, and she looked up.

Blair Colm was standing with his foot atop her, several of his men at his side. "Get her up. And bring her with us. I'm getting a strange feeling there's a relationship between this bitch and the convenient arrival of Red Robert." He leaned low, until his thin face and cold eyes were uncomfortably near her own. "What do you say, dear Bobbie? Is there perhaps a romance between you? Am I right?"

She spat at him. He retaliated by slapping her with the swiftness of a serpent's strike. Her head reeled.

It continued to spin as he dragged her upright. She dimly heard him snap, "Where are the other two captives?"

"They must have been taken out on the first boat, Cap'n," someone responded. "They aren't with her."

"Walk," Colm commanded.

But the world was still spinning, and she couldn't.

She couldn't even protest when he threw her over his shoulder.

She simply lost consciousness.

THE SUN ROSE QUICKLY.

Logan was barely out of the water when he cried, "Fire at will at the ship. Red and the Bethanys aren't aboard. "

Brendan quickly turned to the crew and ordered, "Fire on the ship! Fire at will!" Then he turned to Logan and said, "I know. I saw them ashore."

Logan gripped his shoulders. "You saw them? Were they—"

"They were running inland."

"A glass! I need a spyglass," Logan said. Peg-leg quickly supplied one, and Logan focused on the beach.

With black powder filling the air, it was difficult to make out details, but then he saw two boats, both of them riding dangerously low in the water, thanks to Red.

"Their boats! Fire on their boats!" he yelled.

"Calculate fire!" Brendan shouted. "Aim for the tenders."

And then Logan felt as if an ice cold hand had reached out from the cloud of smoke and closed around his heart.

"Stop!" he roared.

"Cease fire!" Brendan commanded. Then he turned to Logan and asked, "Why?"

"He has her. Blair Colm has Red," Logan said, feeling physically ill.

As Brendan lifted his own spyglass, Logan stared, then slumped against the rail. Walking in easy view, Blair Colm was making his way down the beach to the third longboat, Red thrown over his shoulder. She was unconscious.

Unconscious? Oh, God, please let her only be unconscious, he prayed.

Because Blair Colm was the kind of man who would keep Red's dead body, knowing full well that they would not strike while there was a prayer she was alive.

Someone muttered an anguished, "Oh, God!"

And then Logan realized he was the one who had spoken.

He looked toward shore again and saw her hand move. She *was* alive, he realized with an overwhelming sense of relief.

He watched as Blair and his men got into the last of the tenders.

The second boat was just ahead of the one Red was on, six men aboard, the distance between the boats too narrow for Brendan's men to fire without fear of killing Red.

The first began to sink in earnest, still a good distance from Colm's ship.

Bless her, Red had done her work well.

The men began yelling, cursing, and several started to swim, trying to reach the other two boats.

Blair Colm never sat. He balanced easily, even in the small rowboat, with Red's weight over his shoulder.

He stared toward the *Eagle,* and Logan would have sworn that, despite the distance, the man's eyes met his.

His very look defied them. He smiled in satisfaction as his men rowed.

One of the men from the first boat was struggling in the water. Finally he slipped beneath the surface and drowned, but Colm didn't appear to so much as notice. He was returning to his ship, presumably to sail away to regroup and repair.

With Red as his prisoner.

"Where are the other two?" Brendan asked, almost as if he spoke to himself.

Logan looked around. Neither Lord Bethany nor Cassandra were anywhere to be seen, though he was pleased to see that the second boat was sinking rapidly.

He lowered the glass. "She led them to the caves," he said, praying he was right and that the other two weren't dead. Unfortunately, he knew that Lord Bethany would have fought to the death to save his daughter, just as Cassandra would have died before letting harm come to her father.

He swung the glass back to watch Blair Colm.

From the crow's nest, Jimmy O'Hara shouted down, "Survivors! Eight o'clock!"

"I see them, Jimmy, send a boat to the side, quick, get a good swimmer out there, too!"

As Brendan gave orders to rescue the remains of Blair's crew, Logan thrust the glass toward the other man and gripped the rail. "I'm going after her. I can't let him—"

"Wait!"

Logan almost punched Brendan when the other man reached out and stopped him.

"Treat your wounds first, while we see what his next move will be."

"His next move will be to hurt her."

"His next move will be to try to bring down this ship. We must stop him, and *then* we will rescue Red," Brendan told him.

"Keep her angle fair to fire and escape a volley in return," Logan said. "He lost powder after your first shot, so he'll be hampered. But we won't have much time. I think he'll want to take a few shots, then limp away, and we can't let him do so with Red in custody."

"I know how to sail a ship and how to fight," Brendan told him quietly.

Logan nodded painfully, then felt a hand on his shoulder. It was Silent Sam. "Come on. The surgeon will stitch you up. Hagar is fixing up a fine bag of tricks for you."

Logan allowed himself to be led away. He even accepted a bottle of rum and swigged deeply when the ship's surgeon came with his needle and thread to patch up the worst of his wounds.

After the surgeon left. Logan was still seated on the bunk in the captain's quarters when the door opened and Cassandra burst in, falling to her knees before him.

"Oh, God, Logan!"

"Cassie," he said, touching her wet hair gently. "Your father…?"

"Is well, thank God. They are tending to him, dry clothes, warmed rum…"

He nodded, smiling at her. His fingers trembled. "I'm so glad you're alive. Were you…? Did they…?"

She shook her head, taking his hand, kissing it.

"I'm so sorry this happened to you," he said. "You were coming for me. I pray that God forgives me the harm I've caused you. More, I pray that *you* forgive me."

"Of course I forgive you. How could you ever doubt?"

"You are a generous woman, Cassandra Bethany. And I…I must go and save another."

"Bobbie?" she asked with an understanding smile.

"Aye," he said, and looked away, wondering how much of his feeling for Red she had discerned in his eyes.

"Friends should always seek to save their friends," she told him, then blushed. "Oh, Logan, time is short, and…and this may be the only chance we have to speak of this, so I pray you will indulge me. You are a wonderful man and my dearest friend, but...I have come to realize that I do not love you as a wife should love a husband. And—" She looked up and smiled again, this time radiantly. "I believe you do not...love me as you once thought, either." She waved him to silence when he would have spoken, then went on. "Oh, I know that you do love me. But you are not *in love* with me."

"Cassandra," he murmured, "you are a beauty. You possess a brilliant mind. You have compassion, courage—"

"I am indeed quite wonderful," she told him, laughing now. "And I will be loved. As I believe you are already loved. And I believe you love her in return, do you not?"

He knew she could read the truth both of her words and his feelings in his eyes.

"You are a rare woman, Cassandra Bethany," he said. "And someday, I pray, I will be able to tell you so at length. But now...now I *must* go and rescue... Bobbie."

"Of course. I would expect you to do no less."

She rose and started to leave. "I'll see to my father. And we will be here when you return." She paused, frowning. "Logan?"

"Aye?"

"Just who is she?"

He smiled awkwardly. "She is Red Robert."

RED WAS DIMLY aware of a familiar rocking sensation and knew she was aboard a ship.

More specifically, she was on a bed, in a ship's cabin.

She heard an explosion.

There were shouts, followed by another explosion, this one farther away.

Ships...

Ships at sea, exchanging cannon fire.

She struggled up, hope in her heart that somehow a miracle had occurred and she was in her own cabin, safe, and far from the reaches of Blair Colm.

But she knew immediately that it was not so.

She was in enemy territory. Stretched on the length of what must be Blair Colm's bunk, judging by the size and opulence of the cabin. She caught her head between her hands, still dizzy. When it seemed the cabin was at last standing still, she got to her feet. At first she staggered, but she managed to make her way to the captain's table, where she steadied herself. The remnants of a dice game and mugs half-filled with grog were sitting there. Even pieces of gold had been left behind.

She must have been unceremoniously dumped here, she decided, because the fight for survival took precedence. She might well have a chance to escape.

She moved to the door. If she could slip out, if she could find a weapon...she wouldn't hesitate this time. She would kill Blair Colm without hesitation.

She breathed deeply, gathering her strength, making certain she had her balance. Then she tried the door.

And found she had been bolted in from the outside.

She cursed, slamming her fist against the wood. There had to be a way out!

Again she heard the boom of a cannon, and an explosion very close by, then felt the repercussion as Colm's ship fired in turn. She moved to the window and saw so much black powder filling the air that she wondered whether either of them could even see the other as they continued to fire.

Had Cassandra and her father made good their escape?

She prayed that they had, because no matter what Logan said, Cassandra was a fitting match for him.

As she herself would never be.

She had to stop feeling sorry for herself and forget the pain that was swamping her heart. She had much more to worry about now.

Like killing Blair Colm, for starters.

She looked around the deck and saw that it was slick with blood. Men were sliding in it as they rushed around to protect rigging and move barrels. Several men were working on the mainsail, and they were having tremendous difficulty finding their footing.

And there were bodies, men who had been killed not by cannon shot but by the sword and the knife, which could only mean that...

Logan had been here.

But where was he now?

Again, it seemed her heart sank.

Had he been killed as he fought and his body tossed overboard to become food for the fish?

The sails were rising high against the morning sky.

She watched as they began to billow, and she felt the breeze quicken as the ship began to move.

It occurred to her that she could break a window and escape. But the panes were small and set in broad wooden frames. She would have to break several to manage her escape.

She went to the captain's chair behind the desk, attempted to lift it and realized she would never be able to swing it hard enough to break anything. She hurriedly looked around the room and settled on a stool. She was on her way toward the window when the door burst open with a resounding bang.

She froze.

Blair Colm was back.

"I'LL ENGAGE HER in battle until I've given you fair time." Brendan lowered his voice. "This is…well, suicide, you know," he said, and swallowed painfully.

Logan shook his head. "I learned a little bit about her. I know several places where I can hide." He smiled. "And I'm well-armed." He lifted the satchel Hagar had given him. "Grenades. Four pistols. Lots of shot. Six knives… And a flare. When I've got Red and we've jumped ship, I'll set off the flare."

"And we'll blow her out of the water, I swear it," Brendan vowed.

"Follow closely, as closely as you dare," Logan said.

"Aye, Captain Laird Haggerty. That I will," Brendan promised.

"If we're going, we've got to go," Silent Sam said.

Logan didn't look around. He simply hoisted himself to the rail, then followed Silent Sam down the slide rope to the waiting longboat, the one that had been sent to rescue Cassandra and Horatio.

Once in the boat, they might have been in the midst of hell. So much fire had raged between the two ships that the air itself had turned black.

Silent Sam rowed strongly.

Silently.

The powder began to disperse. "She's just ahead," Sam said.

"Aye, thank you Sam."

"God go with you, Logan."

"And with you, Sam."

"Logan? Bring her back, both of ye alive."

"Aye, Sam. I intend to."

He left his boots in the bottom of the boat, then dove into the water. The heavy, waterproof bag dragged him down, and the saltwater stung his wounds.

Good. The pain gave him strength.

He swam hard, squinting against the salt and the acrid powder in the air.

The ship was ahead, and it was moving. Picking up speed. He gritted his teeth and swam harder. He had to catch it. And yet, despite his determination, he began to fear his strength would fail.

He would drown.

And Red would die.

Die as his mother had died all those years ago.

Die fighting…

He strained harder, harder. He thought of letting his weapons go but knew that would be folly.

He tasted salt as a wave poured into his mouth. He coughed hard, but kept swimming. The ship was ahead, just ahead....

He grasped for a bracket on the hull. It eluded him.

He kicked with all his strength and reached, and that time he caught the bracket, though his arm felt almost ripped from the socket.

But he held. He held fast and breathed. Then he adjusted the weight of the bag over his shoulder and began to climb.

It was slow and tedious. He inched his way up, and all the while the ship picked up speed and the wind tore at him.

He was climbing up the stern, and now he strained and pulled himself up the railing just far enough to see what was happening on board, seeking the proper moment to pull himself over the rail on board and head for a place to hide. The crew were center ship, working to repair the sails and rigging that had been damaged by cannon fire.

At the first opportunity he crawled over the rail and leapt down silently to the deck.

Burnt and ruined canvas and rigging lay in a pile near the hoist of a longboat. Logan hurried over and ducked below the canvas, where he began to slide his knives into sheaths fastened about his arms and ankles. He buckled on a brace of pistols, then tucked the last two knives beneath the gun belt. He drew out the flare and hooked it to the belt, then stuffed a waist bag with the grenades.

He took a deep breath and waited. So long as the crew

was going about the business of securing the sails and setting their desperate pace, there was no way he could hope to slip silently past and find Red, held captive either in Blair Colm's cabin or somewhere in the lower decks.

One way or the other, he *would* find her, but he had to bide his time....

So he waited.

And it was by far the most difficult thing he had ever done.

CHAPTER SIXTEEN

BRENDAN STOOD AT the helm, his eyes hard on the ship they followed, taking care to keep the vessel in sight, taking equal care to make sure she didn't suddenly veer and bring her guns back around in an attempt to knock them out of the water.

His ship had more guns, but it was also more vulnerable, being built for speed. His guns were not as efficient against the thick hull of the merchantman as Colm's guns would be against his lighter ship.

It was a careful cat-and-mouse game. He didn't intend to lose sight of the ship carrying Red, but he would be no good to her if he let Colm sink the *Eagle*.

A tap on his shoulder startled him, he had been holding so hard to the wheel with such great concentration.

"Lad, you've got to give yourself a rest. I can take her."

It was Hagar, and Brendan stared at him blankly for a moment.

"Trust me, lad. I've never let you down."

Brendan inhaled deeply and exhaled slowly. He looked at his own fingers, which were white with tension as he clasped the wheel, and nodded. "Crow's nest?" he asked.

"Silent Sam is keeping the best watch any man can."

"He'll save her," Brendan muttered. "If he made it aboard."

Hagar smiled. "He made it."

Brendan frowned at him. He had sounded so certain.

"Sam saw him with a glass from the crow's nest. He made it. Take a rest now, Brendan. If you break the wheel, we'll all be doomed, you know."

Brendan nodded in grim acknowledgment and gave up the helm to the other man. "Is there coffee?" he asked.

"I'll see some is sent to you. Rest. I know you won't sleep, but get off your feet. There's bound to be a battle soon enough, and you need to be ready for it," Hagar advised.

Brendan nodded.

"Thank you."

"Aye, mate."

Brendan headed into the captain's cabin, rubbing his eyes as he walked straight for the bunk and sat down on the edge of the thin mattress.

A scream startled him, and he vaulted to his feet and stared down at the bed in confusion.

Cassandra, Lady Bethany, was peering at him in terror that turned quickly to embarrassment. Apparently the crew had seen to her comfort while he had been at the helm. Her torn and damaged clothing was gone, and she was dressed from Red's supply of shirts and breeches. She sat up, and he saw that she was barefoot, with her hair streaming down her back in a glorious tangle. The clothing clung to her body in provocative ways, and he quickly raised his gaze to meet her eyes, which were wide and now registered her own confusion.

"I am ever so sorry," he apologized hurriedly. "I had no idea you were here. Forgive me. I'll leave you."

"No, no…" she said quickly. "I never intended to fall asleep. *How* did I fall asleep when… Oh, God, Logan… How could I? I must be the most horrible person."

"No, you're not horrible," Brendan protested. She was so distressed that he quickly went down on his knees in front of her, taking her hands. "You were a prisoner. You endured days of hell with that bas— That scourge of sea and land. If you found some rest, you mustn't condemn yourself in any way. Instinct is helping you to survive, even though your heart and mind are fighting it."

She looked at him, her eyes seeming even larger than they had been a moment ago. "Are you…Bobbie's brother?" she asked.

"Cousin," he said. "Are we that alike, then?"

"Yes, you are," she said gravely. "Except that Bobbie is…well, I'm not sure how she convinced the world she was a *male* pirate. Whereas you are so much more… I'm sorry. I'm rambling. I need to stop—"

"You need to rest and nothing more," he assured her.

"But…I must ask. Are we going to survive?"

"Aye, Lady Cassandra! We will survive. I will not let Red die."

"And neither will Logan," she said.

"He, uh, has proven to be a very good man," Brendan said awkwardly. He didn't know exactly when it happened, perhaps on that island, but he couldn't deny the fact that Logan had acquired something more than admiration for Red, despite whatever understanding he might have with Cassandra.

She looked at him curiously, tilting her head at an angle. To his surprise and consternation, she reached out and touched him. "Please do not fear to wound my feelings. Logan is...my best friend, but he is free to love wherever he chooses."

"But...you and your father. You risked your lives."

"I know, but..."

"But?"

"Brendan, I know I am supposed to be a lady, that I should be reserved and not speak of such things, but...two people who should be right for one another, who may even think for a while that they *are* right for each other, are not. So it is with Logan and me. I shall always love and admire him, but I am not *in love* with him." She met his eyes and blushed. "And so I told him before he left to rescue your cousin, for I felt he had to know."

"You...you are so beautiful and brave and—"

"Thank you," she interrupted, flushing. "But the point is, whatever it is that must lie between a man and woman for a true lifetime of passion...it doesn't exist between us, though I hope and pray I shall find such passion one day."

Brendan didn't know what to say. He felt awkward and uneasy. They were so close. She was touching him.

She was beyond beautiful, and though he knew she was afraid, she spoke and acted with nothing but courage, courage that was all the more amazing *because* she was afraid.

He stood quickly, almost knocking his head on the low ceiling. "I should leave you to your rest."

"Wait, please."

He looked at her quizzically, once again at an uncharacteristic loss for words.

She straightened her shoulders. "I would be eternally grateful if you would teach me something about self-defense. I doubt if I could learn to master a sword in a matter of hours, but perhaps… I don't even know the mechanism of a pistol."

"It will be my pleasure," he assured her, grateful for something useful to do. And it might well prove useful indeed, for as much as he longed to, he could not promise her that she would never need to know the workings of a firearm.

He pulled one of the pistols from his belt. "The sad truth is that pistols must be reloaded—even those with several barrels. This one will allow you five shots, but you must take care and count as you fire, for you don't want to be wondering how many are left. But here…" He paused and drew a dagger. "Here is a weapon that you should keep upon your person. A pistol is best at a distance. When a man is rushing you, a dagger is what you need. If it comes to a hand-to-hand combat—if a man were to come through that door, for example—you would shoot first, then discard your gun, and be ready with a blade. If a man doesn't know you've got a dagger, you can allow him to come close, pretending fear, and then…strike. You must aim below the rib cage, and be hard, fast and certain."

Her hand curled around the dagger, and she frowned. "Like…this?"

She demonstrated a hard thrust into the air.

He slipped his hand over hers. "Aye, but see…" He used his body to show her where to strike. "You must bring him down quickly and completely."

His hand was still on hers when she looked up and nodded. And then he stared down into her eyes and was lost.

RED STOOD face-to-face again with the man who had turned the beauty of life into a sea of death for her, with years of hell to follow. She could throw the stool, but she knew he would barely notice, and it would only serve to make him angrier, which would not bode well for her future health—or life.

She set the stool down.

She needed a better weapon. She desperately needed to get her hands on a knife. She had to play for time so she could find…something.

"Wise move, my dear," he said, then walked toward his desk, keeping his distance from her, which surprised her. Then, with a small jolt of pleasure, she realized he was wary of her.

There was a half-full rum bottle sitting on the desk; he picked it up, his eyes on her, and took a long swig. She didn't move.

"You killed one of my men," he said at last. "Well,

you killed several, since I imagine those who drowned can be credited to you, as well."

"I killed men who should have been hanged. You killed men who only wanted to live in peace."

"I killed vermin who opposed their rightful king," he said pleasantly.

"Do you really believe that?" she asked.

He pointed a finger at her. "You have found a way to influence this wretched Red Robert."

"I have," she agreed.

He set the rum bottle down. "The question is, what shall I do with you now?"

"There is no question," she said.

"Oh?"

"Red Robert's ship is bearing down upon you even now. One way or the other, his crew will sink you."

"You haven't studied ships, my dear. If you had done so, you would know that my hull is thick and can ward off cannon fire."

"And the sloop following you can sail circles around you."

His face darkened with anger. "Even as a child, you were ill-tempered and stubborn, and you did not know your place."

"I knew my place very well. I watched as you murdered my parents, and delighted in killing small babes and wee children. I watched you set fire to my *place*. I watched it burn down. I smelled the roasting of human flesh."

"'Tis a pity you are such a pleasing package—in shape and from a distance. On the one hand, I think I should deal with you quickly—hang you from the yardarm. On the other hand, I think I should have you hog-tied, and then delight in cutting strip after strip of flesh from your body, adding salt as I slice. Then again…I am a greedy man. And you are worth a great deal alive. I know men—in Morocco, for instance. Men of the most…intriguing tastes. They do manage to get full use out of a young woman before she ages…or dies. So…what shall I do?"

She almost shrank back when he lifted his hand.

"See this scar?" he asked, indicating the angry red marks across his hand. "Do you remember how I got that?"

"No."

"Your teeth, my dear. I almost bashed your head into a rock then and there. But…revenge was so much sweeter. Selling you to Lady Fotherington as I did, knowing she would extend your indenture over and over again… Then, that dear gentleman in France, with all his diseases, which you certainly would have come to share… He paid me such a handsome sum to see you brought to him. So no doubt you see my dilemma now. Hang you quick—or perhaps not so quickly, I believe I would want to watch you strangle to death— or delight in sentencing you to years of total humiliation and servitude. And where I would sell you now…they don't endure obstinacy from any woman. You would learn that quickly. Minus a hand, an ear, an eye…oh, when they tire of you, they simply use you as slave labor."

She tried very hard to keep her eyes fixed on his,

trying hard not to betray any weakness. She needed to keep quiet.

She had hope, didn't she?

What hope? Her heart sank.

Brendan wouldn't sink the ship with her on it. And surely he knew that if he attempted to board her, Blair Colm would slit her throat before entering the fray himself.

He suddenly started walking toward her. "What I think would be most amusing is to see you so totally humiliated that all pride within you is killed first. Now, this is something you probably don't know. I can inflict tremendous pain without leaving any evidence. I can hurt you..." He smiled cruelly. "And I think I will."

She backed away from him.

For so long she had hoped this moment would come—but not like this. In her mind's eye, she had not been at the mercy of a shipload of murderers. In her fantasies she had simply faced him and killed him— and she hadn't cared that she would no doubt be killed in the next moment.

Now, though she indeed faced him, it was without weapons.

And now she longed to live.

How had she managed to find such a desperate desire to live after all this time, when now...

She circled around the desk, and her eye was caught by the bottle from which he had just taken that long swig.

Unaware of her intent, he followed her slowly, in no hurry to capture his trapped prey.

She reached for the bottle and smashed it against the edge of the desk, then brandished the jagged edge.

He laughed. "Oh, Roberta. If you draw so much as a drop of my blood, you will be sorry. You will simply increase my rage."

"I'm not certain anything I can do will increase the horrors of what you intend for me," she replied.

"Put it down."

"Are you daft?"

A vein pulsed at his throat.

"I am fond of this coat. You had best take care."

They could circle each other for a very long time, she thought. He seemed unhurried in his efforts to torment her.

Good. She, too, longed for time.

Then, subtly, he increased his pace, and she knew he was about to lunge.

Time had run out—and long before she was ready. Still, she had no choice.

She made the first move, spinning and swiftly leaping toward him.

Desperation was her ally. Her lunge was true, and she aimed for his throat. She was certain that she hit him, hit him hard, but he was strong and cunning. He wasn't quick enough to deflect her blow entirely, but he threw up an arm in time to save his jugular and send her flying across the cabin with the speed of a cannonball to smash against the rear wall.

He clasped a hand to his neck, staring at her with pure venom.

"You bitch." He breathed slowly.

She scrambled up, bracing herself against the wall for strength as he came straight toward her.

His hand shot out, pinning her to the wall, his fingers lacing around her throat. Her air was instantly cut off.

She clawed at him, raking his face, feeling his blood beneath her fingers.

Then, just when she was losing consciousness, something thundered in the night, the ship shuddered with the force of the explosion, and they both went flying across the cabin.

LOGAN HAD WAITED. He'd watched.

At first the decks were busy with men everywhere trying to capture the wind and increase the ship's speed. Then, once the sails were set, most of the activity had died down and the crew had dispersed to other tasks.

He'd peeked out from his cover and had seen men repairing canvas, while others replaced broken decking. Others went below, presumably to clean and prepare the cannons.

He'd seen at least two dozen men.

But he hadn't seen Blair Colm.

And he hadn't seen Red.

He had a sick feeling that both of them were in the captain's cabin. There would be far too much activity below for the captain to be able to enjoy his vengeance there.

But the helm was near the captain's cabin, with a huge man at the wheel, and it would be impossible to get by him unnoticed.

There were still barrels of gunpowder topside, and

he decided to try to buy himself entry to the cabin with a diversion.

He watched for his moment and seized it, slipping from cover and racing to grab a length of match cord near a rear swivel gun. As soon as he had it, he hurried to a barrel of gunpowder, set and lit the fuse, and returned to his hideout.

In seconds, the barrel exploded. Flames shot everywhere, inciting chaos.

"COLM'S AFIRE!" Jimmy O'Hara shouted down from the crow's nest.

Brendan heard him from the master's cabin. With Cassandra following, he burst out on the deck to see that Colm's ship was indeed on fire. They could see the flames shooting higher and higher, until the sails, too, were ablaze.

"More sail!" Brendan ordered. "Man the guns!"

"We've not seen the flare!" Peg-leg cried out.

"I don't give a damn," Brendan responded. "Close in on her. Hard!"

STUNNED, GASPING for breath, Red blinked furiously and tried to clear her head. She saw that she had landed next to the desk.

She didn't see Blair Colm at first, and then she watched in shock as he leapt to his feet and rushed to the door, heedless of her presence.

He didn't even think to shut it as he raced out.

She flew after him, hesitating at the doorway. There was a man down right outside the cabin—and he was *burning*. She reached down quickly for the knife at his waist, then looked around to see men everywhere, many of them screaming with pain. She heard a noise and looked up to see the mainmast crack and start to fall.

She quickly leapt away from the cabin just in time to save herself.

Fires were burning everywhere.

More men were screaming.

"Bobbie!"

She heard her name and was sure she was dreaming....

But she wasn't.

She shouted his name in return.

Logan suddenly burst through a wall of fire and smoke, racing toward her. A man, his face so blackened with smoke that he was unrecognizable, stepped between them and drew a sword.

Logan drew a pistol and shot him dead, then stepped over the body to reach her. "We have to get to the stern and jump. It's dangerous, but it's the only way," he told her.

She stared at him, still fighting off disbelief that he had come for her.

She had been dying, literally dying, with her enemy's hands closing around her throat, and then...

"Blair Colm," she said.

"Forget him! We have to get off this ship. Now!"

He drew her back into the smoke, which helped to camouflage their escape. Logan had a sword, and he slashed their way through anyone who accosted them.

When someone grabbed her from behind, she remembered her own weapon and broke his hold with a wild cut.

At last they reached the stern. She was stunned when Logan set off a flare. He had just lifted her to the rail when she cried out a warning. A man was looming behind him, a boarding ax raised high to strike. Logan ducked, and the ax thudded against the rail. Red let out a long scream as she lost her balance and went flying overboard.

She hit the water, which was like breaking through a hard floor from that height, and plunged into the depths. Then the survival instinct took over, and she kicked with all her strength, her lungs burning as she fought toward the firelight that marked the surface.

She made it, gasping, and heard the roar of a cannon. Treading water, she saw that a cannonball had struck hard and true, toppling the mainmast of Blair Colm's ship.

Another struck, and another....

And then Blair Colm's ship fired back.

She swam hard, knowing she had to get out from between the ships or risk being crushed. As she swam, she looked desperately around, praying with each rise and fall of the waves that she would see Logan's face.

But she did not.

THE MAN WHO had wielded the ax stepped back, seeking another weapon. He grinned, hoisted a spar and flew at Logan.

Logan danced away, calculating his opponent's reach

and weapon. He didn't think he could shatter the spar with his sword, so he kept dancing, allowing his opponent to tire himself out following. Then he lunged, ducking beneath the spar to skewer the man through the middle. With shock in his eyes, the attacker fell back, clutching his gut, and sank down to the deck. Logan turned quickly and raced for the aft rail. Then a knife hurtled past him from behind, so close that he felt it brush by.

He turned.

Blair Colm stood mere feet away across the deck.

He stared at Logan and slowly unsheathed his sword.

The man's ship was afire, his crew running about in a panic...

But the man looked completely calm. Heedless of the insanity around him.

"And who might you be?" he asked Logan.

"Logan Haggerty. *Laird* Logan Haggerty."

"I know that name," Blair said. "A young pup—grown older now, but I'd recognize you anywhere, Haggerty, you're the spittin' image of your father!—who thinks he's quite the man. Well then, *Laird* Haggerty, come die like a man."

"I won't be the one dying," Logan warned.

"You'll die, just as all the little rats who oppose me die. You had it all, you ungrateful whelp. A man who raised you well. An inheritance you never deserved. *I* gave you all that."

He was circling as he spoke, taunting Logan.

"You gave me all that?" Logan echoed. "No, what

you *gave* me is the memory of my mother murdered, my land betrayed."

"I gave you the will to fight!"

"My father, who defended his land and his people, gave me the will and the strength to fight. My mother, who had courage against all odds, showed me that a man is lost only when he has lost his soul."

"Your father was a fool who could not see the truth of what was. And your mother... Ah, what a poor, defenseless little wretch she was. She died so easily, and so quickly. I can still remember the feel of my blade in her flesh."

Rage soared within Logan.

He fought it.

They were both playing games of the mind now, trying to make each other forget that a duel to the death had to be fought with a clear head.

Blair strode forward, and Logan quickly parried the man's first thrust, jumping over a pile of rigging. Then he caught his balance and attacked.

Their swords clashed hard, then clashed again. As they disengaged to strike again, Logan saw that the other man was bleeding. His coat was ripped, and a bloodstain had appeared on his arm, matching the red rivulets that had trickled down his face and neck to his collar. Logan pressed his advantage and came on hard.

Again, steel met steel, and again both men backed away.

"So she's *your* whore now," Colm taunted. "I shall finish her off as soon as I've dispatched you—or perhaps you'd like to kill her yourself? You've been sharing her, you know—with that…bloody pirate, the wretched Red Robert."

Blair Colm slashed down hard at him as he spoke, but Logan merely smiled and easily parried the blow.

"She does sleep with Red Robert. Every night," he said.

His amusement seemed to touch off something in the other man.

Blair Colm strode forward, swinging hard.

Logan caught the blow with his own weapon.

They were locked together, both straining to shove the other off, to seize the advantage. Then, out of the corner of his eye, Logan saw that Blair Colm's men were regrouping.

They should have been saving the ship.

But it was as if hatred was contagious. Blackened with soot, bleeding, limping, they were coming forward with swords to join their master in battle.

Logan gave a mighty shove, forcing Blair Colm to stumble several feet back, then leapt to the rail, knowing it was his only chance.

As he shot into the sea, he heard the cannons roar even louder than before and knew that a true battle to the death had begun.

THEY WERE FAR from shore, where the waves were large and just staying afloat took an almost superhuman effort. But to survive, Red knew she had to reach her own ship and somehow attract someone's attention, but her strength was waning quickly.

She heard another roar, and a cannonball fell short,

slicing through the water near her. She gasped and drank in seawater, then gasped again and couldn't breathe.

Forcing herself to ease to her back and float, she found her breath again. Once more she scanned the sea, trying to position herself and choose a course to avoid both ships' fire and take her to the *Eagle*. She knew Brendan would be firing fast and furiously now, trying to keep the heavier merchantman from causing more damage to their ship. He would board her if he could not sink her. Even now, the men were no doubt prepared with their grappling hooks and boarding axes, ready to wage hand-to-hand combat.

Where was Logan?

She kept swimming, her strength restored as she spotted the *Eagle*. The air around her was now with smoke and black powder, but she didn't care, because her ship's sails were still flying hard and proud.

And Blair Colm's ship was crippled. She was limping, both masts and every sail destroyed.

But her cannons were still alive.

Red swam harder. She closed in on her own ship, and tried shouting for help, but water filled her mouth and drowned her words in her throat.

And then she saw someone looking over the rail at her.

Cassandra.

"It's Bobbie!" the other woman cried. "Bobbie is in the water!"

A rope ladder was thrown down. Red grasped for it and missed. She tried again, but the ship was moving and the waves were high, and she was thrown hard against the hull.

She caught hold of the ladder and managed to climb a few rungs.

Then the ship swung hard, and she was tossed back into the sea.

Dazed, she sought the ladder again, but it eluded her.

"Oh, no you don't! You're not drowning. I won't allow it!"

She turned.

Logan!

His face was running with soot and seawater, but his eyes were burning bright.

"Logan!"

"Get up that ladder," he commanded.

She climbed, and he climbed right behind her, his chest bracing her when she feared she would fall.

She didn't have to climb all the way to the top. Strong arms reached down for her. Brendan was there. And Peg-leg, Hagar, Silent Sam...even Jimmy O'Hara. Lord Bethany and Cassandra watched as she was dragged aboard.

She heard Logan clamber aboard behind her as she went from embrace to embrace, but then she pulled back.

"There can be none of this!" she cried quickly. "We're engaged in battle!"

"The guns are manned," Silent Sam assured her.

"And the grappling hooks are at the ready," Hagar added.

She was weaving, she realized. Exhausted, relieved and trembling, she was near to falling.

Just then the swivel guns let out a resounding volley, and she staggered back, falling against Logan.

"Get her into the cabin," Brendan ordered Logan.

Brendan saw her start to protest and said, "I can captain the ship for now."

She stared at her cousin, who was her blood and her dearest friend, the only soul who shared her past, who knew her completely, who had loved and served her, no matter what her madness. She hugged him tightly, her emotions beyond words.

"Aye, Brendan, you can captain this ship," she managed to say at last.

Then she was pulled from his arms and swept up into the embrace of a soaking wet man in filthy, blood-stained clothes who started carrying her toward her cabin. She allowed herself to relax in his arms and close her eyes.

If only for a moment.

CHAPTER SEVENTEEN

HE SET HER down on her bunk and smoothed a sodden lock of hair from her forehead.

She stared at him. "I was so afraid for you," she whispered.

"I'm so sorry I was detained," he apologized lightly. Then he rose and hurried to the desk, where he seemed to know she kept a bottle of rum in the lower right-hand drawer. He brought it to her.

"Take a long swig."

She did so, making a face. The liquor burned.

"I never really did like straight rum," she told him.

He grinned, swigging in turn. "Right now," he said, "it will sustain you."

She brushed her fingers along his face. "Did you see…Colm?" she asked.

He nodded.

"Did you…kill him?"

He inhaled deeply. "No. I'm afraid that our battle was interrupted. I chose to live to fight another day and jumped."

He was watching her intently, and she wasn't sure why.

"I was so afraid when I didn't see you in the water…"

"I already apologized for being late," he teased, but then his expression grew serious. "I...did what I could as quickly as I could," he said softly, then frowned, a finger touching her throat. "You're...bruised. Oh, God. He—"

"He was in the midst of strangling me when an explosion sent us both flying," she told him. "There has never been anything quite so timely in my life."

He looked down, smiling, but she could see that he was trembling, as well. His eyes met hers again. "His face and neck were bleeding when we met," he told her.

"Good," she said emphatically.

He nodded gravely. "You had a knife?"

"Sadly, no. I was out of traditional weapons. But some fool left a bottle atop the desk."

"Bless the drinkers," he said, then took her hands. "You're shaking, wet and cold. And the real battle is imminent. I'll leave you to change, but be...careful when you stand. You're not at full strength."

She nodded, then said, "Logan...Cassandra, and Lord Horatio. They need to be below, or even here, in this cabin. They aren't fighters."

He nodded. "I will see that they head to safety." He hesitated. "Is there a prayer that you will do the same?"

Something in his eyes was still searching for something inside her.

"Logan, I—"

But he was gone.

OUT ON DECK, Logan found Cassandra at Brendan's side, loading pistols with shot. He looked from her to Brendan with surprise.

"She learns quickly," the other man said.

"I wanted to be of use," Cassandra informed him.

"When the fighting starts, you must head to the captain's cabin or go below," Brendan told her.

"Aye, you must," Logan agreed, but neither of them was looking at him.

"Brendan, you might need—"

"Cassandra, if I am worrying about you, I will not be focused on my efforts," Brendan said.

"Then I will head to safety, as you wish," she told him.

"If the ship begins to sink—" Brendan warned.

"I will find a solid piece of timber, and I will let the current and the waves carry me to the closest shore," she said. She spoke as if she were repeating something she had already told him a dozen times before.

They were closing in on Colm's ship. A cannon spat flame from the opposing deck, and they all staggered for balance. This time they had been hit, and hit hard.

"Fire!" Hagar shouted.

Their eight starboard cannons roared in unison. The sound was deafening. But each ball made a direct hit on the opposing ship. She was already on fire, and now she had started listing.

But her crew was topside, shouting and raising their weapons.

Logan turned to Cassandra and asked, "Where is your father?"

"Below."

"You must go to him," he commanded.

She looked at Brendan, who nodded. She turned obediently.

Nearby, the smaller swivel guns began to fire. The men on Blair Colm's ship screamed, some falling, other cursing with rage.

Logan looked at Brendan, and they both grinned. "It is at hand," Brendan said.

"God go with us," Logan agreed.

Then the captain's cabin door opened. Red was dressed in fresh breeches and a clean shirt, a brace of guns buckled about her waist, sword belt in place, and knives at her ankles and upper arms.

Logan felt his heart ache.

And yet, even now, victory was not guaranteed. She needed to be able to defend herself if he and the others failed her. He had no right to ask her to do otherwise.

She looked at the two of them and arched a brow. "It's time," she said.

"Time," Brendan agreed.

"Grappling hooks and axes at the ready! Men, slam her and board her!" he cried.

There was a mighty tremor and the sound of wood groaning as the two ships collided. Both crews began tossing grappling hooks, and men raged forward from both decks, brandishing their boarding axes. Pistols fired, and there were battle cries and screams of agony.

Logan pushed forward with Red's cousin and crew, fending off those who attempted to board their ship. A man leapt from a broken mast to the rigging of their ship. Logan calculated his shot and fired, then watched as the man fell to the deck.

He spun around to battle a man with an ax. He used his second pistol, then drew a knife. He calculated his aim again and let it fly at a man who was leaping toward Peg-leg with a raised hatchet.

The men crashed into the rail, then flipped over it and fell into the sea.

Peg-leg nodded his thanks, let out a roar and boarded Blair Colm's ship.

Within minutes, Red's entire crew had raged over the side, pushing the battle onto the enemy's deck, and now it would be hand-to-hand combat to the bitter end.

Logan brought down two opponents with his sword.

Brendan, at his back, fended off a furious giant, standing dead still, and moving with split-second precision to allow the man to impale himself on his sword as he attacked.

With the full effort of Red's crew, the fighting was soon over. Colm's crew had been reduced by previous events, and though the remaining men fought to the last, only about eighteen had survived to join the battle.

Logan dispatched a man, spun to protect his back and saw that all Red's men were doing the same.

There was no one left to attack them.

Smoke billowed from the deck. The ship was on fire, and he reckoned she had taken grave damage to the hull, despite Blair Colm's insistence that his merchantman could fend off their cannon.

"Abandon ship!" Brendan ordered.

Through the smoke, Logan could see Red. She was standing midship, looking at the piles of enemy dead. Logan knew exactly who she was looking for.

He felt the ship lurch and realized she was going down, stern first.

"Abandon ship!" he called to Red, but it was as if she didn't hear. She was still examining the dead, searching desperately for Blair Colm.

Logan went over to her and caught hold of her shoulder. When she turned to him, her eyes were enormous and oddly clouded.

"Red, we've won. The ship is going down. We have to get off."

She clutched his arms. "I don't see him!" she cried.

"Red, you can't keep looking for him. The ship is sinking. We've got to disengage before she brings us down, too."

"Logan, I have to know he's dead."

He turned. Brendan had given the order to start disengaging. All the men were hastily abandoning the sinking ship, eager to reach their own.

"Red, we have to assume he's dead and save ourselves."

She pushed him away and started searching almost frantically through the dead men once more.

He followed behind her, swearing, then swung her around to face him.

"Don't make me do it," he warned her.

Her eyes widened.

"You wouldn't dare!"

But he did. There was no other choice. He took a swing.

"You wretched bas—"

It was all she got out. She hadn't defended herself quickly enough, and he caught her jaw in just the right place. She slumped forward into his arms.

He raced to the center rail. The lines had all been disengaged. The ships were already easing apart.

"Logan!"

It was Peg-leg.

He didn't ask why Logan had their captain over his shoulder. He just shouted for a line.

A rope swung toward Logan. He caught it, doubled it around his free wrist, stepped atop the rail and leapt. He held Red tightly to him, and together they swung onto the deck of the *Eagle*.

Brendan was instantly at his side.

"She's hurt? What happened to her?" Brendan asked.

Logan stood. "She'll be fine in an hour or two."

Brendan stared at him.

"She wouldn't leave the ship," Logan explained.

A strange sucking sound alerted them both, and they turned. The ship began to rock violently under them as the merchantman started to go down fast, creating a vortex. Several men stumbled, trying to keep their balance.

The ship was gone completely in a matter of seconds. Then broken timbers and bits of wreckage began popping to the surface, as if spat up by a mighty mouth beneath the waves.

There was dead silence for a long moment, and then a cheer went up among the men.

"Victory! Victory!"

For a man called "silent," Sam had a shout that could cause the ocean itself to tremble.

RED, UNCONSCIOUS on the deck, didn't get to hear it.

She was drifting.

And it was so sweet....

She could sense the waves as they gently caressed the ship, and she could almost feel the gentle kiss of the sun and the breeze.

And then...

She felt it.

The twinge of soreness at her jaw. Her throat hurt, too. Most upsetting of all, the pain was pushing away the absurdly pleasant feel of the dream.

She opened her eyes and blinked. She was in her cabin. Her hand rose instinctively to her jaw. The soreness was very definitely real.

"You're awake."

She blinked again, and turned.

Logan was at her captain's desk. In her chair. He looked to be annoyingly comfortable there, too. A bottle of rum sat before him, but he was drinking from a porcelain cup.

His legs, in dry, well-fitting breeches, were stretched out so his booted feet sat atop her desk. He was leaning back in her chair, his hands folded behind his head.

She frowned.

"You hit me," she accused him angrily.

"I did."

"I was looking for Blair Colm."

He shook his head, eyes narrowed in disdain.

"The ship was sinking. Did sink—seconds after we got off her."

"But—"

"You would have gone down with her, you fool."

She swallowed, closing her eyes again. He was right. But he was *wrong,* as well.

"He's still out there."

"Red…"

He moved at last, swinging his legs down. "Blair Colm's ship sank. Every man aboard went down with her."

"But I couldn't find him," she said.

"Because he was somewhere else when he died or had already been shoved overboard." He growled in frustration. "The point is, the ship went down. In another few seconds—if Brendan hadn't given the order to disengage—you might have allowed it to sink your own ship, along with all these men who would so readily die for you!"

She fell silent, because he was right, and she didn't want to think that she had so recklessly disregarded the lives of others in her pursuit of vengeance.

But she was still afraid.

"I didn't see him dead."

"Does it matter so much?" he asked gently. "So long as he is gone, so long as he can't hurt anyone ever again, does it matter so much that you didn't strike the final blow?"

She shook her head.

"Except that…"

"What?" he demanded.

"What if he's not dead?"

She was startled when he strode over and drew her to her feet. His hands were suddenly at the belt that held her pistols. They were off before she knew it, tossed onto the table.

"What are you—"

"Just shut up."

She reached for his hands, but too late; her sword belt was gone, as well.

This was madness. She was still dizzy when she stood.

Because he had hit her.

And now he was acting as if he were master of the universe, master of *her...*

"Logan, this isn't the time or the place—"

"Don't flatter yourself," he snapped.

She stared into his eyes. They were cold, and he was clearly angry.

"I beg your pardon?"

"As well you should."

"What?"

She tried to stop him, but he was stripping her of all weapons. "Logan, stop acting like a madman! This is my ship. *I* am captain here."

"That you are. And as a decent captain, you're going to go out there and thank every man who saved your ship and your hide, and celebrate the victory with your crew."

She couldn't protest, couldn't explain that she was still desperately holding on...

Holding on to what?

Power?

No. She didn't need to be all-powerful.

She was holding on to...

Fear.

But she found herself propelled toward the door, and she couldn't fight him, couldn't even figure out how he managed to keep her moving and open the door at the same time.

As she stepped out, she saw the dear, familiar—and smiling—faces of those who had given her all she possessed: this ship and a means of existence and, several times over in the past days, life itself.

As soon as they saw her, the cry went up.

"Hail our captain!"

And then Brendan stepped forward and gave her a fierce hug. "Bobbie, we've done it! We are avenged. His ship is sunk."

"And that murdering dog who intended to see *me* hang is at the bottom of the sea with it. My girl, this is a tremendous victory," Lord Haggerty said.

"Grog, Captain, just as you like it," Hagar said, coming forward with a mug. "To victory over tyrants, liars, murderers and thieves!"

She took the cup and drank deeply. She noticed that Cassandra was there, too, and even in men's clothes, she was beautiful. Her face was so alive, her enthusiasm sincere. She stood at her father's side, her arm tucked through his, and she seemed completely at ease in the company of a pirate crew.

"Thank you." At first Red's voice was soft, choked

with emotion, so she forced herself to speak more loudly. "Thank you. There could be no victory without you. My life was in your hands, and you kept it for me when I was convinced myself that it was lost. You are the finest crew who have ever sailed these seas. I am sincerely indebted to you, and I will remain so for the rest of my life."

A cheer went up again. Brendan threw his arm around her and squeezed her tightly.

"We have taken the liberty of plotting a return to New Providence, as our own vessel is now truly in sad need of repair," he said.

She nodded blankly, then looked to Cassandra and Lord Bethany. "But our guests..." she said, and thought, our guests—who now include Laird Haggerty among their number.

"We'll be fine, lass," Lord Bethany said. "You cannot bring me home in this ship, in any case, unless it is well camouflaged. I'm afraid you would be blown out of the water."

"But, New Providence?"

"Oh, we know it's a den of pirates and scurvy rats," Cassandra said cheerfully. "But we are protected," she said, smiling and looking around. "And my father has offered to see to it that a fair and legal pardon is given to any man here who asks, and he will finance those men in finding livelihoods of their choosing, as well."

Another cheer went up.

Were they really all so happy at the thought of becoming law-abiding citizens? she wondered.

With a life span of only a few more years in their current occupation, could she blame them?

Wasn't that what she should want for herself?

She had wanted to live today, had desperately wanted to live. Because of Logan. But in any respectable manner, she could not be a part of his life.

However, she owed these men.

"Lord Bethany, you are truly an honorable man. The finest—as I have been told." She smiled at Cassandra. The woman could not help being perfect.

"Dinner is served!" Jimmy O'Hara announced into the proceedings.

Again, a cheer went up. She became aware of the smell of fish being fried and realized that while she had "slept," others had attended to all the necessities. The men began talking again, toasting each other with an air of celebration.

"Men," she said, in an authoritative tone, "we are, as ever, in dangerous waters. We must keep a lookout."

"Aye-aye, Captain!"

She looked up. Silent Sam was grinning down at her from the crow's nest.

"We are good sailing men," Brendan informed her. "We would not forget to keep watch."

She smiled at him. "Of course, you are. My mistake." He looked at her with such pride and pleasure that she hugged him again fiercely—to yet another cheer.

OVER DINNER, the conversation was loud and lively, some men talking with great pride of their achievements, others looking to the future. Jimmy O'Hara produced a plate of fresh-caught fish and fruit they had bought in New Providence, and someone suggested that he needed to open a public house back in the colonies.

Red listened more than she talked and discovered that every man among them had dreams. Even the ship's surgeon and the carpenter—who had come to them from Black Luke's crew—were ready to settle down to legal activities. Emory, the carpenter, told her that he had been seized from a tavern in Savannah and had never intended to lead a pirate's life.

And Grant, the surgeon, said he had been in the royal navy, but when his ship had been taken and his calling discovered, he had been allowed to live and compelled to serve. When she had killed Black Luke, he had felt himself indebted to her.

"You have long ago repaid any debt to me," she assured him.

The day had long ago become night. In the end, as she watched them drink and laugh and plan so eagerly for the future, she slipped away.

Logan had remained with Cassandra and Lord Bethany. They had seemed to have much to discuss, so she retired to her cabin, where she was undisturbed through the night.

LOGAN KNEW he should have been exhausted, but he couldn't sleep. Around midnight, he took over the helm. They were moving slowly, because it was dark and hazards invisible, but they had to keep moving, because they had a slow leak and were taking on water.

They had to limp into a friendly port soon, and as the *Eagle* was a known pirate ship, New Providence was ~~~~st safe haven.

/as still angry with Red; she had risked too hen they had fought so hard for their lives.

he was worried. There seemed to be something e of piracy that she couldn't let go. He had b⸱⸱⸱⸱⸱d her quest was to ensure the death of the man who had ruined her life and slain her family. He understood that desire far too well.

But while the others had spoken of the future, she had remained silent. She had still been thinking of the battle when she had regained consciousness. She couldn't focus on *life*.

Or on love.

Good God, he really was a fool. All of his life, he had enjoyed the company of women. High-born, low-born, friends and lovers. But he had never felt what she aroused and awakened in him. Cassandra was a perfect friend, and had he not met Red, perhaps they could have been lovers…. But he *had* met Red.

Why, when he finally let down his guard and gave his heart, had he given it to Red? The one woman who would never turn to him?

"Anything out there?"

Logan had heard Brendan coming and was glad of the company to take his mind off his thoughts. "No, thank God," he said. "I have no need of further excitement."

They stood in companionable silence for a few minutes.

Logan broke it first. "What will you do now?" he asked the younger man.

Brendan shrugged. "That will depend on Red. Bobbie."

"Let's pretend that Red decides she wants to build a life on shore somewhere. What would you want for yourself?" Logan asked.

Brendan arched a brow and gave the question some thought. "Ships," he said at last.

"What?"

"I once thought about being a merchantman, but I think I'd prefer to be a shipbuilder. I've studied ships for a long time. I know what makes them fast and what makes them strong." Then he shrugged in self-deprecation. "I haven't the necessary formal education, of course."

"Education is something that can be acquired," Logan pointed out.

"Aye, perhaps." He clapped a hand on Logan's shoulder. "I will never be able to repay you for all you have done."

"Oddly enough…I will never be able to repay you."

"Oh?"

"I have been searching for Blair Colm for a very long time myself."

Brendan nodded. "I wonder how many out there will rejoice to learn of his death," he mused.

"Quite a few, I should imagine." Logan looked at the other man and smiled. "So…a shipbuilder. I imagine you will be wanting a wife."

"Well…yes…of course." Brendan's discomfort was almost palpable.

"Cassandra is an extremely fine woman," Logan pointed out as if the idea were only now occurring to him.

"The finest," Brendan said fervently.

"And lest you be laboring under a misconception, I feel I must point out that she and I have mutually decided that we should not spend our lives together."

Brendan looked out to sea. He swallowed fiercely.

"I am not... I could never... I could never hope to be good enough."

"Good enough?"

"Her father bears a title."

"Aye, well, riches and titles were of concern to me once, too," Logan said. "Perhaps they even meant something to Horatio at one time."

"He remains a lord."

"And a colonist."

"But—"

"I cannot answer for Lord Horatio or Cassandra, of course," Logan said. "But I think perhaps they are more egalitarian than you suspect."

"Still, I cannot accept her father's largesse and hope to... I could never... We haven't actually attacked many ships," Brendan explained.

Logan suddenly laughed.

"Are you mocking me now?" Brendan asked. "I am not a rich man, whatever you might believe of Red Robert and...her crew."

"I am not mocking you. It is just that...I have thought of a way for this crew to reap some benefit from all that has occurred."

"What is that?"

"I had a moment alone last night aboard Blair Colm's ship. I don't know from whom he stole his bounty, but as we know how he operated, the rightful owners are beyond caring. Last night I threw a fortune overboard in relatively shallow waters."

Brendan stared at him blankly, then blinked.

"When the ship is repaired—and reoutfitted, as there will be no more pirating, even in pretense—we will go back. And you will all be rich men indeed."

"I could kiss you!" Brendan exclaimed.

"Please, don't," Logan said.

Brendan laughed and slapped him on the shoulder instead. Logan tried not to wince, as the blow fell on the stitches he had received not so long ago.

"You would take us to it? You…would share?"

"Aye, and easily."

Brendan nodded. "Once again, I will be forever in your debt."

"No. I have given you nothing. The future is something you must make yourself."

Brendan nodded. "Aye," he said softly. "But…" He shook his head. "I'll take the helm. You deserve some rest."

"No, go see if Cassandra is awake, watching the stars…hoping that you will come to her. I cannot rest just now. I am fine where I am."

"I will send someone to relieve you in an hour."

"As you wish."

Brendan moved away, whistling softly.

They were alive, Logan thought.

They had all survived.

And Blair Colm was dead.

So why, when this should have been a night of great celebration for both himself and Red, did he suddenly feel so...

Bereft?

CHAPTER EIGHTEEN

"YOU BROUGHT DOWN Blair Colm?" Sonya said incredulously.

She was lying on the bed in her private space—a room she had earned and paid for—in the tavern. She seldom brought men here; for the most part, she had taken on a managerial role rather than being a provider of services these days.

But she'd always had a weakness for Jimmy O'Hara. He'd never been much of a pirate, but then, he hadn't chosen the life. He'd been taken off a ship years ago by a fellow known as Elegant Elam—long gone now—and rather than be marooned, he had joined the crew. From there he had come to New Providence, where he had spent most of his days drinking. Even so, he had a certain charm about him. He had a lilt to his voice and always called her "darlin'."

Jimmy, lying at her side, nodded with pure pleasure. "Ah, Sonya, what an adventure."

Sonya rolled over. "But who killed him?"

"What?" Jimmy turned to her, frowning.

"Blair Colm. Who killed him?"

Jimmy shrugged, and his grin deepened. "I wish I

could tell you, darlin', that it had been me. Ye'd love me all the more! But I did fight—I honestly fought. And hard. There was something about the righteousness of that battle—not that I'd want to be doing it again! Nay, not I. And that great Lord Bethany, he's of a mind to give us all a new start, a pardon, says he can do it, I swear it. And I believe it. I'm telling you true, that I am, darlin'. And when I am a rich man, ah, well, a man of means, at the least, well then, darlin'..."

Sonya didn't hear him as he rambled on. She was still thinking about his assertion that Blair Colm was dead. She couldn't believe it, much as she wanted to. She would never forget what the man had done to her, how he had made her feel.

And she had never stopped fearing him. Hating him.

She caught Jimmy's face between her hands.

"Jimmy, I have to know. Who killed him? How? Did you see his body?"

"Well, no, that I didn't. But I did see the ship go down. Now, darlin', you're not listening to me. What I want to talk about is—"

"Did Red come ashore?" Sonya demanded.

"What?" Jimmy said.

"Did Red come ashore?"

Jimmy frowned fiercely. "Now, Sonya, I'm a patient man. Here we are, lying all fine and sweet and naked and enjoying one another, and you're worryin' about a dead man, and the captain."

Sonya rose. "We're not lying here sweet and naked anymore, Jimmy O'Hara. I asked you a question. Did Red come ashore?"

Jimmy pouted. "No, Red remained aboard ship. A slew of carpenters are out there now, checking on the damage, trying to make her seaworthy without havin' to careen her."

Sonya was already dressing. "Stay, Jimmy. I'll be back soon enough. Don't go down and be getting yourself drunk, I'll not be having it, you getting all soused and passing out on me."

"Sonya!" he cried.

But she was already closing the door.

She had to know.

RED HAD SENT Hagar ashore to buy her a supply of black wigs, so she would have had no difficulty going into town had she so desired. The only man who had ever dared to pick a fight with her there had been Blair Colm, and even he had been too cowardly to face her himself. Besides, now he was gone. Red Robert was a known friend of Blackbeard, who was growing ever more powerful, so it was likely that—unless a terrible falling-out between the two of them was rumored—she was perfectly safe walking around New Providence.

Far safer than she might be in any legal port.

But though they had been in port for two days, she had chosen to remain with her ship. She had slept. She had awakened, cried for no reason and drunk herself back to sleep again. She was, at the least, rested. Then she had begun the arduous task of trying to decide just what she wanted to do with the rest of her life.

Logan hadn't come near her again.

No matter what he had said, he lived in a different

world. He had no doubt finally realized that himself. He had saved her life. He had…cared for her. And now…

Now he despised her.

Because I can't be a proper woman, she told herself.

And yet, sitting at her desk, trying to pretend she was dealing with how to break up the crew and what in God's name to do with herself, she wondered if that was the truth.

It had to be.

Despite his words, the world was what it was. She had last seen him with Cassandra and Lord Bethany. He was probably still with them, showing them around the town Cassandra had so badly wanted to see.

She was staring down at the papers on her desk and watching them blur before her when the door opened.

Closed.

And was bolted from within.

And he was there.

He didn't speak to her, only walked over to the desk and stared down at her.

She was in full pirate captain garb, minus her weapons, and those were all within easy reach. She had a wig nearby, as well, just in case it should prove important that she be Captain Red Robert at any given moment. Had someone come, seeking to see the captain, she would have been warned by Hagar, who was guarding her door.

Hagar would never have stopped Logan, of course.

"What?" she asked.

He didn't reply, only continued staring at her.

"I had...I had thought you were ashore. With Lord Bethany. And Cassandra."

She tried to speak lightly.

He set his hands on the desk and leaned down until his face was only inches from hers. "Do you think I am a liar, Bobbie?"

She flushed.

"A liar? I don't recall labeling you as such."

He didn't say anything else, only came around the desk and jerked her to her feet.

"What are you doing?" she cried.

He answered by pulling her forcefully into his arms. When she opened her mouth to protest, he silenced her with a deep and penetrating kiss. When she struggled against him, he merely lifted her off her feet, and when she fell back, it was upon her bunk. Before she could rise, he came down upon her, his weight pressing her into the poor comfort of the thin mattress. She felt his hands beneath her shirt, felt the lightning streak of desire his touch evoked, such a burning within, and still the pressure of his lips on hers, the absolute hunger they shared. He moved for a brief moment, casting aside his own shirt, but she only lay stunned when she might have spoken. And then his mouth was on hers again, his hands on the tie of the breeches, and his were already open. Flesh was against flesh, and it seemed as if he were touching her everywhere, creating magic, and she wasn't sure how he managed it, but their clothing seemed to be melting away.

Whatever came, she wanted this, wanted to hold him one last time, know the incredible wonder of his body in hers, the feel of his lips, teeth and tongue against her, all over her. Wanted to touch him, know his powerful and vital presence, the ripple of muscle and sinew, the vibrant heat of his skin. She wanted so badly to press her lips against him and feel the volatile contractions within him, the trembling of his frame because of her...

But she couldn't stop herself. As his mouth trailed from hers to her collarbone and breasts, she gasped out, "What are you doing?"

"What I want," he told her. "What I want more than anything in this world." He pulled away from her, arms bracing his weight above her, as he stared down at her. "What do *you* want?" he demanded.

She swallowed hard and trembled. She knew that she should deny him. Deny herself. But she couldn't.

"What you want," she whispered.

His mouth found hers again. She kissed him wildly in return, and when they pulled apart to breathe, she gasped, then played her fingers down his chest, following those tender strokes with a cascade of kisses and the caress of her tongue. He lowered his weight onto her, finding her mouth again, ravishing it, only to leave her gasping again while he followed her lead, lips against her breasts, her belly, below. She writhed in sweet anguish, her need for him allowing her mind little room for thought and reason. Ecstasy swept over her as she arched beneath him, caught in the moment of pure sensation, but then he was with her again, his mouth claiming hers, his body driving into her with slow and powerful conviction, and he was the most exquisite lover, teasing her with the slowest strokes, then moving like a storm at sea, raising a fire inside her that seemed to scream in silence for the ultimate release. It burst through her and took her breath away, momentarily stilled the thunder of her the heart, then burst like a million flares across a velvet sky, and finally the soft, midnight feel of wonder come sweeping down upon her as she trembled in the aftermath.

She was startled when he immediately and abruptly rose, then donned his breeches before turning back to face her.

"Listen to me. I want to *live,* not just survive. I want to live a life with a future and children and Christmas. I want to know that I will always sleep in the same woman's arms. I want to be with someone who loves life and *me* more than any specter from her past, especially when I have been haunted by that same specter. That is what I want. You ruled the seas with a righteous hatred, but that is over now. And you are not by nature a killer or a thief. Think about it, Red. You can have me and the future, or you can spend your days still haunted by the past. So if you *really* want what I want," he said, "then you have to come for me in town."

And then, throwing on his shirt, he opened the door and left.

She lay there for long minutes in complete shock. Then, slowly, she rose and began to dress. When her clothes were on, she looked at the black wig on the desk. Her hands shaking, she started to put it on.

She couldn't go into town without it.

But what in God's name had he really meant? Did he want to...

Marry her?

SONYA HURRIED down the street. At the dock, she saw a boat just coming in. The man rowing it wore a hat, and his head was low. She wondered if perhaps he was ill, because he had a scarf tied around his neck.

"You there!" she cried. "Take me out to the ship anchored there—I will pay you well."

The man hesitated, but finally he nodded. Sonya stepped down into the boat.

She had to see Red Robert. She had to know the truth, had to know if Blair Colm was really dead.

"You're off to see the pirate?"

"Aye. Red Robert."

"He be on his ship?"

"Aye, obviously."

The man began to row, but she barely glanced at him. Her eyes were on the ship. Then she realized that he had rowed in a circle and taken them into the shadowy waters below the dock.

"What are you doing?" she protested in annoyance.

He looked up then.

And she knew the truth.

No, he wasn't dead. It had been too good to believe.

She never had a chance to scream.

He struck her with an oar. She saw a burst of light. And then...nothing.

LOGAN STILL HAD so much pent-up energy that he had waved off the crewman who offered to row him in. He was eager to put his muscles into the rowing of the little boat.

Would she come?

Would she don the wig of Red Robert one last time to come into the tavern and find him? He'd done nothing but wait for the last several days, but she'd made no attempt to find him nor even to summon him....

What had been left to do?

His thoughts so preoccupied his mind that though some part of him heard the noise while he was tethering the longboat, it didn't seep through at first.

It had just been a mewling sound at first. Like a kitten.

Then it was a voice. Horribly weak. Hardly a whisper.

"Help."

He looked around and saw nothing suspicious. Some workmen were busy farther down the dock; men were walking the streets. A carpenter was repairing a sign that advertised rum.

He stood still, and heard nothing. He started to walk, then thought that he heard it again.

There were other boats tethered at the dock, but they were all empty.

Then it came again. Barely a whisper, so weak. And it seemed to be coming from beneath him.

He dropped down on his stomach by the edge of the dock and looked underneath, where he saw a woman barely hanging on to one of the pilings.

He swore and, barely taking the time to doff his

boots, jumped into the water. She was just keeping her head above the surface. He caught hold of her and realized that she was naked. He also realized that he knew her.

"Sonya!" He almost dropped her, he was so shocked.

Men often grew angry with whores and used them cruelly, but Sonya was the no-nonsense queen of the island. Who would have done this to her?

He hoisted her high, fiercely treading water as he found the strength to push her up on the dock. Then he crawled up beside her and threw his jacket over her. A huge gash marred the right side of her face.

"Sonya, I'll get help for you. Just hang on," he said, and started to move away. But she caught his arm and pulled him back with a surprising surge of strength.

Her mouth worked. He leaned low to hear her.

"He is alive."

"Who is alive, Sonya? Let me get help for you!"

"Blair. Blair Colm." She couldn't open her eyes. She could barely whisper. "He is heading…"

Her words trailed away.

Logan stood, and bellowed loudly enough to be heard on the street. "Somebody help this woman! Get over here and help her!"

He waited a split second, just long enough to see that someone was heeding his call, then jumped back into the tender and started to row.

BLAIR COLM was stopped when he reached the ship and went for the ladder. He had expected as much. He pulled his scarf more tightly about his head and silently cursed the wretched skirt, which was going to make movement difficult.

"Is the captain aboard?" he called out in the highest pitched voice he could summon.

"Aye, what be the problem?" the fellow at the rail demanded.

"There's a row in the tavern among his men. I must speak to him, and quickly."

He was sure the sailor thought he was the ugliest whore imaginable, but he knew well enough that many a whore was not a beauty.

"I'll tell him."

"No, please, I must tell him what's been said, what's happened."

"Come up, then, woman. Be fast. He's in his cabin and not wantin' to be disturbed."

He *was* fast. The minute the crewman helped him aboard, he knifed him in the gullet and let him fall silently to the deck.

There were others aboard. He could hear men calling orders to one another. He had no intention of dealing with them. He strode instantly for the captain's cabin.

DOWN IN THE TAVERN, Jimmy was bemoaning his luck with women.

Blimey, he couldn't even propose properly to a whore.

A hand fell hard upon his shoulder. "O'Hara, you rutting little dog. I heard tell you went off and served under Red Robert. And I'm hearing that you fought a battle and didn't go hiding beneath any sheets, neither."

Jimmy turned. The massive pirate known as Black-beard was standing behind him.

"Aye, it's all true."

"So that bastard Blair is dead, is he?"

"Must be, for the ship went down to Davy Jones's locker," Jimmy said cheerfully.

Teach had always treated him like scum. All right, so perhaps he had been scum. But he wasn't anymore. He was going to be an honest man.

"So why do you look like a man drinking his woes away?" Blackbeard asked.

"I want to marry Sonya," Jimmy said.

"Aye?" Blackbeard gave out a mighty laugh. Then, looking at Jimmy, he sobered. "She turned you down?"

"She went racing off to see Captain Red. Wanted to know if it was true that Blair was dead. She must have had a mighty hatred of the man."

Just as he spoke, they both heard the cry in the street. "They found her down at the docks! They found Sonya!"

Jimmy actually pushed past the giant of a man to run all the way to the docks.

And then he saw her.

WHEN THE DOOR opened again, Red expected Logan.

He wasn't making her come to him, she thought in relief. And she wanted to talk to him; she needed to admit that she was afraid—and why. Pirates weren't supposed to be afraid, but she was terrified. Maybe she wasn't a pirate after all, she thought with a wry grin.

Maybe she had hated too long.

Maybe…

But it wasn't Logan. It was a woman. "What is it?" she asked.

The woman closed the door behind her, then seemed to stagger and fall. Red rushed forward to help her, but as she bent down to help, she felt steel fingers grasp her wrist. She tried to rise and free herself, started to shout out an alarm, but she was silenced and forced back, an arm like a steel pipe against her throat.

And then she saw who it was.

He eased his hold just long enough to lock both hands around her throat, still forcing her to move backward. She tried to raise her hands to fight him, but he was too strong.

And still he pushed her back.

Back to the bunk.

Where she had just lain with Logan.

She stared at him, struggling, trying to scratch and claw, but she was weakening, losing air, seeing the room grow dim. She could feel the wig slipping and expected him to squeeze harder, certain that whatever happened after, he had come to kill her, and kill her quickly.

But first he took one hand off her throat to rip the wig from her head, and then he smiled in a combination of disbelief and amusement, still keeping just enough pressure on her windpipe that she was rendered powerless.

"*You* are Red Robert?" he said.

She struggled fiercely. With his free hand, he was ripping at her clothing. She realized that he meant to rape her, then kill her. Debase her, take away all her pride. Hurt her.

His hands were on her. The hands that had slain her mother, her father. Little children. Hands that were covered in blood.

She had to find a way to fight. He was touching her breasts, ripping at the linen of her breeches. His hand was between her thighs.

No.

She knew he had a weak spot, and she managed to raise a hand and claw at his throat where she had cut him with the bottle.

Startled and in agony, he let out a scream but quickly rallied, bringing a knife that was wet with blood straight to her throat. She went still, but his hold on her had eased. He was relying on the blade to control her.

"Kill me now," she told him. "Because I will never let you touch me."

He smiled. "Dead or alive, my dear, I will debase you. I will use your dying flesh, and when I'm done, I'll hang you out for the crows."

It was over. Her life didn't flash in front of her eyes.

She just waited for the blow.

It didn't come.

He was suddenly wrenched away from her and thrown across the cabin.

And Logan was facing him with murder in his eyes.

Blair threw the knife. Logan barely ducked in time to miss the deadly missile, as Blair turned and flew out the door. Logan followed him, and Red jumped to her feet, straightening her clothing as she raced after the men...

And plowed straight into Logan's back.

She caught her breath, looked around and saw that Blair Colm had been stopped.

They were not alone on deck.

Blackbeard was there, like a living wall of fury. There was nowhere for Blair Colm to run.

"Give me a weapon!" Blair Colm bellowed. "I demand my right to fight like a man."

"You want a weapon, man? You think you should receive a fair fight?" Blackbeard asked.

"Aye, pirate's honor, I demand it."

Blackbeard hiked a bushy brow.

"Bull," he said simply.

Then, he smiled, drew his pistol and shot Blair, point-blank.

The man stared at the huge pirate.

Slowly, he fell to his knees.

Blackbeard shot him again.

And he pitched forward.

There was silence for a moment. The air reeked with the spent powder and shot, a strange contrast to the beauty of the day.

Then Blackbeard shrugged, looking at the two of them.

"I suppose I should have allowed one of you the honor," he said.

Red stepped around Logan and smiled at Teach.

"No, he is dead, and that is all that matters." She walked over and put her arms around his giant girth.

"Thank you," she said softly.

"Get this rubbish off the deck!" Blackbeard roared.

Two of the carpenters hurried forward and quickly took the body.

"Not overboard! His like rots in a gibbet, even in New Providence!" Blackbeard looked over Red's head to Logan. "A lot of people will want to know he's truly dead and gone."

Logan nodded, still silent.

Red pulled away from Blackbeard. "Want another ship?" she asked.

He bellowed with laughter.

Then she turned and walked over to Logan. "I have just one question."

"Aye?"

"Was that…a proposal?" she asked softly.

He grinned, going down on a knee. "Is this better?"

"You want me—*me*—to *marry* you?"

"Aye, that is what I want."

It couldn't work. He was a *laird.*

"Well?" he said.

"Well, lass?" Blackbeard prompted.

"I want what you want," she told the only man she had ever loved.

THE BREEZE WAS SOFT as it drifted in off the water.

Magnolias dripped moss that gently swayed in the glory of the afternoon sunset.

"Are you nervous?"

She turned. Brendan, in a brocade vest and matching jacket, was at her side. He looked glorious. But then, he was attending the College of William and Mary up in Virginia, and he had learned a bit about attire from some of his classmates.

He grinned. "And you… You look like…a girl!"

She elbowed him.

"Truly, Red, you're stunning."

"Thank you."

"But are you nervous?" he persisted.

In her own mind, Red had been married since that night in New Providence.

That was when Blackbeard had decided that, as a ship's captain—and a pirate with a swiftly growing reputation—he needed to marry her and Logan then and there, that night. And so they were married, with a court of pirates and whores and thieves—and amazingly good friends—around them.

That had been easy.

She had a new friend in Cassandra. And it had been Cassandra then—as it was now—who stood up for her as maid of honor. Word had gone out that Red Robert had died in the fight with Blair Colm. Red Robert, being an upstanding member of the pirate community, had been buried at sea, while Blair Colm was placed in a gibbet.

Red didn't need to see it done.

But Sonya was still at death's door, with Jimmy O'Hara keeping watch over her, tending to her every need.

The crewman from her ship had miraculously survived, as well, though at first they had not thought he would. He had gone overboard—mostly dead, in his own words—and clung to the hull until Logan had arrived and pulled him in.

Red meant for Blackbeard to have her ship to add to his fleet.

He accepted.

So Roberta was married to Logan in a ceremony many didn't understand but were still pleased to celebrate. And when it was over and they were alone, she had voiced all her fears for the future, and he had shushed her. He loved her. She loved him. And they would make it work.

It helped, of course, that once they were taken to an island near Charleston and "rescued," they were quickly able to commission a ship and return for the treasure Logan had tossed overboard.

It had helped a great deal. In fact, Lord Bethany had merely rolled his eyes in amused surrender when Brendan and Cassandra had asked permission to marry. His time with the pirates had broadened his mind indeed.

But today...

Today she was to walk, on her cousin's arm, down the aisle arranged in the garden of Lord Bethany's very impressive Savannah estate. And she was nervous. For Logan's sake, she prayed she might be accepted by society. Not that he cared. He assured her that they could go to the Highlands at any time, but she wanted to make a place in the New World, for theirs was a new life.

The music began.

"This is it, Red," Brendan said softly.

She nodded, and they walked out. She saw so many wonderful people.

Jimmy O'Hara.

And his new wife. Sonya.

And there, unbelievably, was a happy if somewhat

plain woman: Lygia. Lygia, who had made her own life bearable when she had been young.

Lygia, who appeared to be a bit tipsy, was on the arm of Silent Sam, and given how wealthy she was, society had no choice but to accept her flouting of convention.

She smiled as Red walked by her. And giggled.

Red kept moving. There was an altar in the gazebo, where a minister—a real minister, Lord Bethany had assured her—waited.

And there was Logan.

Tall, smiling, assured. And waiting for her.

She vaguely heard the minister asking who gave her hand in marriage, and she heard Brendan's reply.

She turned and clung to him for a minute.

Then she met Logan's eyes and took his hand.

The last mist of the past rolled away with an explosion of cannon fire from out at sea.

She saw Logan's smile.

Blackbeard's salute, sent from as close to the harbor as he wished to come.

The minister spoke, and she and Logan answered in turn.

Then they were being told to kiss.

Before his lips touched hers, she whispered to him, "I want what you want."

He drew her into his arms. "I have what I want," he said.

And she laughed, for they were alive, and they were in love, and the future was theirs.